Also by Jennifer L. Schiff

SOMETHING'S COOKING IN CHIANTI

Jennifer Lonoff Schiff

Shovel
& Pail
Press

This is a work of fiction. Names, characters, businesses, places, events, and incidents are either the products of the author's imagination or used in a fictitious manner. Any resemblance to actual persons, living or dead, or actual events is purely coincidental.

SOMETHING'S COOKING IN CHIANTI
by Jennifer Lonoff Schiff

https://www.ShovelAndPailPress.com

Cover design by Rita Sri Harningsih

Formatting by Polgarus Studio

ISBN: 978-0-578-34834-6

Library of Congress Control Number: 2022901228

Cooking is at once one of the simplest and most gratifying of the arts,
but to cook well, one must love and respect food.
—Craig Claiborne

One cannot think well, love well, sleep well if one has not dined well.
—Virginia Woolf

Life is a combination of magic and pasta.
—Frederico Fellini

CHAPTER 1

Guin stared out the window, taking in the Tuscan countryside as they drove from Pisa to Greve. It was just as she had imagined it: rolling hills, rustic-looking stone houses topped with terracotta roofs, and cypress and olive trees as far as the eye could see. And she was pretty sure that was a vineyard they just passed.

"We're almost there," said Glen, glancing over at her.

"I still can't believe we're really here, in Tuscany," Guin replied, still gazing at the scenery.

"Believe it."

And to think she had initially said no when Glen asked her to join him for the cooking course. Of course, that was partly because she didn't think their boss at the *Sanibel-Captiva Sun-Times* would allow Guin to take off two weeks in a row, even though it was the slow season.

But then Glen had used his powers of persuasion on Ginny to convince her that doing a piece on the cooking course and Chianti would be the perfect way to test out that Travel section Ginny had been thinking about adding to the paper. And she had bit.

So now here Guin was, with Glen, driving through Tuscany in a little red convertible, on a beautiful July day. And soon they would arrive at their home for nearly a week, a restored Tuscan villa turned boutique hotel, where they would learn to cook authentic Tuscan food from Glen's old

Wall Street friend, Bridget, who had given up finance and New York to move to Italy and become a private chef.

She glanced over at Glen, who was humming along to the radio. He looked happy and relaxed, like he belonged there, his ash-blond hair whipping around his tanned, chiseled face, his aviator sunglasses and open-neck polo shirt giving him a kind of devil-may-care Italian air.

She tried to picture what he had been like when he had worked on Wall Street. He always seemed so relaxed. At least since she had known him.

He had left New York and his job at an investment bank after a painful divorce, moving back to Southwest Florida to take care of his elderly parents and pursue his passion, photography. And he had found plenty of work, including a steady freelance gig at the *Sanibel-Captiva Sun-Times*. That's where he and Guin had met.

Like Glen, Guin had left the Northeast after losing her job and her husband (to another woman) in the space of a few weeks, settling on Sanibel after visiting the island for a freelance assignment. And after being on assignment together a few times, she and Glen had struck up a friendship, which had almost turned into something more.

As Guin stared out the window she thought again about the kiss they had shared. They had both had a bit too much to drink, and Guin had been heartbroken at the time, her on-again, off-again relationship with Detective William O'Loughlin being off just then. Or so she had thought. But that relationship was permanently off now, the detective having moved to Boston and made it clear he wasn't interested in having her join him or in a long-distance relationship.

But was she ready for a new relationship with Glen? She quickly glanced his way. She couldn't deny he was attractive. And sweet. And kind. And had been there for her when things had been rough. And it was easy being around him.

But they worked together and were friends. And she didn't want to mess that up. Especially when she wasn't entirely over the detective.

"A euro for your thoughts."

"Hm?" said Guin.

"You've been very quiet."

"Just admiring the scenery. It really does look like the photos you see on Instagram."

"Wait until you see the hotel."

"I saw it online."

"Not the same. The pictures don't do it justice."

"Probably because you didn't take them," said Guin.

She smiled at him, and he smiled back at her.

"Oops, almost drove right past it," he said, making a sharp right turn.

"I didn't see a sign," said Guin, looking at the dusty, nondescript gravel driveway.

"There's a small one, but it's hard to see from the direction we came."

"Then they should put up a bigger one."

"You can tell them that when you check in."

Guin gazed out the window again. The driveway was lined on both sides with cypress trees, which looked a bit like sentinels. A few seconds later, they pulled up outside of a large stone building with a terracotta roof. It looked old, like it had been there for hundreds of years. Which it had, according to the history of the hotel Guin had read online. But the place had been fully renovated and updated over the last three years, going from a crumbling estate to a modern boutique hotel, a true Cinderella story. Or however you said *Cinderella* in Italian.

"Welcome to l'Albergo Dell'Incanto," said Glen.

"It's lovely," said Guin.

"So, shall we go check you in?" (Glen had arrived the day before.)

Guin nodded, and Glen went to retrieve her suitcase out of the convertible's tiny trunk.

He had just wrestled it out when a young man came dashing out of the building.

"Please, Signore, allow me."

"It's okay, Matteo, I got it."

Matteo frowned.

Glen turned to Guin, who had been watching the exchange.

"Guin, allow me to introduce you to Matteo. Matteo here is the hotel's valet, bellhop, and Guy Friday. And he takes his job very seriously."

Matteo gave Guin a little bow.

"*Piacere, Signora.*"

"Nice to meet you, too, Matteo. But Glen and I can handle my things."

Guin had been studying Italian online, though she hadn't gotten very far. Mostly just memorizing the words for *please* and *thank you* along with some basic phrases and directions. Fortunately, the cooking course was taught in English. Still, Guin always tried to learn a bit of the language wherever she went. And she knew that *piacere* meant nice to meet you, or a pleasure.

"*Bene.* If you would follow me, I will help you check in."

"*Grazie,*" said Guin. Then she and Glen followed him inside.

As they made their way, Guin took in the stone walls, tile floors, and artwork. The lobby, or whatever the area was called in Italian, had a warm, understated elegance to it.

"Didn't I tell you?" said Glen.

"You were right. The pictures don't do the place justice."

"Wait until you see the rest of it."

Matteo stopped in front of a large antique-looking wood desk. Seated behind it, staring at a very modern-looking laptop computer, was a woman Guin guessed was somewhere in her fifties judging by the streaks of silver in her otherwise black hair, which was pulled into a bun at the nape of her neck. At their approach, the woman looked up.

"This is Signora Lombardi, the manager," said Matteo. "She will check you in."

"Please, call me Rosa," said Signora Lombardi. "Welcome to l'Albergo Dell'Incanto. You must be Ms. Jones."

"I am," said Guin. "How did you know?"

"Signora Lombardi knows everything," said Matteo in a low conspiratorial tone. "Some say she is a witch."

Rosa spoke to him in Italian, no doubt chastising him. But Matteo continued to smile. Clearly, this wasn't the first time they had had this exchange.

Rosa turned back to Guin.

"It is my job to know all of our guests, and you are the last to check in."

"Ah," said Guin.

Rosa then asked Guin for her passport and a credit card and said she would be right back.

As she waited, Guin walked around the reception area, taking a closer look at the furniture and artwork.

"They did a good job renovating this place," she said to Glen. "It feels old yet new."

He nodded.

Rosa returned a minute later, handing Guin back her passport and credit card.

"You are in La Lavanda."

"La Lavanda?"

"The Lavender Suite."

"All of their suites are named after flowers, vegetables, or herbs that are grown in their garden," Glen explained.

"Sì," said Rosa.

Guin had known that from reading about the hotel online, but she had forgotten.

"Here is your key," said Rosa. "Matteo can take your bags and show you the way."

Matteo reached for Guin's bags.

"I can take them," said Glen.

"Let Matteo," Guin said gently.

"*Grazie, Signora.*"

"It's actually *signorina*," she said. Though she smiled as she said it, to let him know he hadn't done anything wrong.

Matteo lifted the handles of Guin's suitcase and carry-on bag and began to head off.

"If you need anything," said Rosa, "just call the front desk."

"Thank you," said Guin. Then she and Glen followed Matteo outside.

The Lavender Suite was located in a building a short distance from the main one and looked very similar. As Matteo explained, there were four suites there and an additional four suites in a building on the other side of the building they had just been in.

He stopped in front of a door with a plaque decorated with a sprig of lavender and the words *La Lavanda*.

"I'm in La Salvia, the Sage Suite, just there," said Glen pointing to the door across the way. "So if you need anything, just knock."

"Good to know," said Guin.

Matteo then opened the door to Guin's room and turned on the main light.

Guin stepped inside and took in the small but charming living area. The walls were made of the same stone as the main building and were hung with photographs of lavender fields. There was a comfy-looking love seat with a coffee table; a wooden desk and a chair, where she would set up her laptop; and a couple of armchairs. There was also a big window on one side and an antique-looking mirror on the other, filling the room with light.

"I love it! It's perfect."

Matteo smiled.

"And through here is the bedroom."

Guin stopped and stared at the sight of the enormous four-poster bed.

"That bed is huge!"

"I have one just like it in my room," said Glen. She hadn't realized he was right behind her and felt her face grow warm.

"It is okay to put your suitcase here?" said Matteo, gesturing to a luggage stand positioned at the foot of the bed.

"Yes, fine," said Guin.

He hefted her suitcase onto the stand. Then he walked over to a door.

"This is your bathroom," he said, turning on the light.

Guin went to look and was not disappointed. In addition to a shower and toilet, there was a claw-foot tub and a large marble-topped vanity.

"Signorina Jones?"

It was Matteo.

"Hm?" she said, turning to look at him. She had been imagining soaking in the claw-foot tub.

"Is everything to your liking?"

"Yes, very much."

"*Bene.* Then I go now."

Guin walked him to the door and reached into her bag to give him a tip, but he stopped her.

"*Non è necessario.*"

Guin knew enough Italian to know he was refusing her offer of a tip.

"But…"

"Please. It is my pleasure to serve you. The hotel takes good care of us. Enjoy your stay. And let me know if you need anything."

"Okay," said Guin. "*Grazie.*"

"*Prego.*"

Matteo left, and Guin turned to Glen.

"Wow. Can you imagine someone in the States turning down a tip?"

Glen smiled.

"Welcome to Italy."

Guin glanced around the room again, taking it in. Then she looked up at Glen.

"You don't need to stay."

"I just wanted to make sure you were good."

"I'm good, though…" she said looking around again. "I don't recall seeing a closet."

"That's what that big armoire in the bedroom is for."

"Ah. I guess I was too busy looking at the bed to notice."

She saw Glen looking at her and felt her face start to grow warm again.

"I should unpack."

"Okay. I have a meeting with Bridget, but I'd be happy to give you the guided tour afterward. The meeting shouldn't take long."

"What are you meeting with her about?"

"I told her I would help her with her new website, take some photos of her and the class."

"That's very nice of you. Is she paying you?"

"In a matter of speaking."

"What does that mean?"

"I told her I would do it in exchange for comping you the class."

"What?!" Guin had had no idea.

"Don't be mad. It's really no big deal."

"It is a big deal, to me. Do you know how much this class cost?"

Though obviously he did.

"Bridget is a friend. And you are my friend. And there's nothing wrong with helping friends." Guin was on the verge of saying something, but Glen stopped her. "And you can always help Bridget with the web copy."

Guin was going to say something snarky but changed her mind.

"Fine. I'd be happy to."

"I'll let Bridget know. We'll be in the kitchen. Come find us when you're ready."

CHAPTER 2

It didn't take Guin long to unpack, but she wasn't ready to meet Bridget. While deciding what to do, she checked her phone, which she hadn't done since Glen had picked her up at the airport in Pisa.

There was nothing urgent or requiring her immediate attention, it still being early morning back in the States. Though her brother Lance, who was vacationing in the South of France, had sent her a message asking if she had made it to Chianti. She messaged him back, saying she had and was at the hotel. Then she wrote to her mother and her best friend Shelly, letting them know she had safely arrived, and sent an email to Sadie, her neighbor on Sanibel who was taking care of her cat, asking if everything was okay.

Guin hadn't heard from Sadie in a few days and was trying not to worry. Sadie was older and not very tech-savvy, though her husband Sam loved nothing better than to sit in front of the computer, surfing the internet and watching the surveillance footage from the cameras they had mounted on both sides of their house. Maybe she should write to him instead.

She put her phone down and gazed out the window. She had been in a car or a plane since early morning and wanted to stretch her legs. But she had told Glen she would go find him and Bridget, so a walk would have to wait.

She stepped outside, breathing in the warm Tuscan air.

(It was much warmer here than it had been in Bath, where she had spent the last week, celebrating her step-aunt's birthday with her family.) Then she looked around. She had no idea where the kitchen was. Though it was likely somewhere in the main building. So she headed that way.

She arrived at reception to find Rosa still seated at her desk.

"Can I help you?" she asked Guin.

"Where would I find the kitchen?"

Rosa was about to reply when an angry-looking man came storming over.

"The internet isn't working again."

"I am sorry to hear that, Signore Oliveira. It appears to be fine here."

"Well, it's not working in my room."

"Again, my apologies. But as I informed you and Signora van Leyden when you checked in, the Wi-Fi does not always work so well in the guest rooms. But we have a good connection here, and you are welcome to use the computer reserved for guests," she said.

Signore Oliveira frowned.

"I prefer to work on my own computer."

"You are welcome to bring it here."

That did not seem to make him any less annoyed.

"How can you expect guests to stay here when you don't provide reliable Wi-Fi?"

Guin watched the exchange, marveling at how Rosa maintained her cool.

"Many of our guests come here to turn off the outside world," Rosa began. But Signore Oliveira cut her off.

"Well, some of us have to work and need Wi-Fi. Reliable Wi-Fi," he huffed as he saw Rosa about to object.

"I will have Matteo take a look," said Rosa.

"Do that," he snapped. "I have a very important business deal I'm negotiating for Signora van Leyden and need to have internet access."

Before Rosa could say anything, Signore Oliveira turned and left.

"Wow," said Guin, watching Signore Oliveira storm off. Then she turned back to Rosa. "Is the Wi-Fi in the rooms that bad? I didn't notice."

Rosa sighed.

"The walls are quite thick, so it is difficult to get a strong signal. But we let guests know that on the website. And we have a computer they can use here in reception that is directly connected to the internet."

"Good to know," said Guin, who had missed that tidbit. Hopefully, it wouldn't be a problem. "So that man, Signore Oliveira, is he here for the cooking class?"

Rosa nodded.

"And is Signora van Leyden his wife?"

The name *van Leyden* sounded vaguely familiar, but Guin couldn't place it.

"No, Signora van Leyden is his boss."

"His boss?"

"Maybe that is not the right word." Rosa looked thoughtful. "Signora van Leyden writes cookbooks, and Signore Oliveira works for her. He is her agent."

Now Guin knew how come she recognized the name.

"Wait. Vera van Leyden, the cookbook author, is staying here? Is she taking the cooking class?"

"*Sì,*" said Rosa.

"But why would she need to take a cooking class?" Guin said, more to herself than to Rosa.

"I believe she is here doing research."

"So she's writing a cookbook on Tuscan cuisine?"

Vera was known for publishing cookbooks on different regional cuisines. She had risen to fame after publishing a cookbook of Polish recipes she claimed had been passed down from one generation to the next in her family. Then she had gone on to publish cookbooks on Bavarian,

Scottish, and Provençal cuisine and had become a bit of a food celebrity, appearing on the morning talk shows and the Food Network. Though Guin didn't recall seeing her on TV recently.

"She did not say, but…"

That reminded Guin. "Speaking of food, where would I find the kitchen? I told Glen I would meet him and Bridget there."

"It is on the other side of the dining room, down that hallway," Rosa said, pointing.

"*Grazie.*"

Guin stopped in the hallway to glance out the window. There was a garden outside. And although she knew Glen and Bridget were probably waiting for her, she figured there was no harm in taking a quick look at the garden.

She searched for a door and found one nearby. Then she walked over to the garden. It was filled with colorful vegetables, herbs, and flowers.

She knelt to smell some basil, closing her eyes as she breathed in the fragrance.

"All you need are some tomatoes and mozzarella."

Guin opened her eyes and turned to see a man in his mid- or late sixties smiling down at her. He looked dressed to play golf, though the hotel didn't have a golf course.

"I'm John… Adams. Like the president. You a guest?"

"I am," said Guin, getting up. "Guinivere Jones."

"Guinivere, eh? Like that queen in King Arthur."

Guin smiled politely. She frequently got that response.

"Yes, though I go by Guin to avoid the confusion."

"Ha!" he said. "Well, nice to meet you, Guin. So, you here to attend the cooking class?"

"I am. And you?"

"Yup, here with my wife."

Guin glanced around but didn't see anyone.

"She went into town to do a little shopping."

"Ah."

"But you'll meet her at the dinner tonight."

Guin was about to say something when she saw Glen walking towards her.

"There you are!" he said. "I was starting to get worried."

"Sorry, I was on my way to the kitchen when I saw the garden. Then I ran across Mr. Adams."

"John, please."

Guin smiled at him.

"So I take it you two know each other," John said.

"Yes, Glen and I work together."

"Ah, yes. He did mention a colleague was coming. I was telling Glen here that the wife and I used to vacation on Captiva when the kids were little. Have some fond memories of the islands."

"Captiva is a great place," said Guin. "So where are you and Mrs. Adams from?"

"Boston."

Guin tensed. The detective was from Boston. Though Boston was a big place. And she doubted John Adams knew him.

"John's a lawyer," said Glen. "And his wife Julia's a doctor."

"Though we're both retired now."

"And is this your first cooking class?" Guin asked him.

"Oh, no. This is actually our third one. The first time we went to Ireland. Then last year we went to France. And next year we're thinking of doing one in Asia."

"Wow!" said Guin. "I'm impressed."

"Don't be. We're still not very good cooks. We just enjoy eating and getting to visit different places. What about you?"

"I took a cooking class years ago, back when I lived in New York. But I haven't taken one since."

Glen touched Guin's arm.

"We should go. Bridget's waiting."

"Of course," said Guin. She turned to John Adams. "It was nice meeting you, Mr. Adams."

"John," he corrected.

"John," Guin repeated.

"See you at dinner!" he called as they walked away. "Julia and I will save you two seats!"

They entered the kitchen and Guin immediately recognized Bridget from the pictures she had seen of her online. She was speaking with a young man and a young woman, probably her helpers. They waited for her to finish. Then, when the young people had left, she and Glen went over to her.

"You must be Guin!" Bridget said, smiling down at her. (She stood a good head taller than Guin.)

"That's me," said Guin. "And you must be Bridget."

Guin didn't realize how tall Bridget was until she stood in front of her. While Guin was on the petite side, Bridget had to be at least five-nine. And she had a mass of thick red hair piled atop her head, making her even taller.

"That I am," said Bridget. "Welcome! Delighted you could join us."

"Glen wouldn't take no for an answer."

Bridget grinned.

"He can be quite stubborn and persuasive when he wants something."

She looked over at her friend, continuing to grin.

"Yes, well," said Guin, not sure what to say. She looked around. "I love your kitchen."

"It's not technically mine, but I love it too. And it's saved Dante having to build me a new one. For now," she added with a twinkle.

"Dante?" said Guin.

"Bridget's husband," Glen explained. "He owns a restaurant in town."

"Actually, he owns two now," said Bridget.

Right. Guin knew about Dante from her reading.

"So, Glen said you're redoing your website."

"That's right. And he promised to take lots of photos while he's here."

"And he said you could use some help with the copy."

Bridget nodded.

"I'm not much of a writer. Numbers were always my thing. And cooking."

"Well, I'd be happy to help."

"Bless you," said Bridget. "So, do you enjoy cooking?"

Guin thought for a moment. Did she enjoy cooking? Sometimes. She enjoyed making food for others.

"I like eating," she said.

Bridget smiled.

"I don't *dislike* cooking," Guin continued. "I just find it hard cooking for one. And my knife skills could use some work. It takes me forever to cut up stuff."

"I was the same way," said Bridget. "But after the course, you and Glen will be able to chop with the best of them. And you can cook for each other," she added with a grin.

"Do most of the people you teach know how to cook, at least a little bit?" Guin asked, ignoring Bridget's innuendo.

"Most of them. Though some of them know little more than how to boil a pot of pasta and heat up a jar of sauce when they get here. But by the time I'm done with them, they can make a four-course Tuscan meal."

"Wow. You must be good."

"I'd like to think so."

"So, do you ever get serious cooks or professionals?"

"Occasionally. Typically they're curious about Tuscan cuisine."

"And you do all of this on your own?"

"Goodness, no. I'd be lost without Leo and Francesca. Leo's my sous chef, and Francesca's our assistant. She works at the hotel, but when we run the course, she helps us out."

"Still, it must be a lot of work teaching a cooking course."

"It is, but I enjoy it. And speaking of work, I need to start prepping for dinner."

"So soon?" said Guin. It was just one o'clock.

"I'm afraid so."

"We'll get out of your hair then," said Glen. "Dinner's at eight?"

"It is. With cocktails and nibbles at seven."

Just then Guin's stomach let out a low rumble. All this talk of food had made her hungry.

"Have you two had lunch?" Bridget asked them.

"I haven't eaten since last night," said Guin. No wonder she was hungry. All she had had that morning was a mug of coffee before heading to the airport.

"I'd offer to make you something but…"

"Please," said Guin. "Don't worry about us. I know you need to start preparing for dinner."

"You like pizza?" asked Bridget.

"Is that a trick question?"

Bridget smiled.

"There's a good place in town, La Cantina. They make the best pizza around here. You should go there for lunch."

Guin and Glen exchanged a look.

"Sounds good to me," said Guin. "Though I'd like to interview you at some point for my article—and for the website."

"Happy to chat when I'm free," said Bridget. Guin's stomach let out another low growl. "Now get the woman some pizza before she passes out from hunger," Bridget told Glen.

CHAPTER 3

"Well?" said Glen.

"Well, what?"

"What did you think?"

"About?"

"About Bridget."

"She seems great. I can see why you two got along. She has a very earthy quality to her."

Glen smiled.

"She does. Though don't let that smile of hers fool you. She can be cutthroat."

"Really?"

Glen nodded.

"I think half the traders on the floor were afraid of her. Just don't cross her and you'll be fine."

"Huh," said Guin. "I'll keep that in mind. So, she and Dante... I know they met when she came here on vacation and then wound up getting married. Do they have kids?"

"No, though Dante has two children from his previous marriage."

"Do they get along?"

"You'll have to ask Bridget."

They were nearly at the car park.

"Hey, I never got the guided tour."

"I'll show you around after we get back from lunch."

"Oh my God. This pizza is so good!" said Guin, polishing off a second slice.

"It's not bad," said Glen, taking a sip of his beer.

"Not bad? Are you kidding me? Compared to Sanibel…"

"Well, compared to Sanibel, it's amazing. But I prefer a good New York slice."

Guin stared at him.

"You can't compare the two. New York pizza is… New York pizza. But this, this is the real deal."

"New York pizza is the real deal. And who do you think brought pizza to New York? People from Italy."

"I'm not going to argue with you about pizza. Just admit that this pizza is pretty good."

"Fine. It's pretty good."

Guin shook her head, then looked at Glen's plate. Despite the pizza being only "pretty good," he had eaten most of his pie.

"Had to choke it down, eh?"

"Didn't want to insult the chef."

"Uh-huh."

She reached for another slice but stopped herself.

"Something wrong?"

"I've already had nearly half a pie."

"A very small pie. Have another slice. You said you hadn't eaten since yesterday. Indulge."

He had a point.

"Okay," she said, placing another slice on her plate. She cut off a piece and began to chew. "I could live on pizza," she said, her mouth half full.

"Just save room for dessert."

She swallowed.

"Dessert?"

"There's a gelato place I want to check out."

"Now you tell me!"

Guin looked down at her pizza.

"Can we get the rest to go?"

Glen signaled to their server and asked for a to-go box and the check. The server returned a minute later, placing the box in front of Guin and handing Glen the bill.

"How much do I owe?" Guin asked.

"Nothing. It's on me."

"You don't have to pay for me."

"I know. I want to. Besides, it's just pizza."

"Fine. Then I'm paying for the gelato."

"Do you have euros?"

Guin frowned.

"No, I didn't have time to get any. Is there a bank around here?"

"There's one by the gelato place."

"How convenient."

Glen paid and they took the pizza box with them.

"So where is this gelato place?"

"Just a few blocks away. We can put the pizza in the car and then walk over there."

Guin stared at the cases full of gelato. How did one choose? They all looked so good.

"You can always get more than one flavor," said Glen, reading her mind.

"I may have to."

There was a family in front of them, and Guin watched as they were handed their gelati. Then it was their turn.

Glen ordered a small cup of *cioccolato* (chocolate) and *noce di cocco* (coconut), and after some debate, Guin ordered a small cup of *pistacchio* and *bacio* (dark chocolate with hazelnut).

They went outside and Guin took a bite of her gelati.

"Mm…"

"You like it?"

"What's not to like? Though I wonder if I should have gotten the strawberry. It looked really good. As did the tiramisu."

"We'll just have to come back another day and try them."

"Hm," said Guin, taking another bite. "If I keep eating this way, I'll need to go on a diet when we get back."

He looked at her.

"What is it with women and diets? You look great, and we're on vacation. It's okay to indulge yourself. It's just gelato."

"Gelato still has calories."

"That's barely anything," he said, looking at her small cup. "Just enjoy yourself."

They walked around Greve as they ate, passing a small park where children were playing.

"You ever regret not having kids?" Guin asked him.

"No. Why? Do you?"

"A bit. Art and I tried for years. But it just didn't happen for us."

"You ever think about adopting?"

"We did. But by the time we got to thinking about it, we were both so busy with work we didn't think it would be fair."

"There's Dante's place," said Glen a few minutes later, pointing at a stone building.

"I'm looking forward to going there," said Guin. "Though I'm not sure I can eat that much meat." Dante's was famous for its all-meat, multi-course lunches and dinners.

"I know, but the courses are pretty small."

They continued walking until they arrived back at Glen's car. He opened the door for Guin, then he got in and drove them back to the hotel.

"So, would you like the guided tour?" he asked her after he had parked.

"Sure. Lead the way."

They started in the lobby. Glen recited the history of the hotel, describing the renovation.

"Did you memorize that from the website?" Guin asked him teasingly.

"Maybe."

Guin smiled.

"And this is the dining room," he continued. "There's also an outdoor dining terrace where we have breakfast and dinner if it's nice out."

"Sounds great."

"It is," said Glen. "And you can see the sunset from there." He turned to face her. "As you've already seen the kitchen and the garden, shall we head down to the pool?"

"Sure."

He led Guin down a path that led to a lower level where there was a rectangular pool surrounded by lounge chairs and canvas tent-like cabanas. Guin thought it looked straight out of a travel magazine.

"Wow," she said. "I could spend all day here."

The pool wasn't large, but it was perfect for doing short laps. And the view... Everywhere you looked there were rolling hills dotted with limestone villas, gardens, and lush greenery. And speaking of lush...

"Who's he?" asked Guin, eyeing a man who looked like a model from one of those old Bain de Soleil ads.

The man had clearly been in the pool a few minutes before, and the water was beading off of his tanned and toned chest. He was dressed in a black Speedo or the Italian equivalent, and his hair, which looked to be dark and wavy, was slicked back. He was wearing sunglasses, but Guin guessed he was in his thirties.

"That's Domenico Conti," said Glen. "His family owns a number of boutique hotels."

"Do they own this one?"

"Not yet."

"Are they thinking of buying it?"

Glen shrugged.

"So why is he here?"

"Supposedly to take the cooking class."

Guin found that hard to believe but didn't say anything.

"And what about her?"

Lying on a chaise next to Domenico was a woman who was his visual opposite, her skin the color of cream and her hair a rich blonde. (Guin wondered if it was natural or dyed.) She was wearing a one-piece bathing suit that showed off her curves. Guin couldn't see the woman's face as she was wearing a large straw hat and sunglasses, but she guessed that she was a beauty.

"That's Beatrice Krueger," said Glen. He pronounced it *BAY-ah-TREE-chay*. "She's a widow."

"Isn't she a bit young to be a widow?"

"Her husband Klaus was quite a bit older. He was a German industrialist."

"So she's German?"

"No, Italian."

"She doesn't look Italian."

"Northern Italians can be quite fair."

"And are they together?"

"I don't think so. I think they're just friends."

"Huh," said Guin.

"Would you like me to introduce you?"

Guin hesitated.

"I'll probably see them at dinner."

"Okay," he said. "So, you interested in going for a swim?"

"Now?"

"Unless you had something else planned."

She didn't. But she was suddenly feeling self-conscious.

"Come on. You can work off that gelato you were so worried about."

"Fine," said Guin. "Let's go get changed."

Guin looked at her bathing suit and wished she had brought a different one. Not that there was anything wrong with her swimsuit. It was just that after seeing Beatrice in hers, she wished she had brought something a little… sexier. Though she immediately chastised herself. This swimsuit was perfectly fine and functional, and that was all that really mattered.

She grabbed a towel from the bathroom and wrapped it around her waist. Then she took her card key and her phone and left. She didn't see Glen, so she knocked on his door. He emerged a few seconds later dressed in a pair of board shorts and a t-shirt.

"You ready?" he asked her.

"As ready as I'll ever be."

They walked down to the pool, Guin privately hoping Domenico and Beatrice wouldn't be there. As luck would have it, they weren't.

Guin placed her towel on a chair and dipped her toe in the pool. The water was cold.

"It feels warm after you get in."

"Is that so?"

"You don't believe me? Come on, we can jump in together."

Guin examined the pool. It didn't look very deep.

"It's perfectly safe," Glen reassured her.

He went around to the deep end and jumped in, emerging a few seconds later.

"It feels warmer already."

Guin looked skeptical.

"Come on. Don't be a chicken."

"I'm not a chicken," she said, taking another step into

the pool and shivering as the water reached her knees.

"You'll never warm up that way."

Guin gritted her teeth and went down another step.

Glen swam toward her.

"Come on," he said, holding out a hand.

Guin shook her head, but Glen didn't stop moving. Now he was standing directly in front of her, water streaming off of his chest. Guin tried not to stare.

The next thing Guin knew, he had picked her up and was moving toward the deep end.

"Stop!" she squealed. "What are you doing?"

"Getting you used to the water."

"Put me down this instant, Glen Anderson!"

"If you say so," he said.

Guin's eyes went wide as Glen let go of her. She felt the water closing around her and began to panic. It was cold. Then she began to swim, and the water suddenly felt a little warmer. She swam to the other end of the pool and poked her head out, glaring at Glen who was waiting for her.

"That was a dirty trick."

But he didn't seem the least bit sorry.

"But I was right, wasn't I?"

Guin scowled. She wouldn't give him the satisfaction.

"I'm going to swim a few laps."

"Be my guest."

Guin closed her eyes and plunged back into the water, all of her tension melting away as she swam.

CHAPTER 4

Guin showered as soon as she got back to her room. There was a blow-dryer in the bathroom, but she didn't use it, preferring to let her curly hair dry naturally. Though she applied a generous amount of styling gel to ensure it didn't frizz.

That done, she went into the armoire to choose a dress for dinner. Attire was supposedly casual, but she got the sense that this wasn't a jeans-and-a-t-shirt kind of place. She had brought a few dresses with her from Sanibel, but she couldn't decide which one to wear. Finally, she selected her blue maxi dress, the one that matched her eyes.

She put it on and looked at herself in the mirror. Every time she looked at her face, it seemed she had acquired more freckles. The perils of having fair skin and living in Florida. Though she always made sure to wear sunblock. Still, a little foundation wouldn't hurt.

She applied makeup and took another look at herself. Maybe she should blow-dry her hair, so she didn't look like a wet poodle. She was about to reach for the blow-dryer when she heard a knock on the door. Though it could have been someone knocking on the room next door. Then she heard it again.

She walked to her door and opened it to find Glen standing there. He looked quite dapper in a blue button-down shirt and a pair of chinos. He eyed her and smiled.

"You look beautiful. Is that a new dress?"

"No. I've had it for a while."

"Well, it looks good on you."

"Thanks. Are you early?"

"I said I'd get you around seven."

"What time is it?"

"A little after."

Guin frowned. She hadn't realized.

"Can you give me a minute?"

"Of course."

She went into the bathroom and picked up the blow-dryer. Then she put it back. She would go just as she was.

She picked up her bag, placing her card key inside.

"Let's go," she told Glen.

It had cooled off a bit since the afternoon, and Guin wondered if she should have brought a sweater.

"Is everything all right?" Glen asked her.

"I was just wondering if I should go back and get a sweater."

"You'll be fine," said Glen.

Easy for him to say.

He led them down to the pool where cocktails were being served. It was a beautiful evening, with the sky growing pale and the clouds turning cotton-candy pink, and a beautiful setting.

"It's so beautiful and peaceful here," she murmured.

"Glad you came?"

She nodded.

They walked down the steps and spied Francesca offering guests hors d'oeuvres.

"*Buona sera*," said Matteo, coming over to them. "May I get you a drink?"

"Could we get two Aperol spritzes?" said Glen.

"*Certo!*" said Matteo.

"What's an Aperol spritz?" Guin asked Glen after Matteo left to get their drinks.

"It's a local cocktail made with prosecco, Aperol, which is a kind of bitter, and club soda or seltzer."

"Sounds refreshing."

"It is."

Matteo returned with their drinks then excused himself.

"To Italy," said Glen, raising his glass.

"To Italy," said Guin.

They clinked glasses and Guin took a sip of her drink.

"It's a little bitter, but I like it."

Glen smiled.

"Glen!"

They turned to see Mr. and Mrs. Adams coming towards them. Glen made introductions.

"Nice to meet you, Guin," said Julia Adams. "Glen told us you're here to write about the cooking class."

"That's right."

"And that you live on Sanibel."

She nodded.

"We used to stay on Captiva," said Julia, "and would visit Sanibel. Though it's been years now."

"You should come back."

"I'd like to."

"So, how was shopping?"

Julia looked confused.

"John said you had gone into town to shop when I saw him earlier."

Julia glanced at her husband then back at Guin.

"It was fine. Do you like shoes?"

"What woman doesn't?"

Julia smiled at her.

"Well, there's this marvelous little place in Panzano, the next town over, where they custom-make shoes. I had read about it before we came here and had to go check it out."

"She wound up buying two pairs," said John.

Julia gave her husband a look.

"What kind?" asked Guin.

"A pair of driving loafers and a pair of sandals. I couldn't resist. They're shipping them to me."

"How long does it take?"

"He said a few weeks. This is their busy season. But once they have your measurements, they can make more shoes without you having to be there."

"Are the shoes expensive?" asked Guin.

"Considering they're custom? I don't think so."

John coughed, and his wife gave him another look.

"It's my money, and if I want to spend it on shoes..."

John held up his hands in surrender, then he turned to Guin.

"So is it true you helped solve a couple of murders?"

Guin turned and shot a look at Glen.

"It's true."

"So you're a crime reporter?" said Julia.

"I'm technically a general assignment reporter. But I also cover crime."

"I didn't think Sanibel had a lot of crime," said Julia.

"It doesn't. Or didn't," said Guin.

"Not until Guin moved there," Glen said.

Guin shot him another dirty look.

"Well, hopefully, there won't be any crimes to investigate here," said John.

"I'll drink to that," said Glen.

Just then Guin spied Signore Oliveira, the man who had complained about the hotel's Wi-Fi. He was with a woman who looked vaguely familiar.

"Is that Vera van Leyden, the cookbook author?" said Guin.

"It is," said Julia.

Was it Guin's imagination or was Julia glaring at the woman?

"Do you know her?" Guin asked.

Guin saw a look pass between the Adamses.

"We've met," said Julia.

Guin was going to ask her about that, but her attention was diverted by Domenico and Beatrice entering. They both looked quite glamorous. Beatrice was dressed in a diaphanous dress, her golden hair falling in waves down to her shoulders. And Domenico was dressed in form-fitting black jeans, a button-down shirt, and a jacket.

Just to their right was Rosa. She was talking to an elegant-looking man with a full head of silver hair and a beard. He was dressed in a suit and his skin was tanned. He reminded Guin of the man from the Dos Equis ads, "the most interesting man in the world."

"Who's that?" Guin asked, continuing to look at the man.

"That's Giovanni Cassini," said John. "He heads up the investment group that owns the hotel."

"Ah. Do you know what he's doing here?"

She saw Domenico and Beatrice go over to Signore Cassini. They were all smiling.

"He's probably here to greet everyone," said John. "Or perhaps Signore Conti will try to get him to sell."

Guin watched as Signore Cassini chatted with Domenico then shook his head and excused himself, going over to Vera van Leyden and Signore Oliveira. Finally, he came over to their little group.

"I am Giovanni Cassini, the owner," he said. "Thank you for staying at our little hotel."

"Our pleasure," said Julia, clearly taken with the handsome Italian.

Signore Cassini smiled at her, and Guin heard John clear his throat.

"Nice place you have here."

Signore Cassini turned to look at him, that practiced smile still on his face.

"*Grazie*. We put a lot of love into it."

"And a lot of money too, no doubt."

"*Sì*," he replied. "To renovate a beautiful place like this requires much time and patience—and money."

"Well, you did a wonderful job," said Julia.

He smiled at her again.

"Thank you." Then he turned to Guin, taking her hand. "And you are?"

"Guinivere Jones."

"Guinivere," he said, pronouncing it with an Italian accent. "It is a beautiful name for a beautiful woman." He was giving her a flirtatious smile, and Guin felt herself blushing. "And you are here to cook?"

"*Sì*," she replied. "I'm writing about the course for my paper."

"I hope you will give us a good write-up."

"I'm sure she will," said John, a bit snidely. Julia shot him a look.

"I am sorry, I did not catch your name," said Signore Cassini.

"John Adams," he said. "And this is my wife, Julia."

"A pleasure," said Signore Cassini, taking Julia's hand and kissing it.

John frowned as Julia let out a small sigh.

"And I'm Glen," said Glen. "Bridget's an old friend of mine."

"Is that so?" said Signore Cassini.

Guin saw the two men eyeing each other, like two bulls.

"Glen and Bridget worked together on Wall Street," she informed Signore Cassini. "But he left his job in finance and is a photographer now, a very good one. He's photographing the class for our paper."

Signore Cassini looked amused.

"You left finance to become a photographer? You must have done well." Glen didn't respond. And Signore Cassini turned to the rest of the group. "Well, welcome to l'Albergo Dell'Incanto. I hope you all will enjoy the hotel and the cooking course."

"I'm sure we will," said Guin.

"Ah, there's Bridget," said Glen, spying their instructor.

They looked over and saw Bridget coming down the stairs.

"If you will excuse me?" said Signore Cassini.

Guin watched as he went over to speak with Bridget. A few minutes later, they heard what sounded like someone tapping a spoon or a fork against a glass. It was Signore Cassini.

"If I may have your attention," he said. "I would like to welcome you all to l'Albergo Dell'Incanto and wish you a pleasant stay." He raised his glass. "*Alla vostra salute*! To your good health!"

Everyone raised their glasses and drank.

Dinner was being served at a single long table on the dining terrace. Guin was seated between John Adams and Signore Oliveira, whose first name was Oliver. Glen sat across from her, surrounded by Beatrice and Julia.

The terrace was lit by lanterns and candles, which cast a warm glow. And there were flowers arranged in ceramic vases along the low wall that hugged the terrace.

The Aperol spritz had gone a bit to Guin's head, and now she was drinking wine. She would need to pace herself if she didn't want to wind up with a headache.

The first course was a variety of bruschetta and charcuterie. It was followed by a wild mushroom risotto. Next came the main course, or secondo, which consisted of roasted wild boar and a medley of vegetables.

Guin wondered if any of the guests were vegetarians. Clearly not, glancing around.

After the dinner plates had been cleared away, a tri-color salad was served. Then came a platter filled with fruit and cheese.

Guin stared at it. She couldn't eat another bite, despite the previous courses not being particularly large.

"Leaving room for dessert?"

It was John.

"You mean this isn't dessert?"

He shook his head.

"This is just the cheese and fruit course."

Guin groaned, and Glen looked over at her.

"Everything okay?" he mouthed.

"Fine," Guin mouthed back.

He had spent most of the meal chatting with Beatrice. Or so it had seemed. Guin wondered what the two of them had talked about. She had heard Beatrice laugh a couple of times and didn't like the way she had looked at Glen.

She went to take a sip of her wine and realized her glass was empty.

A few minutes later, the cheese and fruit platters were taken away and dessert was served. Mercifully, it was just biscotti, or *cantucci* as they were referred to here. Guin asked for an espresso, hoping to counteract all the alcohol she had drunk. Then she reached for a *cantucci*.

Finally, dinner was over. She had been so intent on watching Glen and Beatrice, she hadn't realized Signore Oliveira had left. Though Vera was still there. She didn't look particularly happy. Maybe that was just the way she looked. Though she always seemed happy on those cooking segments she did. But perhaps that was just an act.

Guin turned to John and told him she was turning in for the night. Glen saw her get up and went over to her.

"You heading to your room?"

She nodded.

"I'll go with you."

"You don't have to."

"I know I don't have to. It's just been a long day, and I'm tired."

"You don't seem tired."

He looked at her.

"Is something wrong?"

"Nope."

They started to walk.

"So, what were you and Beatrice chatting about? You looked awfully chummy."

"Oh, this and that. Turns out, Beatrice knows my friend Bella's sister Bianca."

"Small world."

"Indeed."

"Anything else?"

"She asked me if I would photograph her."

"Oh? Would that be with or without clothes?"

"With." He was looking at her.

"What?"

Glen smiled.

"You're jealous."

"I am not." But she was.

"Then why do you care if Bea"—which he pronounced *BAY-ah*—"poses for me?"

"I don't. Go ahead and take her picture."

"You're giving me your permission?"

"You don't need my permission. Though I'm curious. Why does she want you to photograph her?"

"Because I'm a photographer?"

Guin scowled.

"She needs headshots for her new business."

"Her new business?"

All sorts of X-rated thoughts flashed through Guin's head.

"She's launching a marketing company."

"A marketing company?" That wasn't what Guin had expected.

Glen nodded.

"She wants to help market artists. She feels they're underserved, especially the new ones."

"Oh," said Guin. That actually sounded like an interesting business.

They had arrived back at their rooms. Guin yawned.

"I should get some sleep."

"Sweet dreams," said Glen. "You want me to get you up in the morning?"

"What time is breakfast?"

"It's served from eight until nine. Class starts at nine-thirty."

"I think I can manage. But thank you."

"Okay, so I guess I'll see you at breakfast then."

"See you at breakfast," said Guin.

CHAPTER 5

Guin slept poorly. No doubt it was due to all the alcohol she had drunk. Alcohol always affected her. Finally, at six-thirty, she gave up and got out of bed.

"May as well go for a walk."

She got out of bed and went into the bathroom, splashing cold water on her face. She checked the temperature on her phone. It was 70 degrees. Warm.

She got dressed and went outside. She took a few steps then stopped, realizing she had no idea where she was going. Of course, she could just go to the end of the driveway and start walking. She had her phone if she got lost. But she remembered something about there being walking trails. Maybe there was a map at the front desk?

She walked to the main building and headed to Rosa's desk. But there was no one there. Not a big surprise. It was barely seven. She went back outside, thinking she could find the trail on her own, and ran into Leo.

"*Buon giorno*," he said.

"*Buon giorno*," she replied. "Do you happen to know where the trails are?"

He looked confused.

"The walking trails?" Guin clarified.

"Ah, *sì, sì*. They are just over there," he said, pointing.

"*Grazie*," said Guin.

There were actually two trails. One led to a nearby

vineyard and the other led into town. The one to the
vineyard was shorter, so she decided to take that one.

She began to walk, breathing in the fresh Tuscan air and
admiring the scenery. She had lost track of time when she
noticed rows of grape vines up ahead. *This must be the start of
the vineyard.* She took out her phone to take a picture and saw
that it was nearly eight o'clock. If she didn't turn around
now, she would likely miss breakfast.

She turned and hurried back the way she had come,
practically jogging. As she neared the trailhead, she heard
voices and slowed down. It was a man and a woman, and it
sounded like they were arguing. Guin stood still and listened,
even though she knew it wasn't polite to eavesdrop.

"You owe me," said the woman.

Guin strained to hear better. The woman had definitely
spoken in English. But Guin couldn't tell if she had an
Italian accent or not. She didn't think so, but she couldn't be
sure.

"I said I would do it, and I will," snapped the man.

Again, Guin couldn't tell if the man had an accent or not.
But he was clearly annoyed.

"You better," said the woman.

Guin waited to hear more, but they had gone quiet. Had
they left? She counted to one hundred then emerged from
the trail. There was no one in sight. She took out her phone.
It was eight-forty. Still time for breakfast. Though what she
really craved was coffee.

She made her way to the dining terrace. Breakfast was
buffet-style. Guin looked around for coffee but didn't see
any. Though she saw John and Julia, who waved her over.

"Glen was looking for you," said Julia.

"Was he at breakfast?"

"Yes, you just missed him. He seemed worried."

Guin had thought about texting him but hadn't, figuring
she'd be back in time for breakfast.

"I'll let him know I'm okay."

Guin glanced around. There was no one else having breakfast.

"Has everyone eaten already?"

"I didn't see Domenico and Beatrice," said Julia. "But Vera and Oliver were here until a few minutes ago."

"Oh?"

Could that have been who I had heard arguing? Guin wondered. She looked down at the table.

"Where did you get coffee?"

"Just ask Francesca," said Julia.

As if being summoned, Francesca appeared.

"Excuse me," said Guin. "Could I get some coffee?"

"What kind would you like?" asked Francesca.

"I recommend the cappuccino," said Julia.

John nodded.

Guin usually drank her coffee black, but when in Rome—or Greve…

"I'll have a cappuccino."

Francesco nodded and went to get it.

"Would you care to join us?" said Julia.

"I thought you were done."

"We could always stay a few minutes if you'd like company."

"That's okay," said Guin. "I can grab the table over there. I'm fine eating alone."

"Are you sure?"

"Positive."

Guin sat and sent Glen a text. She was gazing at the countryside when Francesca brought over her cappuccino.

"Wow," she said as Francesca placed the bowl in front of her. "That's a lot of cappuccino."

Francesca smiled and asked if she could get Guin anything else.

"Nope, I'm good," Guin replied.

Francesca left, and Guin helped herself to some food.

She had just started to eat when she saw Glen.

"Did you get my message?"

"I did. Though next time you decide to go for an early morning walk, let me know. I was worried when I didn't see you at breakfast, and you didn't answer your phone or door."

"Sorry," she said. "I didn't realize I'd be gone that long. And I forgot my phone was on silent."

"So, where did you go?"

"To the vineyard."

"I've been meaning to go there."

"You can always go after class."

He continued to stand there.

"Would you like to join me?"

He took the seat opposite her.

"Did you want to get a coffee or something to eat?" Though she knew he had already had breakfast.

"Actually, I should get to class."

Guin glanced at her phone.

"I thought class didn't start until nine-thirty."

"It doesn't. But I told Bridget I'd get there early to take some photos."

"Of course. Well, don't let me keep you."

Glen looked a bit reluctant to leave, but Guin shooed him away.

"Go. I'll see you soon."

Guin returned to her room to brush her teeth. Then she headed to the kitchen.

She was right on time, yet only Glen and the Adamses were there.

"Where is everyone?" she asked them.

John and Julia shrugged.

A few seconds later, Beatrice breezed in.

Guin couldn't help noticing how lovely Beatrice looked. She was wearing a chiffon-looking sundress. It was very pretty but not exactly appropriate for a cooking class. Guin saw Beatrice smile at Glen and give him a little wave. He smiled back at her, and Guin felt her jaw tightening.

Domenico entered the kitchen a few seconds later, putting his phone away as he did. He was dressed in form-fitting jeans and a black t-shirt. Guin couldn't help staring at his arms. Then came Vera van Leyden. She looked annoyed. But Guin was starting to think that was how she usually looked.

"Will Mr. Oliveira be joining us?" Bridget asked her.

"He's attending to business."

Bridget waited for her to say more. When Vera didn't, Bridget turned and smiled at the class.

"Welcome to Cooking in Chianti! I'm so glad to have all of you here. I need to go over some kitchen basics, then we can dive into cooking."

At the conclusion of her safety talk, Bridget had Leo give everyone a white two-ring binder.

"The binders contain all of the recipes we will be making this week," Bridget explained. "Plus some additional recipes you can try for extra credit. Please bring them with you to each class. Or, if you prefer, we can hold onto them for you. Just be sure to put your names on them in case they get lost."

Guin immediately began flipping through her binder, as did several of the other students.

Bridget paused while everyone glanced at the recipes. Then she continued.

"Whether you have cooked a gourmet meal for twelve," she said, looking at Vera, "or only know how to make macaroni and cheese," she said, looking at Glen, "by the end of this week, everyone here will know how to make an authentic, four-course Tuscan meal.

"We will start by making antipasti, then cover *primi*, *secondi*, and *dolci*, the courses that make up an Italian meal. Though we may skip around as I like to mix things up. Along the way, I will teach you basic techniques.

"We will also go on several excursions, to visit a local producer of olive oil, a winery, and a cheesemaker. And I have arranged for us to have lunch at Dante's in town. Dante will also be here to teach you how to make several classic Tuscan meat dishes."

"Will we get to make *Bistecca alla Fiorentina*?" asked John. Bridget smiled at him.

"Perhaps. Okay, shall we begin?"

That morning, they made three different kinds of bruschetta and two pasta dishes, making the gnocchi and tagliatelle from scratch. By the time they finally broke for lunch, Guin was hungry and exhausted. Fortunately, there was plenty of food (they would eat what they made), and they didn't have to wait to eat it.

Bridget, Leo, and Francesca brought everything out to the dining terrace, along with some wine and mineral water. The food was served family style at the long table, with everyone helping themselves.

Glen took a seat next to Guin, and Beatrice seated herself on his other side. Domenico took a seat opposite them, and Vera sat beside him. Guin noticed John looking at the empty seat next to Vera and his wife gently shaking her head. Instead, they went and sat next to Domenico. Guin wondered if Vera was saving the seat for Oliver, who had yet to make an appearance.

"Aren't you going to join us?" Guin asked Bridget and Leo, seeing them standing a few feet away.

"We need to clean up and get things ready for this afternoon's lesson," said Bridget.

"But you need to eat," said Julia.

Bridget smiled at her.

"We'll grab something in the kitchen."

"What's this afternoon's lesson again?" asked John.

"*Dolce.*"

"Dessert," translated Julia. "I'm surprised you forgot."

"Oh, yes, wouldn't want to miss that," said John. "What time do we need to be back in the kitchen?"

"Not until three," said Bridget. "You have plenty of time. Now if you will excuse me?"

She left, and everyone dug into the food.

Oliver still hadn't appeared by the time they were nearly done.

"Is Mr. Oliveira all right?" Guin asked Vera.

"I'm sure he's fine."

"It's just, he wasn't in class, and he's missing lunch. Maybe you could bring him a little something?"

Vera frowned.

"Oliver's perfectly able to fend for himself."

Guin was taken aback by Vera's rude tone and said no more.

Finally, lunch was over. Guin wanted to go back to her room and type up her notes from class, but she didn't have much time. Still, something was better than nothing.

"Heading back to your room?" Glen asked.

"Yeah, I need to get down my thoughts on this morning's class. What about you? You must have photos to edit."

"I do, but I'll edit them later. I need to work off lunch."

"You going for a walk?"

He nodded.

Guin would have liked to have gone for a walk too, but duty called.

"Well, have a good walk. I'll see you in class."

"See you in class."

Guin was on her way to her room when she saw Beatrice intercept Glen. What did she want? She stood there for a few seconds watching them, then continued to her room, an unpleasant feeling in her stomach.

CHAPTER 6

As Guin approached her room, she saw Oliver. He was holding up his phone and frowning.

"Is everything all right?" she asked him.

"No. You can't get a damn signal in this place."

"We didn't see you in class this morning or at lunch."

"I've been busy. Some of us have to work."

Guin didn't know why he was snapping at her.

"There's probably left-over food in the kitchen if you're hungry. We made a ton of bruschetta and pasta this morning."

He looked at his phone again and frowned. Then he put it away.

"I could use some food. Where's her ladyship?"

"You mean Vera?"

He gave Guin a look that Guin interpreted to mean, *who else?*

"I saw her at lunch, but…"

But before she could finish, Oliver had removed his phone from his pocket.

"I need to take this."

"Will we see you in class this afternoon? We're making dessert."

He looked like he was thinking about it. Maybe he had a sweet tooth.

"What time?"

"Three o'clock."

Oliver turned away and pressed a button on his phone.

"Yes?" he said. He sounded exasperated. "I told you, I'm in Italy…"

Guin sighed and proceeded to her room.

Guin was so busy writing about the class that she didn't hear someone knocking on her door. Then she heard someone calling her name.

"Guin? Are you in there?"

It was Glen.

She glanced at the clock on her laptop. It was five after three. She was late for class.

She saved her document and hurried to the door. She opened it to find Glen looking concerned.

"Sorry, I lost track of the time."

She grabbed her things, and they headed to the kitchen.

Guin was relieved to see she wasn't the only one late to class, the Italians arriving just after her.

"Now that you're all here," said Bridget. "Let's begin. This afternoon, we are going to make two traditional Italian desserts: a *torta della nonna*, which is a traditional Italian custard tart flavored with lemon and topped with pine nuts, and a tiramisu.

"While I know the Italians in the room are familiar with *torta della nonna*," she said, looking over at Beatrice and Domenico, "the rest of you may not be. The direct translation of *torta della nonna* is *grandmother's cake*. Though every grandmother makes her torta a bit differently. But they all use butter, sugar, flour, eggs, and lemon zest.

"Today we are going to make *torta della nonna* using one of my favorite recipes, which was given to me by my husband Dante's mother, who got it from her mother. Then we will make a traditional tiramisu, which I am sure most of you are familiar with."

Guin could feel her mouth watering.

"Any questions?"

Guin glanced around the room. She had been surprised to see Oliver there. Guess he had finished whatever he was working on or had blown it off.

"No? Then let's begin," said Bridget. "We'll start by making a pastry crust. To do this, you will need to combine all-purpose flour, baking powder, sugar, salt, lemon zest, and unsalted butter…"

Once the dough for the crust had gone into the fridge, they made the pastry cream. Then while that chilled, they worked on the tiramisu.

Guin had never made tiramisu before, though she had eaten plenty. But the recipe looked pretty easy.

They whisked together egg yolks and sugar in a medium saucepan. Then they added milk and continued to whisk, cooking the mixture over medium heat while stirring it. Then when the mixture boiled, they stirred it for another minute then removed it from the heat and allowed it to cool. Once it was cool, they covered it with plastic wrap and placed it in the refrigerator to chill for an hour.

While that was chilling, they whipped heavy cream with vanilla in a medium bowl until the mixture formed stiff peaks. And in a separate smaller bowl they combined the coffee and rum.

Next came the ladyfingers. Bridget had made some beforehand for them to use. All they had to do was split them in half lengthwise, drizzle them with the coffee mixture, and arrange them in the baking dish.

Then it was back to the yolk mixture. They added mascarpone, whisking until it was smooth. Then they spread the mixture over the ladyfingers, adding a layer of whipped cream on top. They then repeated the layers, sprinkled some cocoa powder over the top, and put the tiramisu in the refrigerator.

"Phew!" said Guin when they were done.

She looked around the room. The kitchen was a mess.

Bridget got their attention and told everyone that they had done a great job. As they turned to go, she reminded them that class would start at nine the next morning and that they would be going to a local olive farm for an olive oil tasting in the afternoon.

"Can we help clean up?" Guin asked Bridget after everyone else, except for her and Glen, had left.

"That's kind of you to offer, but we've got this," said Bridget.

"Are you sure?" said Guin, taking in the kitchen.

Bridget smiled.

"Trust me, I've cleaned up worse messes. And with Leo and Francesca to help, it'll go quickly."

"Okay," said Guin. "Though do you have a few minutes to answer a few questions?"

"What kind of questions?"

Guin turned to Glen.

"You can go."

"You're not planning on asking Bridget about me, are you?" he said, giving her a suspicious look.

"Why would I want to ask Bridget about you?" she said with an impish grin. "Now go. I'll see you at dinner."

"Shall I knock on your door?"

"Sure."

Glen looked from Guin to Bridget.

"Be nice," he said.

"Nice costs extra," Bridget replied. Though she smiled as she said it.

Glen gave her a last look and left.

"So, what did you want to ask me?" Bridget said after Glen had gone. "Is it about Glen?"

Guin would have loved to have asked Bridget about Glen, but that wasn't why she had stayed behind.

"Actually, I wanted to ask about you. I read your bio, but how does someone go from a high-powered career on Wall Street to working as a private chef and cooking instructor in Tuscany? That's a pretty big change."

Bridget smiled.

"I know. But it was surprisingly easy. I had always loved to cook. I would throw these crazy dinner parties for my friends during college. Then I started working as a trader and it took over my life."

"Though you managed to squeeze in a trip to Italy."

"Best decision I ever made."

"And you fell in love."

Bridget nodded.

"I did. Italy seduced me."

"And what about Dante? Did he seduce you too?"

Bridget smiled again.

"You could say that."

"How did you two meet?"

"I met him at his restaurant. I was having dinner there with a friend. He flirted with me throughout the meal, though maybe he flirted with everyone. But something about the way he looked at me… Then when dinner was over, he invited me to stay for a drink. I told my girlfriend to go back to our *pensione*. I'd be along later. Though I didn't get back until after one."

"Wow," said Guin. "What did you talk about?"

"Him, mostly. But that was okay. I found him fascinating. He told me he had originally wanted to be a vet. But when his father, who owned the local butcher shop, died, Dante was forced to take it over, being the oldest male in the family."

"That's a pretty drastic change, going from being a vet to a butcher."

Bridget nodded.

"It was. Which is why when he opened the restaurant, Dante made sure that all of the meat he served was humanely raised and slaughtered and that no part of the animal was wasted."

"That's very noble of him."

"I don't know about noble. It's just the way he is."

"But how did he go from selling meat to opening a restaurant?"

"His customers were always asking him how to prepare the meat he sold them. Dante would tell them. Then one of his customers suggested he show them. He did, and it was a big hit. Then the same customer told him he should open a restaurant and offered to bankroll him."

"That was very generous of him."

"It was, but he knew a good thing when he saw it."

"But back to you, how did you wind up moving here?"

"Well, after we spent the night talking, Dante invited me to go on a picnic."

"Did you go?"

Guin could tell from Bridget's smile that she did.

"When it was time for me to go back to New York, I knew I'd be back."

"Because of Dante."

She nodded.

"But also because Italy felt like home."

"So you, what, quit your job and moved here?"

"Pretty much. Though it didn't happen right away. Now, if you will excuse me?"

"Of course. Sorry, I didn't mean to keep you."

She looked around and saw Leo and Francesca were busy doing the washing up.

"Will we see you at dinner tonight?"

"I'll be sure to say hello to everyone."

"You won't be joining us?"

"My place is in the kitchen. Now go. I'm sure you have better things to do."

Guin knew she was being dismissed, so she left.

As she headed back to her room, she spied Vera talking to Domenico. Neither looked very happy. Guin moved closer, trying to keep out of sight. But they were so intent on each other, she didn't think either of them saw her.

"Leave her out of it," said Domenico.

"You know I can't do that," said Vera.

"I'm warning you."

"You're warning *me*? Need I remind you—"

Just then Vera spied Guin and frowned.

"Lovely evening," said Guin, trying to act nonchalant.

They were both looking at her. Then Domenico turned to Vera. The look he gave her sent a chill through Guin. Then his phone rang.

"*Pronto*," he said, answering it. He then moved away.

Guin looked over at Vera.

"Is everything okay?"

"Why wouldn't it be?" she snapped.

Guin was taken aback by Vera's hostile tone.

"I just…"

"Don't you know it's rude to eavesdrop?"

"I'm sorry," said Guin, feeling flustered.

Vera continued to scowl at her.

"I'm doing an article on the class for my paper, and I'd love to interview you when you have a minute," said Guin.

"Unless your paper's the *New York Times*, I'm not interested," said Vera. Then she turned and walked away, leaving Guin looking stunned.

As soon as Guin got back to her room, she popped open her laptop and typed *Vera van Leyden* into the search engine.

There were thousands of references. No surprise,

considering Vera had written several cookbooks and was a food celebrity. Guin clicked on Vera's Wikipedia page and began to read.

She had been born Verna Kowalski, the child of Polish immigrants. But she had changed her name to Vera after she had married prominent Boston art dealer Nicholas van Leyden. *Interesting.*

They had had a son, Christian, an artist, who had tragically died from a drug overdose when he was in his early twenties. Shortly after, she and her husband had divorced. Guin suddenly felt a pang of sympathy for Vera.

After the divorce, Vera, who had learned to cook as a child and had hosted numerous dinner parties for her husband, continued to host dinner parties for her friends, doing most of the cooking herself. The parties typically had a theme, usually a specific cuisine. Though cooking Polish food was her specialty.

After one of these Polish food-themed evenings, a friend of a friend, who was an editor at a large publishing company, suggested Vera write a cookbook. Vera at first scoffed at the idea, but she must have reconsidered as her first cookbook, a collection of Polish recipes, debuted less than a year later. In the cookbook, Vera took classic Polish and East European recipes and updated them, giving cooks a choice of using the original recipe or the modern, less-fattening one.

The cookbook was a hit. And, as a result, Vera went on to do several more cookbooks, each one focusing on a different cuisine using the same model. That led to guest appearances on *The Today Show* and other daytime talk shows. Vera had even been a judge on the Food Network.

Then came the controversy. Several chefs had accused Vera of stealing their recipes, a charge she denied. But the damage had been done, and she no longer appeared on TV.

So why was she here in Tuscany? Was she working on a

new cookbook? That's what Rosa had thought. And what had she and Domenico been arguing about? Guin stared at the computer screen. Then she looked down at the time. She needed to start writing. She closed her browser, opened a new document, and began to type.

CHAPTER 7

Dinner was at eight-thirty on the dining terrace. And because she didn't want to be late, Guin had set a reminder on her computer, leaving herself time to change. She was just putting on lip gloss when she heard a knock.

"Coming!" she called.

She did a final check of herself in the mirror then went to get the door.

It was Glen, looking suave in a pair of dark jeans and a button-down shirt.

"You're early."

"I thought we could have a cocktail before dinner." He eyed her. "I like that dress."

"Thank you."

"So, shall we go?"

"Let me grab my bag."

The evening was warm, but there was a gentle breeze blowing.

"It's beautiful out," said Guin. "The sky looks straight out of an Impressionist painting."

"It does. I should have brought my camera."

"You can always go get it."

"I'm taking a night off from playing photographer. I just want to enjoy myself."

Guin understood. She had already decided she wouldn't

write about dinner this evening. Besides, she still needed to finish writing her article about the day's classes and send it off to Ginny.

They made their way to the dining terrace. The Adamses and the Italians were already there.

"Can I get you something to drink?" asked Matteo.

"I'll have a Pellegrino," said Guin.

"No *aperitivo*?" said Matteo.

"Yes, you must have an *aperitivo*!" said Beatrice. Guin hadn't noticed her make her way over. "It—how you say? —opens the stomach."

"I'll have an Aperol spritz," said Glen.

Beatrice smiled at him. It was what she was drinking.

"Fine. I'll have one too," said Guin.

"*Bene*!" said Matteo. "Two Aperol spritz!" He smiled and went to get their drinks.

"So, Beatrice," said Guin, turning to look at the other woman. Beatrice was wearing a pale, seafoam blue wrap dress that hugged her curves, her blonde hair falling in waves to her shoulders. She reminded Guin of that famous painting of Venus, if Venus had been wearing a dress. "What led you to take the cooking class?"

"I have always loved food. My mother and my grandmother were very good cooks. But I… not so much. My husband did not care if I cooked. But after he died, I wanted to learn."

"But why Tuscan food? Why not German? You were living in Germany, yes?"

"*Sì*. But the German food was not to my liking. And I am from Tuscany. I wanted to learn to cook the food of my home."

"But you said your mother and grandmother were good cooks, why not learn from them?"

"My *nonna* died while I was in Germany, and my mother, she is not well."

"Oh, I'm sorry to hear that," said Guin. "But why take a course taught in English? There must be cooking classes taught in Italian."

"I—"

"Bea wanted to work on her English," said Domenico.

Guin thought Beatrice's English didn't need that much work but didn't say anything.

"*Sì*," said Beatrice. "Also, Nico would be here."

Guin was about to ask Beatrice another question, but Matteo had returned with their drinks.

"*Allora*," he said, handing her and Glen their Aperol spritzes.

"*Grazie*," said Guin.

Matteo looked at Beatrice.

"Can I get you something, Signorina?"

Guin thought he looked a little lovestruck.

"*No, grazie*, Matteo," Beatrice replied, giving him a smile.

He stood gazing at her for a few more seconds. Then at a look from Domenico, he moved away.

Guin took a sip of her drink. She had to admit, it was very tasty. She was wondering where Vera and Oliver were when they appeared at the edge of the dining terrace. She saw Vera glance around then frown as she looked their way. Guin noticed Domenico and Beatrice frowning back at Vera. What was that about? Then she saw John and Julia and excused herself to go say hello to them.

"Beautiful evening," she said.

"It is," said Julia.

Guin noticed that Julia was looking over at Vera.

"Pretty amazing to have a professional cookbook author in class."

"It's amazing all right," said Julia, turning to look at her husband. John looked distinctly uncomfortable.

"What did you think of class today?" Guin asked them.

"Hm?" said Julia.

"I asked what you thought of today's classes. Did they compare with the other cooking classes you've taken?"

Before either Adams could answer, Glen appeared.

"I hope Guin hasn't been grilling you. She has a habit of doing that with new people."

"I do not!" said Guin.

Glen smiled, and Guin realized he was teasing her. Then she saw Julia looking over at Vera again. Oliver was no longer with her.

"She looks a bit lonely," said Glen. "Should I invite her to join us?"

Julia was about to say something but was interrupted by Matteo.

"Could I have your attention, *per favore*? Dinner is about to be served."

Everyone headed to the long table. Guin saw that Oliver had returned. He took a seat next to Vera. However, no one seemed to want to sit on Vera's other side, so Glen took the empty seat. Guin sat next to him. The Adamses and the Italians sat opposite, Domenico sitting across from Guin and Beatrice next to him.

Shortly after everyone was seated, Bridget appeared, dressed in a chef's uniform.

"*Buona sera*," she said. "Tonight, we will be serving you a traditional Tuscan meal. We will begin with bruschetta, followed by homemade potato gnocchi in a light pesto sauce. Then for *secondo* you will be having *cacciucco*, a Tuscan seafood stew. And for dessert, *torta della nonna*. *Buon appetito*! Enjoy!"

Bridget smiled then went back into the kitchen. A minute later, Francesca brought out the bruschetta.

Dinner had been delicious. Though as they had dessert and coffee, Guin swore she would never eat again. She had spent the latter part of the meal speaking to Domenico and had discovered he had studied hotel management in the States, at the University of Central Florida in Orlando. She asked him what that had been like and if he had seen much of Florida.

He told her he had spent most of his time in Orlando and then Miami, where he had worked in two different hotels. Then his father had recalled him to Italy to help with the family business. He had spent the last three years working in the family's hotels in Italy and had recently been put in charge of new business development.

"And what brought you to Greve and Bridget's course?" Guin asked him.

"We are thinking of doing something similar at some of our hotels, offering guests classes in cooking and yoga and other things. My father is not convinced it is a good idea. So he sent me here to investigate."

"Ah," said Guin. "Well, I think offering cooking classes is a great idea. And I have friends who do yoga retreats. Why doesn't your father think it a good idea?"

"He is a bit old-fashioned. He thinks people want to go on vacation to relax and that cooking is work."

Guin smiled.

"Cooking is work. But many people enjoy it. What do you think? Do you like to cook?"

"I was not expected to cook growing up," he said. "And I am always traveling so have no time to cook. But I am enjoying the course."

Just then Beatrice leaned over and whispered something in Domenico's ear. He nodded.

"Would you excuse me?" he said. "It has been very nice talking to you, but I must make a call."

"Of course," said Guin. Though she wondered who Domenico needed to call so late at night.

"I must go too," said Beatrice, excusing herself.

Soon, everyone else got up.

"Shall we head back to our rooms?" said Glen.

Guin nodded.

They got up and said goodnight to the Adamses, Oliver and Vera having already departed. Then they headed across the lawn.

"You and Domenico looked very chummy," said Glen.

It was dark out now, and Guin could barely see in front of her, though the sky was lit with hundreds of stars.

"Jealous?" she said, teasingly.

"Maybe."

They walked in silence for several seconds.

"I saw you talking to Vera van Leyden. Was she nice to you?"

"Why wouldn't she be?"

"She always seems annoyed."

"Well, she was perfectly friendly to me."

"Maybe she just likes good-looking photographers. What did you two talk about?"

"Food mostly. And photography and art. Her son was an artist."

"I read that. He died though. Drug overdose I think."

"She didn't mention that, just that he died too soon. I think it deeply affected her."

"I can't imagine losing a child, especially such a promising one."

They had reached the corridor leading to their rooms, and Guin heard what sounded like two people arguing. It was Vera and Oliver. Vera was standing in Oliver's doorway.

Guin motioned for Glen to be quiet as she pulled him out of the way.

"Don't you know it's not nice to eavesdrop?" he said.

Guin shushed him then leaned in to better hear what Vera and Oliver were saying.

"I told you I'd take care of it, Vera."

"Like you took care of the last deal?"

"That wasn't my fault, and you know it."

"Then whose fault was it?"

There was silence for several seconds.

"If you're not happy with me, you can go find yourself another agent. Though good luck with that."

"Maybe I will," she said. Then she turned and stormed across the hall to her room, slamming the door behind her.

They waited several seconds before moving.

"Sounds like Vera isn't too happy with her agent," said Guin.

"And he didn't sound that happy with her."

"You think she'll fire him?"

"Sounded like he's ready to quit."

They stopped outside of their rooms.

"You want to come in for a nightcap? I have some *amaro*. I hear it aids digestion."

"Thanks," said Guin. "But I'm going to pass. I'll see you at breakfast."

"You going to go for a walk beforehand?"

"I was thinking about it. Depends on when I get up."

She let out a yawn.

"Well, I hope you have pleasant dreams."

She smiled up at him.

"Thank you. You too."

They stood there a minute, neither moving. Then Glen leaned over and placed an errant curl behind Guin's ear. Guin shivered at his touch. Was he about to kiss her? A part of her wanted him to.

"Well, good night," he said.

"Good night," said Guin. When he didn't make a move, she reached into her bag and got out her card key. Then she opened her door and slipped into her room, feeling disappointed.

CHAPTER 8

Guin had set her alarm for six-forty-five. She wanted to go for a walk before breakfast, to work off dinner, and didn't want to sleep too late. But when the alarm went off, she wished she hadn't set it.

She thought about hitting snooze but forced herself out of bed instead. She gazed out the window. It looked to be another beautiful day. She went into the bathroom, then threw on a pair of capris and a t-shirt and headed out, nearly colliding with Glen outside her door.

"You're up," they said in unison then smiled.

"Did you set your alarm?" Guin asked him.

"No, I'm usually up early, and I figured I'd go for a walk. You going for a walk?"

"I was planning on it."

"Where're you going?"

Guin hadn't really thought about it.

"I hadn't decided."

"Would you mind doing the vineyard walk again?"

Guin said she didn't, and they headed to the trailhead.

"I love this place," said Guin as they made their way along the trail.

"It is pretty special," said Glen.

"And so quiet."

"And no dead bodies."

"Thank God for that. I can't imagine anyone being

murdered in someplace this beautiful."

"Though there's always the mafia."

"Aren't they just in Southern Italy? And I thought the mafia wasn't a thing anymore."

They walked in silence for several minutes.

"Can you smell it?" said Guin, taking a deep breath.

"What?" said Glen.

"The grapes."

Glen closed his eyes and inhaled.

"Now I do."

"I wonder if that's the vineyard we'll be going to," said Guin, looking at the nearby vineyard.

"Maybe."

"What time is it?"

Glen looked at his watch.

"A quarter to eight. We should turn around."

"Let me just take a couple of pictures."

Guin took out her phone and took a photo of the vineyard in the distance. Then she turned to Glen.

"Aren't you going to take any pictures?"

"I didn't bring my camera."

"What about your phone?"

"It's okay. I don't always need to take photos. Sometimes it's just good to be in the moment."

Guin felt a bit self-conscious and put her phone back in her pocket. Then they headed back to the hotel.

It was eight-thirty when they arrived at the dining terrace. The Adamses were there, looking as though they had just finished eating. There was no sign of the Italians or Vera or Oliver.

Guin said hello, as did Glen.

"We'd invite you to join us," said Julia, "but we were just leaving."

"That's all right," said Guin. "We're just going to grab a quick bite and some coffee before class."

The Adamses got up and left, and Francesca appeared a minute later. Guin and Glen ordered coffee then went to get some food.

As they were taking their food to a table for two, Beatrice appeared, looking radiant as usual. Guin envied her. She and Beatrice had similar coloring—fair skin, blue-green eyes, and blonde-ish hair, though Guin's was strawberry blonde whereas Beatrice's was pure blonde. Though Guin suspected Beatrice dyed her hair. But there the similarities ended.

"*Ciao!*" said Glen, smiling at Beatrice.

"*Ciao bello!*" said Beatrice, smiling back at him.

Guin frowned.

"Would you care to join us?" Glen asked her.

Just then Domenico appeared. Beatrice looked over and said something to him in Italian.

"We would be happy to join you," she replied.

Francesca appeared with Glen and Guin's coffees. Guin directed her to a nearby table for four. Then Beatrice said something to Francesca in Italian and Francesca disappeared again while Beatrice and Domenico went to get food.

They joined Guin and Glen a minute later. Guin glanced at Beatrice's plate. It contained a mini croissant, a *pain au chocolat*, some prosciutto and cheese, and fruit.

They ate in silence. Then Domenico's phone rang. He excused himself to answer it. Beatrice sighed.

"Is everything all right?" Glen asked her.

"*Sì.* It is just… Domenico, he is always working, trying to impress his father."

"I understand that's why he's here," said Guin.

Beatrice nodded.

"Though I hoped he would take some time to enjoy himself."

"So, how do you two know each other?"

"We grew up together. He was friends with my brother, Alessandro. He is like another brother to me."

Guin got the feeling that Domenico didn't see Beatrice as a sister but didn't say anything.

"We should go," said Glen, looking at his watch. "Don't want to be late for class."

Guin got up, but Beatrice remained seated.

"Are you not coming?" Guin asked her.

"I am not done with my breakfast."

Glen looked like he might stay and keep her company.

"*Andare!*" commanded Beatrice. "Go. I will be there soon."

Guin waited for Glen. Then they headed to their rooms.

"You could have stayed," said Guin.

"No, I need to get to the kitchen and take some photos."

"Where do you think Vera and Oliver were?"

"Who knows? Maybe they had breakfast in their rooms."

"I didn't know that was an option."

They had arrived at their rooms. Guin said she would just be a minute, but Glen said he should get going.

Guin felt a bit miffed as a moment ago he didn't seem to care about being late. But she shrugged it off. She would not let Beatrice get to her.

It was probably a good thing that Glen hadn't waited for her as Guin had wound up messaging with her brother and was late to class. She wasn't the only one. Beatrice, Domenico, Oliver, and Vera were also late. And Guin wondered if anything in Italy ever started on time.

She entered the kitchen and saw a cornucopia of vegetables on the center island. There were purple eggplants, green and purple-spotted beans, bright orange carrots, yellow onions, dark-green zucchinis, and luscious-looking red tomatoes.

"Are we going to use all of these veggies?" she asked Bridget.

Bridget nodded.

"We are!"

"They're almost too pretty to eat," Guin replied.

When everyone was settled, Bridget addressed the class.

"This morning, we're going to learn how to prepare vegetables several different ways. Then this afternoon, we will be going to visit an olive oil farm for a tasting."

"Sounds great!" said Guin.

Bridget smiled, then she went over the dishes they would be making: two salads, one made with beans and the other with tomatoes; a roasted vegetable and pasta dish; and a vegetable soup. As they did the day before, the students would work in teams.

Guin looked over the recipes. None of them looked very difficult, which was fine by her. Then she heard Vera grousing to Oliver that her readers wouldn't be impressed. *Though maybe your readers would appreciate something easy and yummy to make*, Guin thought. But she kept it to herself.

By lunchtime, they had finished making all of the vegetable dishes, and Guin was ready to eat. Bridget told the class to go out to the dining terrace. Leo and Francesca would bring out the food they had made. They also brought out several crusty loaves of bread and two bottles of wine along with some sparkling water.

The food was once again served family-style, with everyone helping themselves, except for the soup.

Guin dipped her spoon into her bowl. She could smell the fresh thyme, sage, and garlic that infused the light tomato broth. She placed the spoon in her mouth and chewed the beans, carrots, zucchini, and onions. It was heavenly.

She watched as the others tried the soup.

"Have you had this soup before?" Guin asked Beatrice, who was sitting across from her.

"*Sì*," she replied. "My *nonna* used to make something just like it."

"And is this as good?"

"Almost," she said with a smile.

Guin helped herself to the pasta and salads.

"Everything is so good," she said to no one in particular. "I could eat like this every day."

"I know what you mean," said Julia. "And this bread..."

"I know, right?" said Guin.

"Tuscan bread is the best," said Beatrice.

"It could use some salt," said Vera, disdainfully.

"Authentic Tuscan bread does not have salt," said Domenico. Vera frowned.

"I'm surprised she didn't know that," Guin whispered to Glen.

As they finished lunch, Bridget appeared.

"I hope you all enjoyed the fruits—or rather the vegetables—of your labors," she said, smiling at the group. Guin groaned. "And I'm here to remind you that we need to leave for the olive oil farm at two-thirty. There is a van that will take us. Just meet at the front of the hotel. And please try not to be late," she added, glancing at the Italians.

Guin looked at her phone. It was two o'clock. She really needed to work, but she didn't have much time. Still, she would use the time she had to get down her thoughts on the morning's class.

"So, what are you going to do with your thirty minutes?" she asked Glen as they headed to their rooms. "Edit photos?"

"I don't really have enough time. What about you?"

"Work."

"Shall I knock when it's time to go?"

He knew Guin lost track of time when she was writing.

Guin was about to say that wasn't necessary but changed her mind and said sure.

CHAPTER 9

Guin heard someone knocking on her door, but surely that couldn't be Glen already, could it? She looked down at the clock on her laptop. Wow. It was nearly two-thirty. Where had the time gone?

"You in there?" Glen called, knocking again.

"I'll be right there!" Guin shouted.

She saved the document she had been working on, then grabbed her bag and her card key.

"Sorry about that," she said, after closing the door. "Got a bit carried away."

"I understand. I get the same way when editing photos. So, you finish your article?"

"Hardly. I just wanted to get down my impressions from this morning before I forgot."

"But you have the recipe book."

"I know. But there's something about getting down your thoughts while they're fresh. Though I guess it's different for photography."

"Actually," said Glen. "I have a little notebook I keep on me when I'm photographing an event. I use it to keep track of all of the people I've photographed."

"That's smart."

"I don't know about smart. It's just my way of remembering."

"Well, I think it's very smart. Who could remember all

of those names? Not me. So, have you sent any photographs to Ginny?"

"Some."

"What did she say?"

"That she wished she was here," he said smiling.

"Did she ask you why she hadn't received anything from me yet?"

"Nope."

Well, that was odd.

"Well, if she does say something, tell her I'll send her something later."

"I will, but I doubt she'll say anything to me."

They had arrived at the front of the hotel and saw Bridget coming towards them.

"Good, you're here."

"Are we late?" said Guin. "I thought we were right on time."

"You are, but… Back in the day, Glen was *always* early for everything, making the rest of us look bad. So when I didn't see him…"

"I didn't do it to make you feel bad," said Glen.

"It's my fault," said Guin. "I was busy working."

"Well, you're both here now. And we're still waiting for Beatrice and Domenico."

Why wasn't Guin surprised?

"I told everyone I'd give them a few more minutes. But if they're not here soon, we'll go without them." She peered around Glen and Guin, but there was no sign of the Italians. "Why don't you two get in the van? I'll message them."

Guin and Glen did as they were told. There were three rows of seats. Vera and Oliver were seated in the first row, John and Julia Adams in the row behind them. So Glen and Guin sat in the third row.

A few minutes later, Bridget got in.

"No sign of them?" said Julia.

Bridget shook her head.

"And I messaged them, but neither got back to me."

"Should someone check on them, see if they're okay?" said Julia.

"I'm sure they're perfectly fine," said Vera. "We should go. We're already late."

Bridget gave one last look then turned to the driver and said something to him in Italian. They had just started to move when Beatrice came running out of the hotel, waving her arms. The van screeched to a halt.

"*Scusami*," Beatrice said to everyone as she peered into the van. "I lost track of the time."

Guin heard more than one huff from her fellow passengers.

"Is Domenico coming?" Bridget asked her.

"No, he has to work. He said to go without him."

"Take a seat," said Bridget.

Beatrice got in and took the seat next to Glen, forcing Guin to move over.

"*Andiamo*! Let's go!" said Bridget. And the driver pulled away.

As they drove to the farm, Bridget told them how the olive orchard had been in the Rossi family for over a hundred years, and that they had been producing olive oil for nearly as long. Guin listened politely, but it was hard to hear as Beatrice kept whispering to Glen.

She was tempted to tell Beatrice to be quiet, but she kept her mouth shut, clenching her teeth.

Fortunately, the olive oil farm wasn't far away.

The van left them off in front of an old stone building. In the distance were rows of olive trees.

They were greeted by a man with brown-black hair and dark eyes, his skin the color of olives. Bridget greeted him as if they were old friends, and they exchanged three kisses. Then she turned to her class.

"This is Luca Rossi," said Bridget. "His family owns the farm. And their olive oil is some of the finest you will have in Chianti."

"In all of Italy," he corrected her.

"Luca, why don't you take it from here?"

"*Certo*," he replied. He turned and looked at the group. "*Benvenuto*. Today, I will teach you how olive oil is made. I will show you where the olives are grown, how they are harvested, and then turned into liquid gold. *Bene*?"

"*Bene*," the group replied in unison.

"Please, follow me."

They followed him out into the olive orchard, where there were olive trees as far as the eye could see. He explained that the olives were picked by hand when ripe to avoid damage, and Guin asked him when picking season was.

"In September, before the weather gets too cold," Luca replied. "Everyone is involved. It is a very labor-intensive process."

"Why not use machines?" asked John.

"Because they can ruin the olives. The olives, they are very delicate." He looked around. "Any other questions?" No one said anything. "*Bene*. Now we go see where the olive oil is made."

They followed Luca into an old stone building. (There were several on the property.)

"Here is where we wash the olives and remove the leaves and stems," he explained. "Then the fruit is placed in *un frantoio*, an oil mill, where it is crushed."

"What about the skin and the pit?" asked Glen.

"Everything goes into the mill," replied Luca.

He then took them over to what looked like a large granite wheel, which Guin figured had to weigh a ton.

"When the olives are ground, it creates a paste," Luca continued. "Then comes the mixing stage. This is very important so must be done slowly, to ensure the proper consistency. Next, we press. When that is done, we separate the water from the oil. The unfiltered oil is then stored in steel tanks until the oil is ready to be bottled. Then we bottle and sell the oil."

"What makes oil extra virgin?" asked Julia.

Luca explained that what Americans called *extra virgin* was what Italians typically called *cold-pressed*, meaning no heat or chemicals were involved—and that most Italians used ordinary olive oil for cooking as it had a higher smoking point and was less expensive than extra virgin or cold-pressed, though still very good.

Next, Glen asked how long the whole process took. And Oliver asked how many bottles they made each year. Then Vera asked if they were ever going to actually taste some olive oil, and Luca smiled and led them into the tasting room.

"Today, I will share with you three different olive oils made here at Azienda Frantoio Rossi. You taste and let me know which is your favorite."

He picked up the first bottle and poured around a tablespoonful into little paper cups. Then he told everyone to take one.

"This first one is our signature olive oil."

"Is it extra virgin?" asked Oliver, sniffing it.

"It is," said Luca. "As you taste it, you will detect some peppery notes. A good extra virgin olive oil should be a bit spicy."

He waited for them to take a sip.

Guin drank hers and immediately made a face. It was very spicy, and she wasn't sure if she liked the taste. Luca smiled at her.

"Americans are often surprised by how real olive oil tastes."

"I like it," said Glen.

"That's because you like spicy food," said Bridget.

Next, they tasted a virgin olive oil, which Luca explained was similar to the extra virgin. It just had more fatty acids and impurities. But it was still cold-pressed. Guin liked this one better than the extra virgin, but she still felt the taste was a bit strong.

Finally, he gave them a sample of their ordinary olive oil, which Guin thought had a fruitier taste and was her favorite.

When they were done, Luca thanked them for coming and informed them that they could buy all of the olive oils they had tasted, along with a selection of balsamic vinegar and gifts, in their shop next door.

"I could go for some balsamic vinegar after that," Guin said to Glen as they made their way next door.

"Maybe they'll let us taste some," he replied. "We should ask."

They entered the gift shop, and Guin and Glen went over to the woman in charge, asking if they could try the balsamic vinegar. She said of course and gave them a taste of two different ones, both made by local producers.

"Wow," said Guin. "These are really good. They don't taste anything like the balsamic vinegar I get at the supermarket. They're almost sweet."

"That is because the balsamic vinegar they sell in American supermarkets is not real balsamic vinegar," said the woman.

Guin asked the woman how much for a bottle and nearly fainted when the woman told her how much a large bottle cost. But, as she explained, there was a reason why this balsamic vinegar was so expensive. And they had smaller, less expensive bottles for sale.

Guin purchased two of the smaller bottles, which were still not cheap. She also bought a couple of bottles of olive oil. She would keep a bottle of vinegar and a bottle of olive oil and give the rest away as gifts.

She glanced around. Everyone seemed to be buying

something. And there were Vera and Oliver, arguing about something. She wondered what it was about this time.

Guin waited for Glen to finish paying for his purchases. Then Bridget announced it was time for them to leave.

On the way back, Beatrice had sat with Bridget. They were conversing in Italian, and Guin had no idea what they were saying. She was just happy to have Glen to herself.

"Well, that was fun and educational," said Glen.

"Mm," said Guin.

"So, you want to go for some gelato when we get back?"

"Aren't you worried about spoiling your appetite for dinner?" Dinner was on their own that evening, and it was nearly five o'clock. "And I should probably work."

"You're turning down gelato?" He looked shocked. "Come on. You can work later. Bridget told me about this place at the other end of town that she said had the best gelato in Chianti."

Guin felt her resolve start to wane. After all that olive oil and vinegar, she could use a little something sweet.

"You can always do a piece on gelato in Chianti."

"Okay, fine. Though just a small cup. I don't want to ruin my appetite for dinner."

"Up to you."

"Just let me drop off my stuff in my room."

"We could save time by going straight to the car. We can put our bags in the trunk."

"Won't the oil and vinegar get too hot?"

"It's cooling off. And we won't be gone for that long."

Guin thought about it for a few seconds.

"Okay."

The van pulled into the hotel, and Guin and Glen went straight to Glen's convertible, putting their bags in the trunk.

The drive into town took less than fifteen minutes. And Glen found a place to park a few steps away from the gelateria. It didn't look like much from the outside. But Guin knew not to judge a book by its cover—or a gelateria by its exterior.

They entered the shop and glanced at the cases of gelato.

"Everything looks so good," said Guin. "How am I supposed to choose?"

"We could each get a couple of scoops like last time and share."

Guin looked at the metal containers, each filled with a different flavor of gelato. She was tempted to get *pistacchio* and *bacio* again, but she wanted to try something different. So she ordered a small cup of *fragola* (strawberry) and *pesca* (peach). Glen ordered a cup of *fior di latte* (a flavor similar to vanilla) and *cioccolato*.

"Really, vanilla and chocolate?" said Guin as she watched the young woman scoop the gelati into a cup.

"Don't knock it till you've tried it," he replied. "And *fior di latte* isn't vanilla."

Guin paid, and they stepped outside.

"Here, have a taste," said Glen, dipping his spoon into his cup.

Guin let the *fior di latte* coat her tongue. It tasted like sweet cream and warm summer days at the beach.

"That is definitely not vanilla," she said.

"See, I told you. Now try the chocolate."

He again dipped his spoon into his cup and held it out for Guin.

"Oh," she groaned, savoring the rich chocolate taste. "This stuff should be illegal."

Glen smiled.

"You want a bite of mine?" she asked him, holding out her spoon.

"Sure."

She dipped her spoon into her cup and held it out to him.

"Mm," he said. "You can really taste the fruit. Bridget was right."

They strolled as they finished their ice cream.

"It's so nice here," said Guin. "I can see why Bridget likes it. It's not super touristy."

"I think that's just because we're not in the more touristy part of town. It's actually the height of tourist season. It's been so busy that Bridget told me she actually has to help Dante out at the restaurant tonight."

"Really?" said Guin. "After teaching all day?"

Glen nodded.

"That's life when you own a restaurant."

"I guess. I feel like a slacker."

They had arrived back at Glen's car.

"What time is it?" she asked.

"Almost six."

"We should go."

"By the way, I made us a reservation for dinner," said Glen as he drove them back to the hotel.

"When? Where?" He hadn't mentioned anything when they were in town.

"A little Italian place down the road from the Incanto."

"Did Bridget recommend it?"

He nodded.

"It's run by a local family. Bridget says the food is excellent. Not many tourists know about it. It's mostly locals who go there."

"Sounds great, but I don't think I could eat a thing."

"After just that little cup of gelato? Trust me, in a couple of hours you'll be hungry." Guin wasn't so sure about that. "Besides, our reservation isn't until eight-thirty, and we probably won't eat until nine."

"Fine," Guin sighed.

Glen parked the car, and they walked to their rooms.

"I'll get you at eight-twenty."

"What's the dress code?"

"I don't know. I assume casual."

"You know what happens when you assume."

Glen smiled.

"I'm sure whatever you wear will be fine."

CHAPTER 10

Guin set a reminder on her computer for seven-forty-five, so she would have enough time to get ready for dinner. Not that it would take her half an hour.

She had immediately begun working on her article on the first day of class as soon as she walked in the door. She wanted to finish it and send it to Ginny before dinner, though she knew it was a stretch. Normally, it would take Guin days to write and polish an article. But she didn't have that luxury. As soon as they had gotten back from town, Guin had found a message from Ginny asking when she'd get something.

She had barely finished the article when her reminder popped up. She thought about sending the article to Ginny right then, but she couldn't bring herself to mail it without giving it another read. She would go over it after dinner then email it to her boss.

She hit save then closed her laptop and walked over to the armoire. She glanced at her dresses, not sure what to wear. Glen said the place was casual, but casual didn't mean the same thing in Italy as it did on Sanibel. Guin thought about wearing slacks and a nice top but wound up choosing a dress.

She was in the bathroom applying makeup when she heard a knock on her door. It must be Glen. She put her makeup away and went to answer it.

She opened the door to find Glen dressed in a pair of cotton pants and a light-blue button-down shirt. He looked good. Then again, he always looked good.

"You look beautiful as always," he said, smiling at her.

"You don't look so bad yourself," Guin replied. "I just need to get my bag and we can go."

Guin enjoyed the feel of the wind whipping through her hair as they drove to the restaurant.

"How far is it?" she asked.

"Bridget said it was just down the road, maybe ten minutes?"

It was dark out, and Guin could barely see beyond the headlights.

"Did we pass it?" Guin asked several minutes later. It felt as though they had been driving for more than ten minutes.

"I don't think so. Wait, I think that's it."

There was a small sign next to a gravel driveway. Guin squinted but she couldn't read what the sign said.

"Are you sure?"

"Bridget said the place was a bit hard to find."

"What is it with hotels and restaurants not putting up big signs?"

"I think they run the restaurant out of their home. So they probably don't want to call too much attention to it."

As they made their way down the long, dark, twisting driveway lined with trees, Guin wondered how many patrons, after a few glasses of vino, had found themselves up close and personal with a tree. Hopefully, that wouldn't happen to them. But just in case, she would make sure Glen didn't drink too much.

Finally, she saw a light up ahead. It was coming from a large stone cottage. There was a parking area to the right of it, and Glen found a spot next to a red Ferrari.

"Nice car," she said as they got out.

"It's a Portofino," said Glen, admiring it. "It has a 3.9-liter V-8 and goes from zero to sixty in under four seconds."

Guin stared at him.

"Did you own one?"

"Oh, no."

He continued to admire the Ferrari.

"Why not?"

"They're not exactly cheap."

"How much does one cost?"

"The base model starts at around $215,000."

Guin gulped.

"I'd hate to see how much the non-base model costs."

Glen turned to her.

"Let's go in."

They went inside and were greeted by a smiling young man who Guin thought looked to be in high school. Was he the son of the family who owned the restaurant? Glen had said it was a family enterprise.

The young man greeted them in Italian. However, seeing their confusion, he quickly switched to English.

"I have a reservation," Glen said. "The last name is Anderson."

"*Certo*, Signore Anderson," said the young man. "This way, please."

He led them to a table for two by the window. As they headed over, Guin was surprised to see John and Julia Adams seated a few feet away. As if sensing someone was looking at them, they looked up and waved for Guin and Glen to come over.

"Would you excuse us?" Guin said to the young man. "Those are friends of ours."

She went over to say hello, Glen and the young man following her.

"Guin! Glen! Fancy running into you here!" said John. "Please, join us."

"We don't want to intrude," said Guin.

"Nonsense!" said John. "We haven't even ordered yet. Pull up a chair."

They were seated at a table that looked as though it could seat four, but it was only set for two.

"Please," said Julia. "You'd be doing me a favor."

Guin exchanged a look with Glen, who seemed to be saying it was up to her.

"Is that all right?" Guin asked the young man.

"Of course, it's all right!" said John. "Bring us a couple more place settings!" he commanded.

Guin looked at the young man.

"It is no problem," he told her.

"If you're sure," she said to John and Julia.

"Positive!" said John. "Now take a load off."

Guin took a seat and Glen followed suit, and the young maître d' went off to get two more place settings.

"So how did you find out about this place?" Guin asked them.

"Bridget," Julia replied. "What about you?"

"Same," said Glen.

"Anyone else from class here?" said Guin, glancing around.

"We haven't seen anyone," said Julia.

"Hm. I would think this was just the sort of place Vera would go," said Guin, "I understand she's here doing research for a new cookbook."

At the mention of Vera's name, Julia frowned, and John looked down. Then the young man returned with two place settings and menus for Guin and Glen.

"Can I get you something to drink, perhaps an *aperitivo*?" said the young man.

"I need a minute," said Guin. "Could we get a bottle of sparkling water while we decide?"

"*Certo!*"

"Why don't we order a bottle of wine?" suggested Julia after the young man had gone to fetch some water.

Glen agreed that that sounded like a good idea.

John studied the wine list and frowned.

"You have a look," he said to Glen. "I'm not familiar with these Italian wines. Though, of course, I know Chianti."

Glen took the wine list and studied it.

"I'm not that familiar with them either. Why don't we ask our server?"

The young man returned bearing a large bottle of Pellegrino, which he proceeded to pour into each of their water glasses.

"Could you help us select a wine?" Julia asked him when he was done pouring.

The young man smiled.

"You should ask my brother Giuseppe," he said, indicating a man a bit older than him who was helping another table. "He will be your server. I am, how you say, just the busboy."

"Fine, fine," said John. "Tell Giuseppe to come over."

"*Sì*, I tell him."

"And what is your name?" Guin asked the young man.

"Giacomo," he replied.

"*Grazie*, Giacomo," said Guin.

Giacomo went over to Giuseppe, whispering something in his ear. Giuseppe nodded and came over a couple of minutes later.

"*Buona sera*," he said. "Giacomo says you would like help picking a wine?"

"That's right," said John.

"Can you help us?" said Julia.

"*Certo!* What is it you are thinking of having this evening?"

Julia looked over at her husband.

"Let me guess, you want us to share," he said.

"You know me so well."

The restaurant had a limited menu, with only a few choices, but everything sounded good to Guin. Maybe she and Glen would share too. That is if Glen was willing.

She looked over at him.

"Let me guess, you're thinking we should share too," he said.

"If you don't mind."

"Not at all."

"So I guess we'll be getting one of everything," said John.

"In that case," said Giuseppe, "I recommend the Chianti Rufina. It is made from local Sangiovese grapes." He pointed to it on the wine menu.

"That's fine," said John. "We'll have a bottle of that."

"Very good," said Giuseppe. "Can I get you something to drink to start, an *aperitivo*?"

"I'll just have the wine," said Guin.

"Same for me," said Glen.

John looked like he was about to order a cocktail, but at a look from his wife, he closed his mouth.

"Very good," said Giuseppe. "I will be right back."

"So, what are you going to order?" she asked Glen.

"Does it matter if we're sharing?"

"I suppose not. But it'll make life easier for Giuseppe."

"Okay," he said. He picked up his menu. "How about I order the duck tagliatelle and you order the wild mushroom risotto to start?"

"That's fine. What about for *secondo*?"

"How about I get the pork and you get the rabbit?"

"I'm down with that."

"What about you, dear?" Julia said to her husband.

"You decide."

Giuseppe returned and presented the bottle of Chianti Rufina to John. He nodded. Giuseppe then uncorked it and poured a little into John's glass.

John sniffed the wine, swirled it gently, sniffed it again, then took a sip.

"Very good," he said to Giuseppe. "Would you like to try it, Glen?"

"That's not necessary."

Giuseppe looked at John.

"Go ahead and pour."

Giuseppe did as he was told, waiting for everyone to take a sip.

"It's very good," Guin said.

Giuseppe smiled and excused himself.

"A toast!" John said, picking up his wine glass. "To Chianti!"

"And to new friends!" said Julia.

Guin smiled, and they all clinked glasses and drank.

"This is really good," said Guin, taking another sip. "I wonder if it's sold around here."

"We should ask," said Glen.

"Let's," said Julia. "I'd love to bring home a case."

"I doubt it will fit in your carry-on, dear."

"I wasn't thinking of bringing it on the plane," Julia retorted. "I'm sure if it's sold at a wine store around here they'll ship it."

"I'm hungry," said John.

He signaled to Giuseppe, who came right over.

"*Sì?*"

"We're ready to order."

They placed their orders and Giuseppe said he would be back with some bread.

"So, what do you think of the class so far?" Guin asked the Adamses.

"I'm enjoying it," said John.

"And you, Julia?"

"I am, too."

"And what do you think of our classmates?"

"I like watching the Italians," said Julia.

"That's because you fancy that Domenico," said John, a bit petulantly.

"Oh, and you haven't ogled Beatrice? Please."

"What about Oliver and Vera?"

Julia frowned, and John looked uncomfortable.

"I take it you don't like them."

"Not particularly."

"How come?"

"John used to work for Vera's husband. Or rather ex-husband."

"Oh?" said Guin. "What did you do for him?"

"Mostly contracts. He's an art dealer in Boston."

"I read that," said Guin. "What is he like?"

"Very patrician," said Julia. "A member of Boston's elite. Vera was his second wife."

"What happened to his first wife?"

"She divorced him after she caught him and Vera *in flagrante*."

"That was just a rumor," said John. "Nicholas said he didn't start seeing Vera until after they were separated."

"I'm sure that's what Nicholas wanted you to believe," said Julia.

Guin didn't know what to say. She couldn't imagine Vera having an affair with a married man. She was about to ask Julia a question about Vera, but Giuseppe had arrived with their antipasti and was busy explaining what was on each plate. There were two different kinds of bruschetta, one vegetarian and one with a kind of pâté; prosciutto with melon; roasted vegetables; a variety of cured meats; and several kinds of cheese. Everything looked delicious, and Guin didn't know where to begin.

"So much food!" she said. "It's a meal in itself."

"I know," said Julia. "I didn't realize there would be so much."

John didn't say anything. He just reached in and helped himself. Glen did the same. Then Guin and Julia each took a piece of bruschetta.

The plates of antipasti were nearly empty. And Giuseppe had come over to see how they were doing.

"You like?" he said.

"We hated it," said John.

Giuseppe frowned.

"He's kidding," said Julia. "Everything was delicious."

"Ah, very good," said Giuseppe. He glanced down at their wine glasses. "Can I get you another bottle of wine?"

"Capital idea!" said John.

Giuseppe took their plates and returned a few minutes later with a fresh bottle of wine. He showed it to John, who nodded. He then uncorked it and began refilling their glasses.

"Just half a glass for me," said Guin.

He finished pouring and told them their main course would be out momentarily.

"So, how are you two enjoying the class?" asked Julia as they sipped their wine.

"I'm enjoying it very much," said Guin. "It's been years since I took a cooking class. The last one I took was just after I got married."

"Oh, you were married," said Julia.

Guin nodded.

"It was a long time ago. Well, not that long ago. It just feels that way. We've been divorced a few years now."

"And what about you, Glen? Have you been enjoying the class?"

"Very much. Bridget is a great teacher. Though I knew she would be. We worked together on Wall Street, and she was always good at explaining things."

Their main courses came out, and conversation temporarily stopped.

"That was so good," said Guin, as Giacomo cleared away their dinner plates.

Everyone nodded in agreement.

"I've never had rabbit," said Julia.

"Me neither," said Guin. "And, I admit, I felt a little guilty. But it was really good."

"Tasted a bit like chicken to me," said John.

"Could I interest you in some dessert and coffee?" said Giuseppe. "Everything is made here in house."

"I don't think I could eat another bite," said Guin.

"Nonsense!" said John, who was a bit tipsy. "One is never too full for dessert!"

"This is true," said Giuseppe, smiling at them.

"What do you have?" asked Glen.

Giuseppe recited a short list, and they ordered *cantucci* and *zuccotto*, a semi-frozen cake with ice cream in the middle, both of which they would share. They also ordered espressos, Guin requesting decaf.

The desserts arrived, and they immediately dug in.

"I thought you didn't want dessert," Glen said teasingly to Guin.

"I never said I didn't want it. Just that I didn't have room. We did have gelato earlier, in case you forgot."

"I didn't forget."

"So, what's the deal with the two of you?" said John.

"What do you mean?" said Guin, looking over at him.

"You two dating?"

"We're colleagues," said Guin.

John shook his head.

"I've seen the way you two look at each other. There's something going on between the two of you."

"Ignore him," said Julia. She turned to her husband. "Can't you see you're making them uncomfortable?"

"You're not making me uncomfortable," said Glen. "I'm very fond of Guin."

"See!" said John triumphantly. "I knew it!"

"But as Guin said, we're just colleagues—and friends."

"Very good friends by the looks of it," said John.

"I think we should get a check," said Julia and signaled to Giuseppe.

He brought over the bill a minute later, and John immediately snatched it.

"Dinner is on me," he said.

"Please," said Guin. "Let's split it."

He shook his head.

"I insist."

Guin looked over at Julia, but she just shook her head.

"That's very kind of you, but you needn't."

"My pleasure," he said. "It's nice having dinner with a couple of young folks."

He signaled to Giuseppe and handed him his credit card.

"Thank you," said Glen. "You must let us return the favor."

But John waved him away.

They stepped outside. The fresh air felt good after sitting inside for over two hours. And it was cooler now. Guin shivered.

"You cold?" Glen asked her. "Here," he said, gently rubbing her arms.

"See! I told you there was something between them!" said John.

Guin felt mortified and put a hand on Glen's to stop him.

"Come along, dear," Julia said to her husband. "Leave Guinivere and Glen alone."

"Guinivere! Like the queen in King Arthur! My queen," he said, bowing to Guin.

Julia looked exasperated, but John wasn't done. He looked up at Glen and made a face. "So are you Arthur or Lancelot?"

"He's neither," said Julia.

"No, that's not right," said John. "Wait, I've got it! I shall call thee Glenivere!"

Guin and Glen exchanged a look, and Julia took her husband's arm.

"I fear John has had a bit too much to drink," she said.

"Have not," said John. "I'm perfectly fine. I'll show you."

He attempted to walk a straight line but stumbled.

Julia sighed.

"I'm sorry," she said to Guin and Glen. She turned to her husband. "Keys, please."

He made to protest, but at a stern look from his wife, he fumbled in his pocket and produced the car key.

"Thank you."

She said good night to Glen and Guin then led John away.

"Good night, Glenivere!" he called.

Guin sighed.

"I rather like it," said Glen.

They waited until the Adamses drove off. Then they made their way to Glen's convertible. Guin noticed the Ferrari was gone.

"Looks like your ride vanished."

"It wasn't my ride," said Glen.

"Who do you think it belonged to? My money's on the silver-haired gentleman with the attractive blonde who left a little before us."

"Could be," said Glen, opening the door for Guin. She got in and yawned.

"Tired?"

She nodded.

"I think it's the Tuscan air. Or it could be all the food I've eaten."

"Well, I bet you'll sleep well tonight."

"I hope so."

She kept her eyes open as they made their way down the driveway, making sure they didn't hit a tree. But as soon as they were back on the road, she felt her eyelids drooping.

"Okay, sleepyhead, time to get up."

Guin opened her eyes and glanced around. They were back at the hotel. Had she really fallen asleep? Apparently so. She got out of the car, and they headed to their rooms.

"I think I had a little too much wine."

"You didn't have that much," said Glen.

They passed by the kitchen, and Guin thought she heard voices coming from inside. But who would be in the kitchen so late? It must have been nearly eleven. She saw there was a light on and stopped to listen.

"What are you doing?" said Glen.

"Sh!" said Guin. "I thought I heard voices coming from the kitchen. It sounded like two people arguing."

Glen came and stood next to her.

"I don't hear anything."

Guin frowned.

"Come on," he said, gently placing a hand on her arm.

"I wasn't imagining it. And there's a light on." Though just as she said it, the light went off.

"Well, it's not on now," he said, glancing at the window.

"It was on a minute ago. And I know what I heard."

She waited by the window, but after not hearing anything more, she reluctantly allowed Glen to lead her away.

CHAPTER 11

Someone was banging on Guin's door. There it was again. Guin cracked open her eyes. What time was it? There was light streaming into her room. Had she overslept? She hadn't drunk that much wine at dinner, though it was more than she normally drank. She picked up her travel alarm clock and was surprised to see it was after eight. She never slept that late at home. Then again, on Sanibel she was usually in bed by ten. Last night she had gone to bed after eleven.

There came the knock again, louder this time. She got up to get it and heard a familiar voice.

"Guin, are you there?"

It was Glen. Was something wrong? Class didn't begin until nine-thirty.

She opened the door.

"Is everything okay?" she asked sleepily.

"No. I need you to come with me to the kitchen."

"But class doesn't start until…"

Glen cut her off.

"It's not about class."

Guin looked confused.

"Then what?"

"It's Vera."

"What about Vera?"

"She's dead."

"Vera's dead? What happened? And why do I need to go with you to the kitchen?"

"Because the police want to interview everyone."

"The police? Why do the police want to interview everyone?" Then the realization dawned. "Vera was murdered?"

Glen nodded.

"How do you know all of this?"

"I was taking pictures around the property when I heard sirens and saw the police arrive and followed them to the kitchen."

"Did you see the body?"

"No, they wouldn't let me inside. They just asked me who I was, then they told Rosa to gather everyone, and I said I'd get you."

"Huh. So who all was in the kitchen?"

"The kitchen staff and Julia."

"Why was Julia there?"

"Probably because she's a doctor."

"Right."

"Get dressed. We should go."

Guin had forgotten she was wearing her nightshirt, an old concert tee, and suddenly felt self-conscious.

"Just give me a couple of minutes."

She shut the door, went to the bathroom, and quickly got dressed. Glen was waiting for her when she stepped outside.

"What about Oliver?" asked Guin. "Was he there?"

"No. At least not when I was."

"Should we see if he's in his room?" It was next door to Glen's.

"He probably knows by now."

"Did you see him when you were coming to get me?"

"No, but..."

"We should knock, make sure he knows." Guin went over and knocked on his door. "Oliver, are you there?" There was no reply. She knocked again. "Oliver, you there?

It's Guin Jones. We need to speak with you. It's important."
Still no answer.

"He's probably in the kitchen, which is where we should
be."

They were nearly at the main building when they heard
sirens.

"I thought you said the police were already here."

"It could be an ambulance."

They entered the building but were barred from entering
the kitchen by a brawny policeman. Guin peeked in and was
able to see a small group of people—Bridget, Leo,
Francesca, and Julia, and an officious-looking man who she
assumed was a detective or police officer—but she was
unable to see the body.

Suddenly, there was a commotion behind her. She moved
out of the way to allow two EMTs to get by. The people in the
kitchen parted. That's when Guin saw the body.

"Whoa," she said.

Glen was standing next to her.

"Whoa is right."

They stood staring at the body until their view was
blocked again. But Guin would not soon forget what she
had seen. Someone had stabbed Vera van Leyden in the
back.

Guin wanted to get into the kitchen, but the brawny
policeman continued to guard the entrance. Then Rosa
appeared. Guin immediately went over to her.

"What happened?"

"I do not know."

"Who found her?"

"Leo. She was lying there when he arrived this morning."

"That must have been awful for him."

"Yes. The poor boy was in shock."

"Was she dead when he found her?"

Rosa nodded.

Guin looked back into the kitchen.

"Who is that man?" she asked, indicating the man in plainclothes who was speaking with the EMTs.

"That is Chief Inspector Manetti of the *Polizia di Stato*."

"Chief inspector? So he's a detective?"

"*Sì*."

"With the state police? Does Greve not have its own police force?"

"We do, but it is very small. And it does not handle crimes such as this."

Guin was going to ask her about the Italian criminal justice system, but she realized now was not the time. She turned back to the kitchen and saw the chief inspector speaking to Julia. Then he led her over to the EMTs. Guin wondered if they spoke English. She guessed not as it appeared the chief inspector was translating. So clearly he spoke English.

It wasn't a very long conversation, and Julia was now heading towards them. Guin saw John out of the corner of her eye. He had been standing off to the side but was now moving towards his wife.

"You okay?" he asked her as soon as she stepped out of the kitchen.

"I'm fine, but I can't say the same for Vera."

Guin and Glen went over to them.

"Do you know what happened?" Guin asked Julia.

"She was stabbed in the back with a chef's knife."

"Is that what killed her?"

"I think so, but I'm not positive. I hadn't fully examined her when the police arrived and told me to move away from the body."

"I saw the chief inspector talking to you. What did he say?"

Julia was about to answer when their attention was diverted by the arrival of Beatrice and Domenico. Beatrice looked a bit wild-eyed. She went over to Rosa and spoke to her in Italian. Guin watched as the three of them spoke and gesticulated. If only she spoke or understood Italian.

"Guin." It was Glen. He gently moved her aside so the EMTs could get through.

As soon as they passed, Guin went over to Rosa.

"Why are they leaving without the body?"

"They are going to get *una barella*, a stretcher," Rosa explained.

Guin was about to ask her another question when she saw Chief Inspector Manetti signal to Rosa. Rosa immediately went over to him. They spoke for a minute, then Rosa led him to their little group.

"I am Chief Inspector Manetti of the State Police," he said in lightly accented English. "As you may have heard, there has been a death of one of the guests. I understand you all knew the deceased and attended the cooking class with her. So I will need to speak with each of you. Please do not leave the property without permission. I will have Officer Bianchi come find you when it is your turn."

Just then, Oliver appeared, followed by Matteo.

"What's going on?" he demanded. "Where's Signora van Leyden?"

"And you are?" said the chief inspector, eyeing him.

"I'm her agent, Oliver Oliveira. And who are you?"

"I am Chief Inspector Manetti of the Italian State Police." That didn't seem to impress Oliver. "I regret to inform you that Signora van Leyden is no longer with us."

"What do you mean, *no longer with us?*"

"I mean she is dead."

Oliver stared at him.

"Dead? But I just saw her last night, and she seemed perfectly fine."

"What time was that?" asked the chief inspector.

"I don't remember," said Oliver, suddenly sounding a bit cagey. He looked around. "Where is she?"

The chief inspector stepped aside, allowing Oliver to see Vera's body.

Oliver immediately covered his mouth.

"No," he said. "It can't be."

Guin thought he looked genuinely shocked. Or else he was a good actor.

Just then the EMTs returned with the stretcher. The group watched as Vera's body was placed on it and covered with a sheet. Everyone moved aside to let them pass.

"Where are they taking her?" Oliver asked the chief inspector.

"To the hospital," he replied.

"I should go with her."

"I am afraid that is not possible."

"Why not?"

"Are you family?"

"I told you, I'm her agent. I'm responsible for her."

"I am sorry, Signore Oliveira, but only family may accompany her."

"That's ridiculous!" said Oliver. "I should be with her!"

"Perhaps you could tell me who her next of kin is?"

"Her sister, Lena. But they weren't close. And she lives in the States, near Chicago, which is miles away."

"Do you know how I may contact her?"

"I'll need to find her information."

"Please do that. Also, I would like to speak with you about Signora van Leyden's whereabouts last night and this morning. And yours also."

"Why?"

"A murder has been committed, Signore Oliveira. We must ask everyone where they were."

"Surely you don't think I had anything to do with it?"

said Oliver, sounding appalled. "I was her agent! I loved Vera! She was like a sister to me!"

Guin heard someone snort.

"As I said, I will be speaking with everyone staying at the hotel."

"Did you speak with *her*?" Oliver said, looking at Bridget.

"Are you referring to Signora O'Brien?"

Oliver nodded.

"She was clearly jealous of Vera."

Guin stared at him. She had never gotten the impression that Bridget was jealous of Vera.

"Is that so?" said the chief inspector.

"Oh, yes," said Oliver, looking smug.

"And why would Signora O'Brien be jealous of Signora van Leyden?"

"Isn't it obvious? Vera was a famous cookbook author. And Signora O'Brien was a wannabe."

Guin looked over at Glen. He looked ready to punch Oliver.

"A wannabe?" said the chief inspector.

"As in she wanted to be a famous cookbook author."

"But if Signora van Leyden was so famous, why was she taking a class from Signora O'Brien?"

"She was researching a new cookbook on Tuscan cuisine."

"Surely a famous cookbook author would not need to take a class from—what did you call her?—a wannabe though, yes?"

Oliver struggled to answer.

"Why don't you come with me, and we can discuss it?" said the chief inspector.

"I have calls to make."

"It is quite early in the States, no? Surely, the calls can wait?"

Oliver looked distinctly uncomfortable.

"Fine," he finally said.

The chief inspector turned and said something to Rosa in Italian. Rosa replied, and Guin heard the chief inspector say *grazie*. It was the only word she had understood. Though his English was quite good. She wondered if he had studied in the States.

"This way, please, Signore Oliveira," said the chief inspector.

Guin watched as Oliver reluctantly followed him.

"I bet he did it," said John.

"What makes you say that?" said Guin.

"The two of them were always arguing."

"I heard them too," said Beatrice. Guin hadn't heard her come over. "They sounded like cats."

"Where are they going?" Guin asked Rosa.

"I told the chief inspector he could use my office."

"Where will you work?"

"At my desk."

Guin glanced down the hall. A part of her wanted to follow Oliver and the chief inspector to Rosa's office and eavesdrop. Though she probably wouldn't be able to hear what they were saying through the thick door. She turned and looked into the kitchen. Bridget was speaking with Leo and Francesca. Guin turned to Rosa.

"Can we go in? We'd like to see if Bridget and Leo are okay."

"Please," added Glen.

Rosa nodded and went to speak with the officer guarding the kitchen. She returned a short time later.

"He says just for a minute, and that you must not touch anything."

"We can do that," said Guin. "Thank you."

CHAPTER 12

They quickly made their way over to Bridget, who was talking with Leo and Francesca.

"How are you doing?" Guin asked them.

"About as well as can be expected," said Bridget.

Guin turned to Leo.

"I understand you were the one who found Signora van Leyden."

He nodded.

"She was just lying there."

"Poor Leo," said Bridget. "I can't imagine. I should have been here."

"Where were you?" asked Guin.

"I was running late. Then I walked in to find Dr. Adams with the body. I mean Mrs. van Leyden. And Leo told me what had happened."

"Do you know what Vera was doing here so early?"

"We have no idea."

Bridget was looking at Leo as she said it, as though silencing him. What was that about?

"What did the chief inspector have to say?" Guin asked her.

"Not much. He asked Leo if he had seen anyone entering or leaving the kitchen."

"Did you?" Guin asked him.

"No, I saw no one."

"He also asked if we knew of anyone who might want to harm Mrs. van Leyden."

"What did you tell him?"

"I said we knew of no one who wanted to harm her."

Though Guin wondered if that was the truth.

"Did you tell him she was a famous cookbook author?"

"No, I just said that she was a student."

"Signora Adams told him," said Leo.

"What did he say when she told him that?"

"He asked me if it was usual to have famous chefs attend my class," said Bridget.

"And what did you tell him?"

"I told him no."

"Did he ask you anything else?"

"He asked me if I had a problem with Vera being here."

"And what did you say?"

"I said it was no problem. I considered her a student like everyone else."

Guin studied Bridget's face, trying to see if she was lying. Guin knew she would have felt a bit intimidated if a famous journalist showed up at the paper and followed her around. But maybe Bridget didn't feel the same way. She continued to look at Bridget, but she was hard to read.

Then she remembered what she had read about Vera allegedly stealing recipes.

"Did you know about the accusations, the chefs who claimed Vera had stolen their recipes?"

"I recall reading something about that. It was all over the cooking blogs at the time. But I didn't pay much attention. I was in Italy, trying to start a business."

"But when you found out Vera had signed up for your class, weren't you worried she might steal some of your recipes?"

"I didn't even know she had signed up to take the class until I saw her here. Mr. Oliveira had made her reservation using an assumed name."

"Did you know she was working on a new cookbook?"

"Not at first."

"But you found out."

Bridget nodded.

"And you didn't kick her out of the class?" asked Glen.

"I couldn't do that," she replied. "They had paid. And the accusations were never proved. Besides, she had signed an agreement acknowledging that all of the recipes taught in class were for private use only. It's stated on the first page of the binder I gave you too. All recipes are the property of Cucina D e B."

"So you weren't concerned about Vera stealing your recipes?" Guin asked her again.

She saw Leo looking at Bridget.

"What is it?"

Bridget sighed.

"Okay, maybe I was a little concerned. We've been keeping it quiet, but Dante and I have been working on our own cookbook. We're planning on publishing it later this year."

"That's great!" said Glen. "You didn't tell me."

"As I said, we've been keeping mum about it. Though Leo and Francesca know. They've been helping me test the recipes. As have you all," she added with a smile.

"It is going to be a bestseller," said Leo.

"I don't know about it being a bestseller," said Bridget. "But we hope it does well."

"I'm sure it will be a hit," said Guin. "So it features recipes from the course?"

"It does—and recipes passed down through Dante's family."

"What's it called?" asked Glen.

"The working title in English is *Cooking with Love: A Modern Take on Classic Tuscan Cuisine*. I know it's a mouthful. But it describes what we do."

"It sounds perfect," said Guin. "But wasn't it risky using recipes you planned to publish in the course? Someone could have shared them online before the cookbook was out."

"I know it was a risk, but it's how we tested many of the recipes. And as I said, there's a copyright on every recipe and everyone signed an agreement. So we felt safe."

Until Vera came along, thought Guin.

"So if Vera published any of the recipes, you could have sued her," said Glen.

"Theoretically," said Bridget. "The problem is that recipe theft is hard to prove. She could change an ingredient or call the dish something else and we probably couldn't touch her."

Guin saw Francesca touch Leo's arm. She was looking past Guin and seemed nervous. Guin turned to see Chief Inspector Manetti standing a few feet away. She hadn't heard him come in. How much had he heard?

"Please, do not let me interrupt," he said.

"We were just checking on our friends," said Glen. "Making sure they were okay."

"Friends?" said the chief inspector.

"Glen and Bridget used to work together on Wall Street," said Guin.

"Ah," said the chief inspector. He looked at Glen. "And now you are a photographer."

"How did you know?" said Glen.

The chief inspector indicated the camera hanging off Glen's shoulder.

"Right. I often forget that it's there."

"So, as a photographer, you must have a good eye," said the chief inspector.

"I like to think so."

The chief inspector smiled.

"And you have been taking pictures of the class and the people here?"

"I have."

Guin wondered where this was going.

"Did you happen to notice anything?"

"Notice anything?" said Glen.

"About this room," said the chief inspector, gesturing around him.

Glen looked around. The kitchen seemed pretty much the same as it did the day before. Well, except for the blood on the floor.

"Not really," he said.

"So nothing appears to be missing?"

"I wouldn't know."

The chief inspector looked disappointed.

"What about the other guests?"

"What about them?"

"Did you notice anything about them as you were taking their pictures?"

"Like what?"

"Little looks, perhaps at Signora van Leyden?"

"They were all too busy making food."

"What about Signora van Leyden? Did you know her before you came here?"

"No. I only met her here."

"Did you speak with her?"

"I sat next to her at dinner the other night."

"What was your impression?"

"Of her?"

"*Sì.* Was she friendly, rude?"

"I…" Glen saw Guin and Bridget looking at him. The chief inspector saw them looking at him too.

"Come, let us talk in private," he said to Glen. He turned to Bridget. "And please let me know if anything is missing."

"Of course," she said.

"Signore Anderson?"

Glen reluctantly followed the chief inspector out of the

kitchen. Bridget watched them leave. She was frowning. Guin saw her pull out her phone. Guin hadn't heard it ring, but perhaps it was on vibrate. Bridget looked down at the screen and sighed.

"Is everything okay?" Guin asked her.

"It's Dante. He heard about Vera and wants to know if I'm okay."

"Wow," said Guin. "That was fast."

"Greve is a small town. Word gets around quickly."

That reminded Guin.

"The chief inspector said he was with the state police. Is there a state police station here?"

Bridget smiled.

"No. There is only a small local police department here. The state police are based in Firenze—Florence."

"So he came all the way here from Florence?"

"Greve is part of the commune of Florence. And Florence isn't that far. Though the chief inspector may have been here already."

"Oh?"

"He's from Greve and still has family here."

"Do you know him?"

"Not well, but Dante does. He likes to eat in Dante's restaurant when he's in town."

"His English seems quite good."

"I think he spent time in the States. Now if you would excuse us, we need to do an inventory for the chief inspector."

"Right," said Guin. But she didn't leave. "Does the chief inspector think Vera could have been killed by a burglar? Do you get a lot of burglaries around here?"

Greve seemed so peaceful. Then again, Sanibel was a peaceful small town too. But there had been several murders on the island since Guin had moved there. Purely a coincidence, of course.

"There've been a few," said Bridget. "I'd hate to think one of the guests was responsible."

Guin felt the same way, but the kitchen didn't look like someone had burgled it.

She turned to go then remembered something.

"One other thing. I happened to be passing by the kitchen last night after dinner. There was a light on, and I thought I heard voices. Were you in here?"

"It wasn't me," said Bridget. "I was at home with Dante."

Guin turned to Leo and Francesca. They both shook their heads.

"Maybe I had imagined it. Okay, I'll leave you to your inventory."

Guin stood outside. The fresh air felt good. She wondered if she should go to reception and wait for Glen or go back to her room. She opted for the latter, sending Glen a message.

She hadn't gone far when she noticed John and Julia. Were they arguing? She made to go around them, but they saw her, so she stopped and went over.

"Is everything okay?"

"Everything's fine," said Julia.

Guin looked at John, who was silent.

"So, what did the chief inspector ask you?"

"What you would expect." Guin waited for her to go on. "He wanted to know when I had got there and if I thought the knife had killed her."

"And what did you say to him?"

"I said it was likely but without a toxicology report, I couldn't say for sure."

"Assuming it was the knife, who could have done it?"

"It would have had to have been someone pretty strong. The knife was pretty deep."

"Could it have been a burglar?"

"A burglar?"

"The chief inspector asked Bridget if anything was missing."

"I guess it could have been."

"I think the agent did it," said John. "I heard him talking on the phone yesterday. He sounded pretty angry. Called Vera the B-word and said he was tired of being her lapdog."

"Did you tell the chief inspector that?" asked Guin.

"I will when he questions me."

Guin couldn't picture Oliver plunging a knife into Vera's back. Though despite what he said about loving her like a sister, she had seen no love between the two of them. More like the opposite. So she couldn't rule him out.

"Well, I should get going," said Guin. "I owe my boss an article." Though she wasn't sure she'd be able to concentrate.

She was about to head to her room when she saw Officer Bianchi walking towards them.

"Signora Jones," he said. "Would you come with me?"

What was she going to say, no?

"Of course," she said. She turned to John and Julia. "If you happen to see Glen, could you tell him I'm meeting with the chief inspector?"

They said they would, then she followed Officer Bianchi to Rosa's office.

CHAPTER 13

"Please, have a seat," said the chief inspector.

Guin did as she was told.

"How well did you know the deceased, Signora van Leyden?" he asked her.

"Not very," said Guin, who continued to be impressed by the chief inspector's English. "I just met her."

"I see," he said. "So you did not know her before taking this class?"

"I mean, I knew *of* her, but I had never met her before I got here."

"So you knew she was a famous cookbook author."

Guin nodded.

"And when was the last time you saw Signora van Leyden?"

Guin had to think.

"At the olive oil farm."

"And when was that?"

"Yesterday afternoon." It seemed so long ago now.

"So you did not see her last night or this morning?"

"No. I didn't see her until... you know."

"And where were you last night and early this morning?"

"I had dinner with my colleague Glen Anderson and the Adamses at a little place down the road. Then we came back to the hotel, and I went to bed."

"What time did you return to the hotel?"

"A little after ten-thirty? I wasn't wearing a watch."

"And you say you went straight to bed?"

Guin nodded.

"Alone?"

"Alone," she replied.

"And did you happen to see or hear anything as you walked from the car to your room?"

Had Glen told the chief inspector that she had thought she had heard voices coming from the kitchen? She studied him. He had thick dark hair and eyebrows and deep brown eyes. He reminded her a bit of a young Al Pacino.

"Actually... I thought I heard voices coming from the kitchen."

"You *thought* you heard voices?"

"There was a light on. And I thought I heard two people arguing. But when I asked Glen if he heard them, he said he hadn't. And then the light went off."

"I see," said the chief inspector.

"May I ask *you* a question?"

He indicated for her to go ahead.

"Your English is very good. Did you spend time in the States?"

"Italians cannot speak good English without spending time in the United States?"

Guin felt embarrassed. She knew many Europeans studied English in school.

"It's just..."

He held up a hand.

"It is all right. I did spend time in the States."

Guin tried not to look pleased.

"Where did you live?"

"In Connecticut."

"Where in Connecticut?"

"In New Haven."

"I lived not far from there before moving to Sanibel.

That's in Florida. They have really good pizza there. In New Haven, I mean. Not Florida. The pizza is just okay there. Did you ever go to Frank Pepe's?"

She knew she was rambling and told herself to shut up. This is what happened when she didn't have coffee. But the chief inspector was smiling.

"I preferred Sally's Apizza."

"I never went there, but I heard it's very good. So what were you doing in New Haven?"

"I went to school there."

"Oh, did you attend the University of New Haven?"

"No, a little place called Yale," he replied. "Perhaps you have heard of it?"

Guin knew her cheeks were turning pink.

"I worked at my cousin Sal's pizzeria, to help pay the bills."

"Sal as in…?"

The chief inspector nodded.

"Well, that explains why you preferred Sally's Apizza."

"No, I preferred it because it was the best. Now, if we could get back to Signora van Leyden?"

"Of course," said Guin.

"These voices you heard in the kitchen…"

"Thought I heard."

"That you thought you heard. Could one of them have belonged to Signora van Leyden?"

"I suppose," said Guin. "I didn't hear them for very long. And they were a bit muffled."

"And could the other voice have belonged to Signora O'Brien?"

"I just told you, I didn't recognize either voice. And Bridget said she was at home with Dante, her husband."

The chief inspector tented his hands.

"What did you think of Signora van Leyden?"

"What do you mean?"

"Was she pleasant, rude? Did she get along with the other guests?"

"She was a bit aloof. But then again, she was a famous cookbook author."

"Famous cookbook authors cannot be friendly?"

She looked at him. He had a point. Guin had met several famous authors and people during her years as a reporter. Most of them had been quite friendly. However, she couldn't say the same for Vera.

"And you did not find it curious that a famous cookbook author was taking a cooking class?"

"I admit, I found it a bit odd. But she was supposedly researching a new cookbook."

"What about her agent, Signore Oliveira?"

"What about him?"

"Did the two of them get along?"

"You wouldn't think so. They were always arguing. But maybe that was their way."

"And what about the other guests? How did they feel about Signora van Leyden?"

"I don't know. You would have to ask them."

He smiled again.

"I thought you suspected it was a burglar?"

"Did I say it was a burglar?"

"No… But you asked Bridget if anything was missing."

He regarded Guin, and she felt slightly uncomfortable. But she refused to let it show.

"May I go now?"

"You may, but I will need your passport."

"My passport? Why? You can't possibly think I had anything to do with Vera's death."

"Your passport, Signora Jones."

They had a staring contest.

"I'll need to go get it from my room."

"That is fine. I will be here."

"When will I get it back? I'm supposed to leave in a few days."

"We will return it once we have determined who killed Signora van Leyden."

"But that could take weeks!"

"Hopefully not. Now please, go retrieve your passport."

Guin fumed as she made her way back to her room. Not that being stuck in Chianti would be the worst thing in the world. But she missed her cat and her friends. And Ginny would not be happy. Guin had already taken an extra week off, albeit she was supposed to be working. And what did she have to show for it? One measly article. She would need to send Ginny an email when she got back to her room.

She was so lost in thought that she nearly collided with Glen. He stopped her by placing his hands on her arms.

"Oh!" she said, looking up at him.

He smiled down at her.

"I saw John and Julia. How did it go with the chief inspector?"

"He wants my passport."

"Mine too," said Glen. "I was just heading up there to give it to him."

"I'll go get mine, and we can go together."

"Okay, I'll wait."

Guin hurried to her room, emerging a minute later with her passport. Then they headed to Rosa's office. The door was closed, so Glen knocked.

"*Avanti!*"

Glen opened the door. The chief inspector was looking down at his phone, but he looked up as Glen and Guin entered.

"We brought our passports."

The chief inspector gestured for them to come closer.

They walked over to the desk and handed him their passports.

He didn't bother to examine them.

"You'll let us know when we can have them back," said Glen.

"*Certo*," said the chief inspector.

"I have a question," said Guin.

"Yes?" said the chief inspector.

"I know we can't leave the country, but are we allowed to leave the property?"

"Where is it you want to go?"

"Into town… around Chianti… maybe to Florence?" Guin didn't really know, but she didn't want to be stuck at the hotel.

"I see," said the chief inspector. "Give me your phones."

"Our phones?" said Guin.

"*Sì*, your phones."

"Why?" asked Glen.

"So I can put a tracker on them."

"A tracker?" said Guin.

"So that I may keep track of you."

Glen and Guin exchanged a look.

"That is the only way," said the chief inspector.

"Fine," said Guin. She took out her phone and unlocked it. "Here."

She handed it to the chief inspector.

"*Grazie.*"

Guin watched as he moved his finger across it. No doubt he was installing a tracking app.

"Now your phone, Signore Anderson," said the chief inspector after handing Guin back her phone. She looked down at it.

"Do not uninstall it," warned the chief inspector. "You may remove it after I have returned your passports."

Guin frowned.

"Signore Anderson? Your phone?"

Glen reluctantly handed it over.

"There now," said the chief inspector when he was done. "You are both free to go."

"Gee, thanks," said Guin.

The chief inspector looked amused.

There was a knock on the door.

"*Avanti!*" called the chief inspector.

The door opened. It was Domenico. He looked over at Guin and Glen.

"We were just leaving," said Guin.

Guin went back to her room to try to get some work done. But it wasn't easy. She had been trying to write for over an hour when she received a group message from Bridget. She had received permission from the chief inspector to take everyone to lunch at Dante's. Then they would go to a local vineyard for a wine tasting.

Guin's stomach rumbled in response. She hadn't had breakfast or even gotten coffee, and she was hungry. Bridget had said they would leave for the restaurant at twelve-thirty. Guin looked at the clock on her laptop. It was only ten-thirty. She groaned.

She looked back at the article she had been working on. It was no use. She needed a distraction. Maybe a walk.

She saved the document then messaged Glen. Did he fancy a walk?

"I'm by the pool," he wrote her back. "Why don't you join me?"

Guin thought for a minute. Did she want to go for a swim? Not really. Glen messaged her again.

"Fine," she wrote him back. "I'll be there in a few."

CHAPTER 14

Guin arrived at the pool to see Glen lounging near Beatrice. She looked like a 1940s movie star in her vintage-looking one-piece, big sunglasses, and straw hat. Glen was wearing board shorts and looked like he had recently gone for a swim. As if sensing Guin's presence, he sat up and smiled at her.

"You made it."

"Though it looks like you were doing just fine without me," said Guin, looking over at Beatrice.

Beatrice didn't move. And Guin wondered if she was asleep, wearing earbuds, or just ignoring her.

"You want to go for a swim?" he asked her.

"Could we talk first?"

Guin wanted to ask him about his interview with the chief inspector.

"Sure, have a seat," he said, gesturing to an empty lounge chair.

"Let's go over there," she said, pointing to one of the cabanas.

He got up, and they headed to the other side of the pool, taking a seat in one of the cabanas.

"What's up?" he asked her.

"How did your interview with Chief Inspector Manetti go?"

"Okay, I guess."

"What did you tell him about Vera?"

"Not much. It wasn't as if I knew her."

"Though you talked with her the other night at dinner."

"It was mostly polite conversation, as I told you."

"Did he ask you about the other guests?"

He nodded.

"What did you tell him?"

"I told him I didn't think anyone here was a killer."

"Did he believe you?"

"I don't know."

"You think it could have been a burglar?"

"I don't know what to think."

"Well, someone shoved that knife into her back."

"I know."

"Did you tell the chief inspector I had heard people talking in the kitchen late last night?"

"I told him that you thought you heard something."

Guin frowned. She was sure she had heard someone.

"Did you message Ginny?"

"Not yet. You?"

"Not yet. But we should tell her we may be stuck here for a while."

"That's not the worst thing, is it?" he said, giving Guin a look that made her face start to grow a bit warm.

"Except that we may be staying with a murderer."

"You don't really think one of the guests killed Vera, do you?"

"You don't really think it was a burglar? Besides, we heard her arguing with Oliver. And I heard her getting into it with Domenico. And did you see the way John and Julia look whenever her name is mentioned? There's something going on there."

"So everyone's a suspect?"

"Well, not everyone. I don't think you killed her."

"Gee, thanks."

"Come on, don't you want to know who done it?"

"Not really," said Glen. "This was supposed to be a vacation."

"A *working* vacation," Guin reminded him. "So let's get to work."

"You don't mean try to figure out who killed Vera."

"That's exactly what I mean."

"This isn't Sanibel, Guin. And that chief inspector isn't Detective O'Loughlin."

"Thank goodness for that. Look, who better to investigate than us?"

"Uh, the police?"

Guin made a face.

"Between my reporter's instincts and your ability to see things other people don't, we'll nail the killer in no time."

"I'm not Superman, Guin. I can't read minds."

"You know what I mean. And Superman couldn't read people's minds. He had x-ray vision."

Glen made a face.

"Come on. It'll be fun."

"Fun? Someone was killed, Guin."

"Okay, *fun* was maybe a poor choice of words. I didn't have any coffee or food this morning. So my brain's not fully functioning."

"I'll say," Glen mumbled.

"Excuse me?"

"Nothing."

"I promise I won't do anything risky. Just say you'll help me."

"Do I have a choice?"

"No, not really."

Glen sighed.

"Fine. What do you want me to do?"

"Keep your eyes and ears open—and talk to Bridget."

"Bridget? Why do I need to talk to Bridget? Wait. You

don't think she killed Vera, do you?"

"No, but…"

"Oh my God. You *do* suspect her."

"It's not that I suspect her. It's just… She had motive and opportunity."

"Bridget did not kill Vera van Leyden."

"Then let's prove it."

"Fine," he said getting up. "I'm going to do a few laps."

"I'll go with you," said Guin.

Beatrice was gone when they emerged from the cabana. Thank heaven for small miracles. Guin was self-conscious enough as it was. She removed the towel from around her waist, placing it on a chaise longue. Then she dipped her hand into the water. It was still cold. Did they not heat pools in Italy?

She watched as Glen dove in. He emerged, water cascading down his chest, and looked over at her.

"Come in."

"I'm working on it."

"Just jump."

Guin looked like she was thinking about it.

"I'll catch you."

Guin made a face.

"I'm not a little kid."

"No, you're not."

There was that look again, the one that made Guin's toes curl.

"Fine, I'll jump. But you don't have to catch me."

"Suit yourself."

Guin walked around to the deep end of the pool. She held her breath and jumped. Just as before, the water felt like ice. She immediately began to swim, hoping it would warm her up.

When she opened her eyes, she saw Glen looking at her.

"See?" he said.

"Yeah, yeah, yeah. I'm going to do a few laps."

"I'll join you."

They swam back and forth. Guin didn't know for how long. She did ten laps, then hauled herself out of the pool. Glen followed her out.

She toweled off and picked up her phone. It was nearly noon. She frowned.

"We need to hurry."

"What time is it?"

"Almost noon."

"We have plenty of time. The van doesn't leave until twelve-thirty."

"Maybe plenty of time for you," said Guin. "But this hair takes more than half an hour to dry." She held out a wet curl.

"I like your hair when it's wet."

"Yes, well, I don't." Though she actually did. The problem was it frizzed when it dried. Which was why she always traveled with a tube of gel to stop her hair from frizzing. But it wasn't always enough.

"I'm heading back to my room."

She wrapped her towel around her, though now it was wet, and left the pool area.

Guin showered and changed as quickly as she could. She combed out her hair and frowned. She glanced over at the blow-dryer, but she was loath to use it. Instead, she grabbed a ponytail holder and pulled her hair back. She looked in the mirror and frowned again, removing the ponytail holder. She grabbed her tube of hair gel, squeezed out a large blob, and ran it through her hair.

"It'll have to do," she said to her reflection.

She looked at her phone. It was twelve-thirty. She

grabbed her bag and her card key and hurried to the front of the hotel.

Bridget was by the van along with the Adamses and Glen. Had he knocked on her door? She hadn't heard anything.

"Sorry I'm late," she said. She glanced around. "Where are the Italians and Oliver?"

"Oliver is taking care of Vera's affairs," replied Bridget.

Of course. He would no doubt have to contact Vera's publisher and the embassy or consulate and Vera's family. Though Vera was divorced and her son had died. But Oliver had mentioned a sister.

"What about Domenico and Beatrice?" she asked Bridget.

Bridget sighed.

"Who knows?"

"I say we go," said John.

Guin was with him, but she stayed silent.

"Let's give them a few more minutes," said Bridget.

Guin glanced around the driveway. She didn't see a police car.

"Did the police leave?"

"They did, but they'll be back," said Bridget.

Guin turned to the Adamses.

"Did the chief inspector put a tracking app on your phones?"

They nodded.

They stood around for several more minutes. There was no sign of the Italians. Bridget checked her phone one last time.

"All right, let's go."

"Hallelujah!" said John.

They got in the van and filled the first two rows.

"Should someone check on Beatrice and Domenico, make sure they're okay?" asked Glen.

"I sent them another message, letting them know we're

headed to Dante's," said Bridget. "They can always join us there."

"What if something happened to them?"

"I'm sure they're fine," said John. "Let's go already."

"I'm with John," said Bridget.

She turned to the driver and told him to leave.

CHAPTER 15

Guin had read about Dante's. The place was famous for its multi-course all-meat lunches and dinners featuring different cuts of meat ("from tongue to tail"). Though meals also included fresh seasonal vegetables, along with Tuscan bread, wine, olive oil cake, and grappa, all for the very reasonable price of €40 (approximately $45).

Guin couldn't imagine eating several meat courses, but she had promised herself she would try everything. If only so she could write about it later.

They arrived at the restaurant and were welcomed by Dante himself. He directed them to the communal table and told them to help themselves to wine. He then whispered something to Bridget, and she excused herself, saying Dante needed some help in the kitchen. Guin didn't believe that. She suspected he just wanted to speak to her in private. But she didn't say anything. Instead, she glanced around the table. It seated a dozen, and there was another foursome waiting to have lunch at the other end.

A few minutes later, a server appeared and placed a bowl of vegetables in front of them, along with a dip, a loaf of bread, olive oil, and salt. Guin immediately reached for a carrot and spread a little dip on it.

She finished the carrot and reached for a piece of celery. She could have eaten the entire bowl she was so hungry.

Guin saw John helping himself to wine. Glen also took some. He looked over at Guin.

"You want some?"

"I'm good with water, thanks."

She saw that Julia was also drinking water.

They made small talk as they waited for the first course to arrive. Guin was tempted to bring up Vera, but she didn't want to spoil the mood.

The first course came out, and the server explained what it was. Guin was so hungry, she barely paid attention. All she knew was that it was some kind of meat ragu on crostini. She eagerly took a piece and bit into it. She practically groaned.

"Oh my God," she said, her mouth partially full. "This is so good." She finished it off then reached for another piece before stopping.

"Go ahead," said John.

"Are you sure?" Guin asked them.

Glen and Julia nodded, and Guin immediately took another piece.

"Did anyone else taste cinnamon?" asked Julia. "I swear the ragu had a cinnamony taste."

"Ask Bridget," said Guin. "I'm sure she'd tell you."

Speaking of Bridget, why hadn't she joined them? Maybe Dante really did need help in the kitchen.

The server removed the now-empty crostini plate and returned a few minutes later with a bone broth soup. Guin dipped her spoon in. Again, she was bowled over by the flavor. It had a rich, umami taste, and there was garlic and onions too, and something else Guin couldn't identify.

"Wow," said Glen. "This is amazing. I don't know how to describe it."

"I know," said Julia, dipping her spoon back in her bowl for another taste. "It's like the best roast you ever had in liquid form."

Guin liked the description and took out her phone to jot it down.

"Are you going to quote me in your article?" asked Julia. "I assume you plan on writing about lunch."

"Hm?" said Guin looking up at her.

"I asked if you were going to be writing about lunch."

"I was thinking about it." Though she still had to write about the visit to the olive farm.

"Send it to me if you do."

"Happy to," Guin replied.

They finished the soup and the next course, which looked like meatballs, came out. The meatballs were flavored with rosemary and other herbs, and again Guin found them delicious, as did Glen and the Adamses. But now she was feeling quite full, and there were two more courses to go, plus dessert.

But instead of another meat course, the server brought out a Tuscan bean salad. The beans were coated with extra virgin olive oil and sprinkled with parsley, with bits of fresh tomato and a splash of lemon juice to brighten it up. Guin took a small helping and tasted it.

"Mm," she said. "It tastes like summer."

"How are you enjoying lunch?"

It was Bridget. She was wearing an apron.

"Everything's been delicious," said Julia. "Did you help make it?"

"I may have helped a bit," Bridget replied with a smile. She looked over at Glen.

"What about you? You enjoying your meal?"

"Everything's great. Though it's a lot of meat."

"I know. Margaux would be appalled."

"No doubt."

The two shared a grin.

Guin look confused.

"Who's Margaux?"

"Glen's ex," said Bridget. "She was a vegan."

"Your wife was a vegan?"

"She wasn't when I married her."

"She became one after she watched one of those documentaries about the big, bad beef industry," said Bridget.

"And did you become a vegan too?"

"I gave it a shot, but it wasn't for me. I think that's part of the reason why she left me. Our lifestyles were no longer compatible."

Guin remembered Glen telling her that his ex had had an affair with her tennis instructor. Guin wondered if he had been a vegan.

"Well, I should get back to the kitchen," said Bridget. "Enjoy the rest of your meal."

"Aren't you going to join us?" asked Julia.

"Can't. One of Dante's assistants called in sick this morning. So I'm on kitchen duty."

"He's lucky to have you," said Julia.

"I tell him that every day," said Bridget.

She headed back to the kitchen, and a few minutes later the server appeared with a platter containing thin slices of meat that looked like roast beef. He placed the platter on the table, and they helped themselves. Guin took a bite. It did taste a bit like roast beef. She didn't catch what the server had called it, but she would ask Bridget to send her the menu later.

"One more meat course to go, then dessert!" said John.

He refilled his wine glass (this would be the second time), and Guin saw Julia give him a look.

The last course was a beef and vegetable salad, which reminded Guin of a Thai dish she used to have back in New York. While all of the courses had been delicious, this one may have been her favorite. And despite being full, she ate every bite.

"I gather you liked the salad," said Glen.

"Mm," said Guin, nodding her head as she chewed and swallowed the last bite. "It's been ages since I had something like this."

"Not a lot of Asian places on Sanibel."

"No, which is surprising. Though there are plenty of Asian restaurants in Fort Myers and Naples."

The server cleared the plates, taking them back to the kitchen. Guin tapped on her phone, trying to describe the Thai beef and vegetable salad. A few minutes later, the server reappeared again, carrying a platter covered with slices of olive oil cake studded with raisins. Everyone took a slice.

Guin pulled off a piece and popped it into her mouth. The cake was incredibly moist, the olive oil coating her tongue. But unlike the olive oil she had tasted at the farm, this olive oil tasted sweet, and the raisins tasted as though they had been soaked in brandy or rum.

"Do you think Bridget would give us the recipe?" Julia asked. "This olive oil cake is divine."

"I agree," said Guin. "It's so moist. It practically melts on your tongue."

"Ask her," said Glen.

"Though maybe the recipe's in the cookbook," said Guin.

"Oh?" said Julia. "Is Bridget writing a cookbook?"

That's right. She wasn't there when Bridget told her and Glen about the cookbook.

Guin nodded.

"She and Dante have been working on it for a while. Bridget says they hope to publish it later this year."

"I'll definitely buy a copy," said Julia. "Do you think it'll be available in the States?"

"You'll have to ask her," said Glen. "But I would think so."

"I'll do that."

The server returned once more, asking everyone if they'd like coffee.

"Yes, please," said Guin. She was beginning to experience caffeine withdrawal.

He returned with four cups of espresso. Guin looked down at hers, then glanced at the others. She could drink all four.

"Could I get some milk and sugar?" asked John.

The server nodded and returned a minute later with a small pitcher of milk and a bowl containing sugar.

Guin had already downed her espresso and asked the server if she could have another one. He immediately returned with another cup.

Now that she had been well fed and caffeinated, Guin's brain started to whir. She thought about the two cookbooks. Could Bridget have been worried about being scooped or plagiarized? She had admitted as much. But to kill Vera? It seemed unlikely. Though Bridget certainly looked strong enough to have done it. And she certainly knew how to use a knife. Though chopping vegetables was not the same as plunging a knife into someone's back.

Bridget reappeared, telling them that the van would be there any minute to take them to the vineyard. Guin had forgotten about the vineyard and would have preferred to have gone back to the hotel. But she didn't say anything.

"Will you be going with us?" Glen asked her.

"Can't," said Bridget. "Dante needs me."

"Did you hear from Oliver or the Italians?" Guin asked her.

She shook her head and saw Glen frowning.

"I'm sure they're okay," she said. "Now I need to get back to the kitchen."

Guin followed her.

"Is everything okay?" Bridget asked her.

"I was hoping I could get a copy of the menu. I want to

write about lunch for my paper."

"I'd be happy to send you it when I have a minute."

Guin glanced around. She saw Dante and another man. They were busy chopping vegetables.

"How are you holding up?"

"Fine. It's probably a good thing that Dante needed me today."

"Is the chief inspector okay with you working here?"

"If he wants his supper, he better be."

"I don't understand," said Guin.

"Dante said he made a reservation."

"I see," said Guin. Her mental wheels were turning again. "Now if you'll excuse me?"

"Of course," said Guin.

CHAPTER 16

The van dropped them off at the small, family-run winery and vineyard. No one had been familiar with the name, but Bridget had assured them that the wine the Bruni family made was excellent, some of the best in Chianti.

They got out of the van and were met by Tommaso Bruni. He welcomed them and asked where Bridget was. Glen explained that she had to stay behind and help out Dante at the restaurant. Tommaso nodded his head. He understood being a part of a family business. He glanced at the group and said that he thought there were to be eight guests, not four.

"The rest couldn't make it," said Guin diplomatically. There was no need to tell Tommaso about Vera.

However, just then they heard the roar of an engine, and a silver Maserati pulled in. Guin thought the car looked familiar, and soon she knew why. It belonged to Domenico. He got out of the car along with Beatrice.

They came over to the group and said something to Tommaso.

"Anyone have any idea what they're saying?" John whispered.

Glen and Guin shook their heads.

"Well, whatever Beatrice just said," said Julia, "he looks pleased."

Guin watched as Tommaso and Domenico shook hands.

What was that about? Finally, they stopped talking and Tommaso turned to face the group.

"*Bene!*" he said. "My name is Tommaso Bruni, and my family has owned this vineyard and winery for many generations. Today, I will take you on a tour of our vineyard and show you how the wine is made. Shall we begin?"

Everyone nodded and followed him to the vineyard.

Tommaso gave them a brief history of Chianti, what made the region good for growing grapes. Then he held up a bunch of grapes.

"A wine can only be called Chianti Classico if it contains at least eighty percent Sangiovese grapes, the grapes we grow here at the vineyard."

"I didn't know that," Guin said softly to Glen. "Did you?"

Glen shook his head.

Tommaso spoke at length about the grapes they grew— it was as though he was talking about his children—and Guin had begun to space out.

"Any questions?" Tommaso asked them.

"Hm?" said Guin.

"He asked if anyone had any questions," Glen whispered to her.

"Oh," she replied.

"I have a question," said Julia. "When are the grapes harvested?"

"The Sangiovese grapes are typically harvested the second half of September." He looked around. "Any other questions?"

No one replied, so they headed into the winery.

"After the de-stemming and pressing, the grapes are fermented in these cement tanks for two to three weeks," said Tommaso, leading them around the production facility. "Then the liquid is transferred to these steel tanks to complete the fermentation process. A few months later, the liquid is transferred to oak barrels where the wine will mature for between twelve and thirty months. Then it is filtered and bottled."

He again asked if anyone had any questions, and Domenico asked him something in Italian. At the looks of confusion from the Americans, Tommaso explained that Domenico had asked him how many bottles they typically made each year.

"How many?" asked John.

"We are a small winery," said Tommaso. "In a good year, we can produce around seven thousand bottles."

"And in a not-so-good year?"

"If the weather is bad or there is a blight, it could be half that. Any other questions? If not, we will taste!"

No one raised a hand, so they headed into the tasting room.

"We will begin with our Chianti Classico. This wine is aged for a year and is one of our most popular."

He poured them each a small glass.

"Please take a sip and let me know what you think."

Guin watched as John sniffed, swirled, and tasted the wine. She copied him, swirling the wine gently in her glass before tasting it. She took a sip and let the wine play on her tongue. It tasted a bit like tart cherries.

"You like?" asked Tommaso.

Guin nodded her head.

"Very much. It tastes a bit like tart cherries and has an oakiness to it."

Tommaso smiled and asked the others what they thought of the wine. They all agreed it was very good.

After they rinsed out their glasses, he held up a bottle of Chianti Classico Riserva.

"This wine is made from the oldest grapes, from vines over thirty years old. After fermentation, the wine must mature for twenty-four months in oak barrels before it can be bottled and sold. Would you like to taste?"

Everyone nodded their heads, and he poured.

As before, Guin sniffed the wine, then swirled it before taking a sip. It had a velvety texture and was a bit spicy. She enjoyed it but liked the Chianti Classico better.

"We must get some of this," Julia said to John, who nodded his head.

"Do you ship to Boston?" John asked Tommaso.

"*Certo*," he replied.

Then it was onto the third wine.

By the time they had sampled the fifth wine, a sweet *vin santo* made from white grapes, Guin was feeling a bit lightheaded, even though they had just had a huge lunch and she hadn't drunk nearly as much wine as the rest of the group.

Once again, Tommaso asked if anyone had questions.

Guin saw Beatrice whisper something to Domenico. He nodded and went over to Tommaso, speaking to him in Italian. Guin watched and again wished she had taken a course in Italian before coming to Italy.

"What is Domenico saying to him?" she asked Beatrice.

"He is telling Tommaso that he will take several cases of his wine for his family's new hotel."

So that was why Tommaso looked so happy.

Guin went back over to Glen.

"You going to buy anything?"

"I'm thinking about it. What about you?"

"Same."

"Which wine was your favorite?"

"I really liked the first one, the Chianti Classico. You?"

"That may have been my favorite too. Though I also liked the Riserva." They watched as John and Julia placed an order.

"I liked the Riserva," said Guin. "But if I'm just going to get a bottle or two, I think I'd go with the Classico."

"How about we split a case? Maybe Tommaso can give

us six bottles of the Classico and six of the Riserva."

"That's a great idea. Do you think he'll do it?"

"Only one way to find out."

He went over to Tommaso and spoke to him as Guin watched. She saw Tommaso nod his head. A good sign. Glen smiled, and he and Tommaso walked over to the cashier. Tommaso said something to her, then Glen handed her his credit card. Guin frowned.

"Did you pay?" she asked him.

"I did."

"I thought we were going to split it."

"You can pay me back when it arrives."

"How much was it?"

"I'll let you know when I get my credit card statement."

"You didn't need to pay."

"Actually, I did. I bought a second case to send to a friend and didn't want you to have to pay for it."

"Lucky friend. Anyone I know?"

"I don't think so."

Guin was about to ask him another question, but Tommaso had begun to speak.

"Thank you again for coming to visit us today. I hope you come back next time you are in Chianti."

They thanked him for the tour and the tasting and went outside. The van was parked a few feet away. Guin was about to get in when she saw Domenico carrying a case of wine to his car. She wondered which wines he had bought. Beatrice was walking beside him, carrying a bag no doubt filled with wine.

Guin got in the van and sat down next to Glen, just behind John and Julia.

"Do you know what Domenico bought?" she asked Glen. "I saw him carrying out a case."

"No idea."

"I saw him this morning, as I was about to leave the chief inspector's office. I wonder if the chief inspector put a tracker on his phone too." She looked out the window at the Maserati.

"Probably," said Glen. "Why wouldn't he?"

"I don't know. Maybe because he's Italian?"

"I doubt that."

"I wonder where he was when Vera was killed," Guin mused. "You know, I saw Vera speaking to him the other day. It sounded like they were threatening each other."

"Threatening each other? Why would they be threatening each other? They barely knew each other."

"I have no idea. But I know what I heard. He seemed angry. They both did."

"What exactly did they say?"

"I don't remember exactly, but I think it had to do with a woman."

Glen didn't say anything, and they were quiet as they drove back to the hotel. It was a quick trip, and when they left the van, John and Julia asked them what they were doing for dinner.

"I don't think I could eat another thing after that lunch," said Guin.

"We were thinking of checking out this pizza place in town Bridget told us about," said John, seemingly ignoring Guin's comment. "You're more than welcome to join us."

"Thank you," said Guin. "But I think I'm going to skip dinner tonight. Besides, I really need to work."

"Glen?" said John. "You up for some pizza later?"

"Thank you, John, but I'm good."

"Well, if either of you changes your mind, give us a shout. We're not leaving until eight."

Guin thanked them again for the invitation but said they shouldn't wait on them. Then she and Glen headed to their rooms.

"Do you think Oliver is back?" Guin asked Glen as they passed by Oliver's room.

"I have no idea."

"I feel a bit bad for him."

"You do?" said Glen, surprised.

"I know he's not the most likable person, but it can't be easy having to notify Vera's sister, arranging to have the body flown back to the States, and who knows what else."

"True, but I'm sure he can handle it."

"I'm going to knock on his door and see if he's okay."

"What? Why?"

"As I said, I feel bad for him."

"What if he's the killer? You heard what John said."

"You think he has a chef's knife in his room and is going to plunge it into me?"

"No, but…"

"I'm just going to knock and see if he's okay. I won't go inside. And you can stand off to the side and make sure he doesn't harm me if you're that concerned."

Glen frowned but didn't move.

"Suit yourself," she said. Then she went to knock on Oliver's door. There was no answer. She knocked again and called his name. Still no answer.

"I don't think he's there."

"Good," said Glen. "I'm going to my room to edit photos."

"I should get some work done too." Though she wasn't really in the mood. The wine had made her a bit sleepy. They headed down the corridor, stopping in front of their rooms. "You tell Ginny about Vera?"

"Not yet."

"I guess I should."

"You don't have to."

"Are you kidding? If Ginny reads about it somewhere, she'll kill me. Besides, we may be stuck here for a while."

"You want me to tell her?"

"No, that's okay. I'll do it."

Guin took out her key and was about to unlock her door when Glen stopped her.

"If you change your mind about food, let me know."

Guin turned to look at him.

"Are you hungry?"

"Not now, but…"

"You could always have pizza with the Adamses," she said with a smile.

"That's okay," he replied.

Guin sat in front of her laptop. She had been trying to compose an email to Ginny, but she was struggling. She tried again.

"Hey, Ginny," she typed. "You'll never guess what happened! Vera van Leyden, the famous cookbook author, who was taking the course with us, was found face down in the kitchen this morning with a knife in her back."

"Ugh," she said and deleted what she had written.

She tried again but was equally dissatisfied with her next attempt. And the one after. Maybe she should go for a walk and try to clear her head. A walk always helped her organize her thoughts. But no, she had work to do. And she needed to tell Ginny what was up.

"Okay," she said, clasping her hands out in front of her and taking a deep breath. She lowered her hands to the keyboard and began to type.

"Dear Ginny," she wrote. "Glen and I continue to enjoy the course and learning about this part of Italy. The food and the wine have been excellent. This afternoon we…"

She described their lunch at Dante's and the wine tour and said she would send Ginny an article on both soon. Then she paused, wondering how to introduce the topic of Vera.

"Unfortunately, I don't know if the class will continue. One of the students, Vera van Leyden (the famous cookbook author, who I told you was taking the course with us), died unexpectedly this morning."

Guin thought about whether she should tell Ginny that Vera had been murdered. Well, in for a penny, in for a pound.

"Actually, she was murdered. Someone put a knife in her back. The assistant chef, Leonardo, found her lying face down in the kitchen when he came in this morning. And when I got to the kitchen, the police were there.

"They interviewed the kitchen staff and all of the guests, including me and Glen. The man in charge, a Chief Inspector Manetti, spoke excellent English. Turns out, he went to Yale and worked at his cousin's pizza place in New Haven."

Guin didn't know why she had written that and thought about deleting it, but she left it in. Ginny would probably be amused by an Italian chief inspector having gone to Yale and worked at a pizza joint.

"Anyway, the chief inspector has asked us all to stay close to the hotel and took all of our passports. Which means we can't leave." Which reminded Guin, she should check in with Sadie, her cat sitter, and let her know she might be gone a few extra days. "Not sure when we'll get our passports back. But I'll keep you posted and will send you more articles.

"How are things on Sanibel? Not too busy, I hope. Ciao for now, Guin."

She read over what she had written then hit "Send" before she changed her mind.

"Okay. Now to get some work done."

She pulled up the article she had been working on, but after an hour she gave up. She glanced at the clock on her computer and saw that it was six-thirty. She looked over at the window. It was still light out. She got up and looked outside. Then she looked back at her laptop.

"Maybe just a short walk," she said.

Guin stood outside, wondering where she should go. There were always the trails, but she didn't want to walk for more than half an hour. She just needed to stretch her legs and clear her head. She could always walk down the driveway and along the road. It wasn't heavily trafficked.

She took out her phone to mark what time it was, determined to turn around after fifteen minutes, and saw that she had a message from Bridget. Everyone was invited to Dante's in the morning for a lesson on meat. The van would pick them up at eight-thirty.

Guin had no problem getting up early, but she wondered about the Italians. And she was a bit surprised to learn that there would still be a class. Though it would be at Dante's restaurant. No doubt the police didn't want anyone using the kitchen just yet.

She immediately messaged Glen, asking if he planned on going to Dante's in the morning. Then she saw she had an email from Ginny. She thought about opening it but decided to wait. She needed to walk. She put her phone on silent and shoved it in her back pocket.

Guin got back to the hotel thirty minutes later. She took out her phone and saw that Glen had replied to her message. He was planning on going to Dante's in the morning—and he was going to have dinner with "Bea" at eight.

Guin wrinkled her brow.

He was having dinner with Beatrice? Had she invited him, or had he invited her?

"Have fun at dinner!" she wrote him back, sounding far

cheerier than she felt. "Where are you going?"

He replied a minute later.

"Some little place not too far from here run by one of her cousins. Was planning on taking our car. Is that okay?"

Well, it technically wasn't *their* car. It was Glen's. And what was Guin supposed to say, *no*? She frowned as she wrote him back.

"Totally fine! Just drive carefully!"

She added a smiley face and hit "Send." Then she headed to her room, all the good feeling from her walk having vanished.

CHAPTER 17

As Guin approached her room, she saw Oliver standing outside his door.

"Oliver!" she called.

He turned and looked at her. He didn't look happy.

"Where've you been?" she asked him. "We were worried about you."

"Florence," he curtly replied.

"Florence?"

"Dealing with the U.S. Consulate there."

Of course, thought Guin. *Duh.*

"How did that go?"

He frowned, and Guin guessed not well.

"They told me I'd have to come back tomorrow."

"Why?"

"Italian bureaucracy."

"Were you able to find out where Vera is?"

"Some hospital, but they wouldn't tell me which one."

"Did you ask the chief inspector?"

He gave her a look that said, "What do you think?"

"I gather he wasn't much help either."

"Apparently, only family is privy to that information," he cynically replied.

"Were you able to reach Vera's sister?"

"I sent her an email."

Guin thought the sister deserved a phone call, but she

didn't say anything.

"But you spoke with the chief inspector."

"Yes, I spoke with the chief inspector. And before you ask, it was a one-way conversation. He wasn't at all interested in helping me, only in discussing Vera and our relationship."

"And what was your relationship with Mrs. van Leyden?"

"We had an excellent relationship." Guin found that hard to believe. "She even paid for this trip."

"She did?"

"Vera could be quite generous."

Guin had a hard time reconciling that with the woman she had seen, but again she didn't say anything.

"Well, if you want another crack at the chief inspector, he's going to be dining at Dante's tonight. He might be more willing to help you after a couple of glasses of wine and some steak."

"As tempting as that sounds, I have far too much to do. Now, if you would excuse me?"

"Of course. Though, if there's anything I can do to help…"

Oliver had opened his door and was about to go in, but he stopped and turned.

"Actually…" he said. "If you really mean it…"

"I do," said Guin. But she didn't like the look in Oliver's eyes.

"You could go to Dante's and speak with the chief inspector."

"Me? Why me?"

"You're a reporter, yes?"

"Yes, but…"

"So you must have lots of practice getting information out of people."

"Yes, but…"

"So I'm sure you'll have no trouble finding out where they're keeping Vera and when they'll allow us to go home."

Guin opened her mouth to argue with him, but she quickly closed it. She was a reporter. And a good one. And she was used to dealing with detectives. And it wasn't as though she needed the chief inspector to reveal any state secrets. She just needed to find out where they were keeping Vera's body and how to get it released. That shouldn't be that hard.

"Fine, I'll do it," she said.

"Thank you," said Oliver. "Now I really must be going."

"Of course," said Guin.

Guin had no idea what time the chief inspector would be dining at Dante's. Though she vaguely remembered something about a set seating. She did a quick search online and discovered dinner was served at eight-thirty. It was now seven-thirty. So she had an hour to prepare and get changed.

Next, she did a search for *Chief Inspector Manetti Firenze.* Most of the results were in Italian, but she found a couple that were in English. They were about cases he had worked on that involved English speakers, one involving a Brit and a Canadian and another involving two Americans. While interesting, neither told her much about him, except that his first name was Marco. Though she knew he had grown up in Greve and had attended Yale.

She looked at the clock on her computer. Time to get changed. She went to the armoire and studied her choices, ultimately choosing another dress and a pair of high heels. She then went into the bathroom to apply some makeup. Satisfied, she picked up her bag and headed to the front desk to arrange a taxi.

Matteo greeted her.

"*Buona sera*, Signora Jones. How may I help you?"

"Good evening, Matteo. I need a taxi to take me to Dante's."

"Why do you need a taxi?" came a familiar voice. It was Domenico. "Where is your friend?"

"He's off having dinner with Beatrice."

Didn't he know? Guin found that odd. Though judging by his frown, she guessed he didn't.

"I will take you," Domenico announced.

"That's really all right," said Guin. Domenico looked like he was on his way out to dinner.

"It is no trouble."

"Thank you. But I don't want you going out of your way. A taxi is fine."

"Actually," said Matteo, "the taxis are very busy right now. There is a big party at the villa down the road."

"Please, allow me," said Domenico. "I was on my way to Dante's."

"Oh?" said Guin.

"*Sì*. I was supposed to have dinner with a business associate, but he unfortunately had to cancel. I was going to dine there on my own. But perhaps now you will join me?"

Guin thought about it. It would definitely look better than her being there alone, especially after just having had lunch there.

"Okay," she said. "If it's really no trouble."

"You would be doing me a favor."

Guin doubted that, but she didn't say anything.

"Shall we?" he said.

Guin nodded and let Domenico escort her out.

Domenico opened the passenger-side door of the Maserati for Guin.

She gingerly got in, worried about somehow damaging the leather seats.

"Is everything okay?" he asked her.

"Sorry, I've just never been in a Maserati before."

"No?" he said, surprised.

"Where I live, on Sanibel Island, you can't go over thirty-five. So there's no point in having a fancy car. Though I've seen a few Porsches."

"That is a shame," he said.

He started the car and pulled out. As soon as they cleared the driveway, he hit the accelerator, and Guin found herself clutching her armrest. She looked over at the speedometer. They were going over eighty. Then she realized that was kilometers. She tried to remember the conversion rate. She thought it was around one and a half kilometers to a mile. She did the math in her head. They were going over fifty miles per hour. Too fast for these country roads, in her opinion. She focused on her breathing, trying to calm down.

"So, how fast can this car go?" she asked him, watching the needle on the speedometer.

"Three hundred kilometers per hour," he said, as though it was no big deal.

Guin gripped the armrest tighter.

"Three hundred kilometers per hour?" That was nearly two hundred miles per hour.

"You like to go fast?" he said, grinning at her.

Before she could reply, he increased their speed.

"Watch out!" Guin practically screeched as a car swerved onto the road in front of them. Her heart was pounding inside her chest, and she thought it might just leap out.

"There is no need to worry," he calmly replied. "I am an excellent driver, and I know these roads like the back of my hand."

Guin glanced over at his hands, too terrified to speak.

"So, I hope I am not being rude, but why were you going to Dante's alone? Did you not go there for lunch with the others?"

"I did," she said, glad for the distraction, though still keeping her eyes on the road—and making sure Domenico was too. "Actually, I was going there to speak with Chief Inspector Manetti."

Domenico frowned.

"And why do you wish to speak with Chief Inspector Manetti?"

"I told Oliver, Signore Oliveira, that I would."

Domenico continued to frown.

"He was unable to find out where the police took Vera's body or when they might release it," Guin continued. "I heard that the chief inspector would be dining at Dante's this evening and…"

"You thought you could seduce him into telling you?"

Guin scowled.

"I wasn't planning on seducing him. I was simply going to ask him after he had a glass or two of wine and some steak."

Domenico smirked.

"It is the same thing."

"It is not," said Guin.

"*Buona fortuna.* The chief inspector is not an easy man to seduce. Though you are a very attractive woman."

Guin felt herself begin to blush, and they didn't speak the rest of the way.

A short time later, they arrived at the restaurant, and Guin sent up a silent prayer of thanks for them arriving in one piece.

Domenico got out and went around to open Guin's door. Then he escorted her into the restaurant.

There was a young woman seating people at one of the two communal tables, which were nearly full. Guin wondered if the young woman was Dante's daughter or a relation.

"Nico?" said the young woman, coming towards them.

Domenico smiled at the young woman, and she said something to him in Italian. It sounded as though she was chastising him. Then he said something to her in Italian, an apology? And they were off. It wasn't until Guin cleared her throat that they seemed to remember she was there.

"I am sorry," said Domenico. "How rude of me. Guin, this is Giovanna, an old friend."

"Who are you calling old?" said Giovanna, who Guin thought to be in her early twenties.

"I meant that I have known you a long time." He turned to Guin. "I was good friends with Giovanna's brother growing up. He told me she was working here over the summer. So I thought I would surprise her."

"You should have told me you were in Greve!"

"I am only here for a short time."

"Still."

"So, are you going to seat us?" Domenico asked her.

"Maybe," said Giovanna. "Do you have a reservation?"

"Of course!"

"Let me check," she said. She made a big deal out of checking her list. "Okay," she said. "This way."

She led them over to one of the communal tables where there were four empty places. Guin glanced around. She didn't see the chief inspector. She turned to Giovanna.

"I have a favor to ask."

"Yes?"

"A Chief Inspector Manetti is supposed to be dining here this evening. Could you seat him near me?"

Giovanna eyed her suspiciously. Then Domenico said something to her in Italian. She listened then looked back at Guin.

"Very well," she said. Then she turned back to Domenico, again saying something to him in Italian before heading back to her post in front.

"What did she say to you?" asked Guin.

"She wanted to know why you wanted to be near the chief inspector."

"And what did you tell her?"

"I told her you had a thing for policemen."

"You did not!" said Guin.

He smiled, and she realized he was teasing her.

"No, I did not. I told her it was personal and none of her business."

"No wonder she looked annoyed," said Guin. "So will she seat the chief inspector here?"

He nodded.

"Giovanna is a good girl." He picked up a bottle. "Some wine?"

"Just a little."

She looked at the table. As at lunch, there were ceramic jars filled with vegetables with smaller jars containing some kind of dip next to them. She took a carrot and bit into it. Then she glanced around the room. The lighting was softer than it had been at lunch, and the room had a more intimate feel, even though the restaurant was packed. She looked over at the door and saw the chief inspector enter, accompanied by an older man. They spoke with Giovanna, then she led them over to their table.

The chief inspector saw Guin and Domenico and frowned. He said something to Giovanna, but she shook her head and gestured at the two empty seats. The chief inspector reluctantly sat next to Guin, his companion across from him.

"Good evening," Guin said to the chief inspector.

"*Buona sera*," he replied. "I did not expect to see you here."

"Domenico invited me to join him for dinner," she sweetly replied.

The chief inspector glanced over at Domenico, who nodded at him.

"Would you like some wine?" Guin asked him, picking up a bottle. "Or are you on duty?"

"I am not on duty."

"Then please have some wine. It's quite good."

He nodded, and Guin poured.

CHAPTER 18

"So, how's the investigation going?" Guin asked the chief inspector as they waited for the first course.

"I cannot discuss the case with you, Signora Jones."

"Please, call me Guin."

She smiled at him, but he did not return the smile. Then his companion spoke to him. The chief inspector sighed and turned to Guin.

"Mayor Rinaldi, allow me to present Signora Jones, a visitor to Greve."

The mayor smiled at Guin.

"*Piacere di conoscerla.* What brings you to Chianti, Signora Jones?"

"I'm here to attend a cooking class."

"A cooking class!" He sounded delighted. "Who is the teacher?"

"Signore Moretti's wife."

"Ah, Signora O'Brien," he said, nodding. "She is a very good cook."

"She is," agreed Guin. "So are you the mayor of Greve?"

"I am!" he replied.

Guin couldn't help smiling. The mayor was so jolly. Though she was finding it a bit hard to hear or understand him, what with his thick Italian accent and the noise from the other diners.

Guin was about to ask him what it was like being mayor

when the first course appeared. It was a selection of charcuterie. Everyone helped themselves.

"Can I pour you a little more wine?" Guin asked the chief inspector.

He nodded, and Guin poured.

"I understand you grew up here in Greve. Is that how you know the mayor?"

"*Sì.* He is an old friend of my family."

"Do you still have family here?" Though Bridget had said that he did. But it was a way to keep him talking.

He nodded and took a sip of his wine.

"Do you often come back to see them?"

"When my job allows."

The mayor leaned over and said something to the chief inspector in Italian. They spoke for several minutes. Then the woman seated next to the mayor said something to him, and he began speaking with her. This was Guin's chance to ask the chief inspector about Vera. But she hesitated. Instead, she asked him about his time in New Haven, feeling that was safer. She was also curious.

"And what did you study at Yale?"

"Guess," he said.

"Hm…" said Guin, eyeing him. "Psychology?"

He shook his head.

She tried to read his mind.

"Political science?"

Another shake of the head.

"International relations?"

"That is the same as Political Science."

"I give up," said Guin.

"You give up too easily."

"Tell me."

"No. I will give you two more guesses."

"Give me a clue."

"When I lived in the States, I watched many movies."

"Everyone in the States watches movies."

She waited for him to say something else, but he didn't.

"Give me another clue."

"I have already given you a clue."

Guin scrunched up her face, studying him again.

"Wait. Were you a Film major?"

"Very good."

But Guin was confused.

"But why study film in the States? They make movies in Italy."

"But not American movies. From the time I was a little boy, I have always been fascinated by American movies."

Okay. She could understand that.

"But why Yale?"

"Why not Yale? It is an excellent university, no?"

"It is, but why not go someplace like NYU or UCLA? Was it because you had family in New Haven?"

He nodded.

"*Sì.* My family did not want me living someplace where I knew no one."

Guin could understand that too. But what she couldn't understand was how he had gone from studying film at Yale to becoming a chief inspector with the Italian State Police in Florence. So she asked him.

"It is a long story," he replied.

Guin was about to say that she didn't mind, but the next course, a bone marrow soup, was on its way over. And the mayor had leaned over to say something to the chief inspector.

"How is it going?" Domenico asked Guin, keeping his voice low. "Has he told you who done it yet?"

"No. And I haven't asked. I'm just trying to loosen him up."

"Loosen him up?"

"Get him to feel comfortable talking to me."

"Ah. This is what reporters in America do?"

Guin ignored him and ate her soup.

When they were done, the busboy removed their bowls. Here was another chance for her to speak with the chief inspector about Vera, but now the woman seated next to the mayor was asking him something.

She was going to interrupt, but then the door to the kitchen opened and Dante appeared, carrying the biggest piece of steak she had ever seen. Bridget was behind him, also carrying a platter of steak.

She saw the mayor grinning as the meat approached. He wasn't the only one. She turned to Domenico, who was also gazing hungrily at the platters of beef coming towards them.

"You would think everyone here had never seen a steak before," she mumbled.

"This is no ordinary steak," he said. "It is Dante's famous *Bistecca alla Fiorentina.*"

Dante put his platter down on their table, next to the mayor, and Bridget placed hers on the other table. The diners watched as Dante and Bridget began slicing the steaks. It was like a piece of performance art. When they were done, they wished everyone a *buon appetito* and returned to the kitchen as a server brought out platters of roasted vegetables. Guin wasn't really hungry, but she took a couple of slices of steak along with some vegetables.

"That is all you are eating?" said Domenico, looking at her plate. He had taken several large slices of steak along with a good helping of vegetables.

"I'm not really hungry," she told him.

He shook his head and took a bite of the steak, closing his eyes and sighing as he did.

"That good, eh?"

"Try it," he told her.

Guin picked up her fork and knife and cut off a small piece, placing it in her mouth. She began to chew and closed her eyes. The meat practically melted in her mouth. It was so tender and juicy. And she could taste the sear on the outside.

"See," said Domenico. Was he gloating?

"I'll admit, it's pretty good."

"Pretty good?" said Domenico.

The mayor now turned to her.

"What do you think of Dante's famous steak?" he asked her.

"It's very good," she replied.

The mayor beamed.

"You must ask Signora O'Brien to teach you how to make it!"

"Actually, Dante is giving us a lesson on meat tomorrow."

"You must ask him to show you how it is done! No man can resist *Bistecca alla Fiorentina*, especially when made by a beautiful woman."

Guin didn't know how to reply. Fortunately, the woman next to the mayor said something to him, and he forgot all about Guin.

Dinner was now almost over, and Guin still hadn't asked the chief inspector about Vera. And time was running out. As they waited for dessert, Guin saw her opportunity. She gently touched the chief inspector's forearm to get his attention.

He turned and looked at her, and Guin couldn't help thinking he had nice eyes. She mentally shook herself. She had clearly had too much wine.

"Yes?" he said.

"I was wondering," she began. He waited for her to continue. "Were you able to contact Signora van Leyden's sister?"

He continued to look at her, and Guin feared he wouldn't answer. But he nodded.

"So you can release Vera's body to Signore Oliveira?"

"Not yet."

"Why not? I thought you said you contacted her sister."

But again they were interrupted, by dessert this time.

Guin was relieved when dinner was finally over. Though she was frustrated. She had been unable to quiz the chief inspector further as he had left shortly after dessert was served. She wondered if he had been called away on business or was just avoiding her.

Domenico insisted on paying for her meal, and Guin was too weary to protest. They stopped on the way out to see Giovanna, and Guin listened as she and Domenico spoke in Italian, even though Guin couldn't understand what they were saying.

They stepped outside, and Guin felt a cool breeze brush by her. It felt wonderful.

They walked to Domenico's Maserati, and he opened the door for her.

"*Grazie*," she said.

"So, did you get what you needed from the chief inspector?"

"No," she replied.

"You should have tried to seduce him."

"I don't think that would have worked, and that's not how I operate."

Domenico shrugged and started the car.

Guin wasn't in the mood to talk, so she asked if he could play some music. He pressed a button and the car filled with the sound of smooth jazz. Soon, Guin found herself nodding off.

"We are here," said Domenico, gently touching Guin's arm.

"Hm?" she said. She hadn't realized she had fallen asleep. She looked around. "We're back at the hotel?"

"*Sì*. You fell asleep."

Guin prayed she hadn't snored.

Domenico got out of the car and went around to open the door for her.

"Thank you," she said.

"May I escort you to your room?"

"That's okay," said Guin. She looked around the parking lot. Glen's car wasn't there.

"Then I will bid you a good night."

"Good night," said Guin. "And thank you for dinner."

"My pleasure."

Then he headed off into the night.

It was dark out, and Guin could barely see. She turned on the flashlight app on her phone and made her way slowly back to her room, trying not to think about Glen and Beatrice.

CHAPTER 19

Bridget had sent a message to everyone after dinner letting them know that the van would be at the hotel at eight-thirty to take them to Dante's. So if Guin wanted to get in a walk before breakfast, which she did, she would need to set her alarm for six-thirty.

She stared at her travel alarm clock. Did she really want to get up at six-thirty? On Sanibel, it wasn't a problem. She was often up at six-thirty, without the aid of an alarm. But there she was typically in bed by ten.

She continued to stare at the clock. She couldn't imagine being hungry for breakfast. Not after all of the food she had eaten. So she set the alarm for seven, then got into bed.

The alarm went off promptly at seven, and Guin fumbled to shut it off. She had not had a good night. No doubt thanks to all the food and wine she had consumed. But she dragged herself out of bed and into the bathroom. No doubt she would feel better after a walk.

She splashed cold water on her face and combed her hair. Fortunately, the frizz was at a minimum. But she put her hair back in a ponytail anyway. Then she got dressed.

It was a beautiful morning, with a light mist covering the grass. Guin took a deep breath, closing her eyes, then slowly letting it out. She loved how it smelled here. She headed to the vineyard trail, pausing near the dining terrace. She thought about getting a quick cup of coffee but decided to wait.

She was nearly at the entrance to the trail when she heard a familiar voice calling her name.

"Guin! Wait up!"

Guin turned to see Glen approaching her. She stopped and waited for him.

"I wasn't expecting to see you so early this morning."

"Oh?" he said. "I'm usually up early."

"I just thought after your night with Beatrice…"

He gave her a funny look.

"You two have a good time? I didn't see you when I got back from Dante's with Domenico."

"What were you doing at Dante's with Domenico?"

Was he jealous? A part of Guin hoped so.

"I had gone there to speak with the chief inspector. I was hoping he might tell me where Vera was."

"And did he?"

"No. Though I know he reached out to Vera's sister."

"And what were you doing there with Domenico?"

"He offered to drive me there as there weren't any taxis. Apparently, his date stood him up. So, how was your dinner with Beatrice?"

"It wasn't a date, and it was fine."

"Just fine?"

"You going for a walk?"

Guin knew he was trying to change the subject and let him.

"Yes. Care to join me?"

He nodded, and they headed off.

"So, what did you and Beatrice talk about over dinner?" Guin asked him.

"This and that."

"Could you be a bit more specific?"

"She asked me if I enjoyed being a photographer."

"And what did you tell her?"

"I told her that I did. That it beat spending all day in front of a Bloomberg machine under fluorescent lights."

"Well, when you put it like that. What else? Did you learn anything about her?"

"A bit."

This was like pulling teeth.

"Such as?"

"She's from a small town just outside of Sienna and wanted to be an artist. But her family disapproved. So she went to university in Florence and bartered with art students."

"What did she barter?"

"She offered to pose for them if they'd let her work in their studios."

"I see."

Guin could' just picture Beatrice in the nude, modeling for art students.

"Did she offer to model for you?"

Glen looked uncomfortable. She would take that as a yes.

"What about her husband?"

"Klaus?"

"Unless she has another one. Where did she meet him? He was older and German, yes?"

Glen nodded.

"They met at an Italian trade show. He took one look at her and wouldn't take no for an answer."

"And now she's a widow. How did he die?"

"Heart attack."

They didn't speak for several minutes.

"We should turn around," said Guin.

"What about Domenico?" asked Glen as they made their way back to the hotel.

"What about him?"

"What did you two talk about?"

"Steak."

"Steak?"

"Dante's famous *Bistecca alla Fiorentina*."

Glen looked confused.

"We didn't really have a chance to talk. I was trying to speak with the chief inspector over dinner. But the mayor kept interrupting us."

"The mayor?"

"Of Greve. He was there with the chief inspector. He kept asking me questions."

"Huh."

They were silent again.

They arrived back at the hotel and Guin said she was going to get some coffee. Glen said he would join her. It was a little after eight, which didn't give them much time. But Guin still wasn't hungry. They saw the Adamses having breakfast and said hello.

"Will you two be joining us for class at Dante's?" Julia asked them.

"I am," said Glen.

"I was planning on it," said Guin. Though the thought of eating more meat made her feel slightly nauseous.

"You don't have much time if you're planning on taking the van," said Julia.

"I just need some coffee," said Guin.

Julia looked up at Glen.

"I, on the other hand, could use some food," he said. "You sure I can't get you something?" he asked Guin.

"I'm sure."

He headed to the buffet, and Guin asked Francesca for two cappuccinos, one for her and one for Glen. Back on Sanibel, she always drank her coffee black. But since coming to Italy, she had switched to cappuccino. Would she go back to drinking her coffee black when she returned home? She wondered.

"So, are you looking forward to class?" Guin asked John and Julia.

"My mouth has been watering just thinking about that beefsteak a la Florentina," said John.

"It's *Bistecca alla Fiorentina*," said Julia, pronouncing it the Italian way.

"Whatever," said John. "As long as we get to eat it."

Glen returned, and they made small talk with the Adamses for several minutes, until they excused themselves. Glen looked at his watch.

"I should go too. I need to get my camera."

"And I should go brush my teeth," said Guin.

"Shall we?" he said, getting up.

Guin nodded, and they made their way off the dining terrace.

As she brushed her teeth, Guin wondered if the Italians and Oliver would be going to Dante's. She hadn't seen any of them at breakfast. Of course, they could have eaten earlier. Though she doubted that.

She finished brushing her teeth and wiped her mouth. Then she went to get her phone and her bag. She paused before putting her phone away. She had unanswered messages from Shelly and her mother and brother. She would need to reply or else they would worry. And she still owed Ginny several articles.

She promised herself she would write to everyone later, as well as work on her articles. Then she put her phone away and hurried out the door.

Guin was surprised to see everyone already by the van, including Oliver. Apparently the lure of learning how to make—really eating—Dante's *Bistecca alla Fiorentina* trumped going back to Florence.

"I was just about to go get you," said Glen.

"Sorry I'm late," said Guin. Though it was just past eight-thirty.

They got in the van, and it headed down the long driveway. Fifteen minutes later, they arrived at Dante's restaurant. The door was closed, and it didn't look as if anyone was there.

"Should we knock?" asked Julia.

A few seconds later, as though sensing their presence, the door opened and Dante stepped outside.

"Welcome!" he said in his booming voice.

Guin was amazed to see him looking so cheerful. He had to have been up until late the night before, cleaning up after dinner. But maybe he was a morning person.

"Please, come in. We have a lot of work to do today!"

They followed him inside, Glen taking a few pictures before going in.

"Didn't you get pictures yesterday?" Guin asked him.

"I did, but the light is much better now."

Dante ushered them into the kitchen.

"Where's Bridget?" Guin asked him.

"She will be here momentarily. Please, take a place."

Guin stood next to Oliver.

"I thought you would be in Florence," she said to him in a low voice.

"No point," he said. "At least until someone at the Consulate answers the phone." He paused. "Were you able to speak to the chief inspector?"

"Yes, but he didn't say much, only that he had contacted Vera's sister."

Oliver frowned.

"But I'm sure she'll give the police permission to release Vera's body to you. Then you can fly her home."

Oliver didn't look convinced.

"Good morning, everyone."

Guin looked up.

It was Bridget.

"Thank you all for coming. I apologize for the change in venue and the early hour."

"We don't mind," said John.

Bridget smiled at him.

"So, is everyone ready to learn about butchering meat?"

Guin saw several people looking confused.

"I thought we were here to learn how to cook steak," said John.

"We will be doing that too. But first, we will teach you about the meat we will be preparing. And with that, allow me to formally introduce my husband, Dante Moretti. Dante, as you probably know, began as a butcher and now owns two restaurants, one here in Greve and one in Panzano.

"And today, after a short lesson on butchery, he will show you how to make his famous *Bistecca alla Fiorentina* as well as porchetta and *peposo*, which is a Tuscan beef stew. Any questions?" Bridget looked around, but no one had raised a hand. "Very good. Let us begin."

CHAPTER 20

Dante began the lesson on butchery by placing two large poster boards, one of a cow (technically a steer) and one of a pig, on the large kitchen island. Each poster showed where the different cuts of meat came from.

He began with the poster of the cow, explaining that most people only ate the meat from the top of the cow—cuts like sirloin, tenderloin, T-bone, and ribeye—which were also the most expensive. However, he believed in using the whole cow, or as much as possible. And he told them that when properly prepared, the so-called cheaper cuts of beef were just as delicious as the more expensive ones, maybe more so.

"But you be the judge," he said, noting that they would be using both types of meat in today's preparations: a T-bone steak from local Chianina cattle to make *Bistecca alla Fiorentina* and chuck meat for the *peposo*.

"Any questions?" he asked them.

Guin glanced around. No one had raised a hand. She thought about raising hers but decided she would save her questions for later.

"*Bene*," he said. Then he moved on to the chart showing the pig.

As he did with the cow, Dante went over the different cuts of pork, where they came from on the pig. Then he explained that they would be using meat from the pig's belly, along with meat from the loin, to make the porchetta, which he told them meant "little pig."

"Any questions?"

"Where does prosciutto come from?" asked Glen.

Dante smiled.

"Prosciutto is made from the hind legs of the pig." He then went on to explain the dry-curing process.

"What's the difference between prosciutto, pancetta, and bacon?" asked Julia.

"A good question," said Dante.

He explained that pancetta, while also cured, came from the underside of the pig and was typically seasoned with juniper berries, coriander, and fennel in addition to salt and pepper.

Bacon, he said, also came from the pig's belly, but it was smoke-cured, as opposed to salt-cured, like pancetta and prosciutto. And that the taste of the bacon varied depending on what type of wood was used.

"What about salami and sausage?" asked John.

Dante smiled and said there were many different kinds of salami and sausage, and that he would be happy to discuss the matter with him and anyone else interested after class but that it was now time to start cooking.

Bridget split the class into two groups. Guin and Glen were paired with Domenico and Beatrice while Oliver would work with John and Julia.

They would begin with the porchetta, then move onto the *peposo*, finishing with the *Bistecca alla Fiorentina*. They would also be making a polenta and roasting potatoes and vegetables.

"That's a lot of food to make in just a few hours," said Guin, feeling a bit overwhelmed.

"Now you know what it is like to work in a restaurant," said Domenico.

"*Sì*," said Beatrice. "My cousin, Gianni, he is all day in

his kitchen, cooking, cooking, cooking. But his food…" She raised her fingers to her mouth and kissed them. "Is that not so, Glen?"

"His food was very good," Glen replied.

"All right." It was Bridget. "Are you ready to start making the porchetta?" The four of them nodded. "Then let's begin."

Bridget watched as they placed the porchetta skin side down then worked salt into the meat and added fresh rosemary, sage, fennel, garlic, and pepper. Then they rolled the porchetta up and tied it with string, seam side down. Next, they placed the porchetta on a baking sheet, rubbed it with olive oil, then added the leftover seasoning. Then it was into the oven where it would cook for an hour at 200° Celsius (400° Fahrenheit), then another two hours at 170° Celsius (325° Fahrenheit), until the center registered 76° Celsius (170° Fahrenheit).

"Now we will make the *peposo*," said Bridget. "As you can see, this is a very simple recipe. The pot does most of the work. But that does not make it any less delicious."

The first step was to brown the beef in a large pot. Then they added a bottle of Chianti along with six whole cloves of garlic, a tablespoon of freshly ground pepper, and a teaspoon of kosher salt.

"Now we let the meat simmer with the lid on for an hour and a half, checking it occasionally. Then you remove the lid and let it simmer for another hour and a half, until the liquid has reduced slightly, making sure to stir the pot occasionally so the meat doesn't stick."

They followed Bridget's instructions. When the meat was simmering, she told them they should take a break and go outside to get some air.

"Just be back in thirty minutes."

"But what about the *peposo*?" said Guin. "Shouldn't someone stay behind to make sure it doesn't burn?"

"I'll keep an eye on it," said Bridget.

Glen and the Italians headed to the exit, but Guin lingered.

"Don't you get a break?"

Bridget smiled.

"No rest for the weary. I need to clean up and prepare for the next part of the lesson."

"Can I help?"

"That's very kind of you, but I've got this. Go outside and get some fresh air."

Guin was about to protest, but Bridget stopped her.

"I'll get a break later. Now go."

Guin reluctantly left. As she stepped outside, she saw that Glen was waiting for her.

"Everything okay?" he asked her.

"Everything's fine. I just felt bad leaving Bridget there to clean up."

"I'm sure Dante and his assistant are helping."

"Maybe."

She glanced around.

"Where are the others?"

"The Adamses took a walk, and I'm not sure where the others went. I saw Oliver and Domenico take out their phones."

Which reminded her.

"I should do the same. I need to return some messages."

"Of course," he said. "I should probably send a couple of emails myself."

Guin found a shady place to sit not far from the restaurant and sent Shelly and her mother and brother quick messages, letting them know she was fine, just busy. She briefly thought about mentioning Vera then decided not to. Why worry them? Though she knew if they found out, they'd be furious at her for not telling them. But she was willing to take that risk... for now.

"We should head back in."

It was Glen.

"Is it time already?"

He nodded.

"Wow, time seems to fly here."

"Tell me about it."

They went back into the restaurant. The Adamses and Beatrice were already there. But Guin didn't see Domenico or Oliver.

"We will give the others a few more minutes," said Bridget. "Then we will make the polenta and the roasted vegetables and potatoes."

Five minutes went by.

"Shall we resume?" she asked the class. Everyone nodded their heads. "We will start with the polenta. Polenta is a staple of many cuisines," Bridget told them. "It is most often made from cornmeal, water, salt and pepper, butter, and parmesan cheese.

"The trick to making a good polenta is time. You must cook the polenta slowly, over a low flame, stirring it every ten minutes or so.

"There are many recipes for polenta, but this one is my favorite. The polenta is smooth and creamy and melts in your mouth—and goes well with the *peposo* you are making. After, we will roast some vegetables and potatoes."

They were busy making the polenta when Domenico and Oliver entered. All eyes immediately turned to them, but no one said anything.

Domenico took his place between Beatrice and Guin. Beatrice gave him a look, and Domenico shook his head.

"Is everything okay?" Guin asked him in a low voice.

"It is this new hotel. Every day there is a problem."

"I'm sorry to hear that. Will you need to go there?"

"I hope not. My brother, he is supposed to be in charge."

When they were finished preparing the polenta, Bridget told them to come up and get a basket of vegetables and potatoes.

"I'll go get us a basket," said Glen.

He brought the basket of fresh vegetables and potatoes to their station and removed everything, placing each vegetable on the island. When everyone had a couple of vegetables, Bridget demonstrated the proper technique for chopping.

"Now you try."

Bridget walked around the kitchen, offering assistance or guidance. Guin was busy cutting up a zucchini when Bridget came over and told her she was doing a good job—and Guin nearly cut herself.

When they were done, they tossed the vegetables in extra virgin olive oil and seasoned them with salt and pepper. Then they placed them on a baking sheet and put the sheet into the oven.

At last, it was time to make the *Bistecca alla Fiorentina*. Guin was exhausted, though none of the recipes had been that hard to make. But she hadn't slept well or eaten that morning and was feeling cranky. Fortunately, the steak was quite easy to make. Most of the work had been done by the cow. As long as you didn't overcook the meat, you couldn't go wrong.

To prepare the *bistecca*, they seasoned the meat with salt and pepper and brushed it with some extra virgin olive oil and herbs (in this case rosemary and sage). Then they grilled it over a hot flame for approximately ten minutes on each side, letting it rest for another ten to fifteen minutes.

Finally, a little after one-thirty, it was time to eat. Dante, Bridget, and Dante's assistant brought everything out to the communal table, along with loaves of bread and bottles of the house wine. Guin was surprised the place was empty and asked why there were no customers.

"The restaurant is closed on Mondays," Bridget told her. "That's why we were able to hold class here."

"Ah," said Guin. She should have known.

Once everyone had sat and had some wine, Dante spoke to them, telling them what a good job they had done and that he would welcome them in his kitchen any time. Guin didn't think he really meant it, but she raised her glass with the others as they toasted him. Then they helped themselves to food.

"This *peposo*, it tastes just like my *nonna*'s," said Beatrice, savoring the rich Tuscan beef stew.

"She must have been a good cook," said Julia.

"*Sì*, she was."

"My grandmother was a horrible cook but a wonderful nurse. That's why I became a doctor. I wanted to be just like her."

The group continued to eat, voicing their opinions on the *peposo*, porchetta, and steak.

Domenico and John both said the steak was their favorite while Guin and Glen said they liked the porchetta the best. Julia and Beatrice voted for the *peposo*. Guin was about to ask Oliver what his favorite dish was, but he had taken out his phone and abruptly stepped away from the table.

"I wonder what's up," said Guin.

Just then Bridget reappeared.

"Did you enjoy your meal?" she asked them.

"Everything was delicious," said Julia.

Bridget smiled.

"So will everything we made be in your cookbook?"

"Cookbook?" said Beatrice. "I did not know you were working on a cookbook."

"It was a bit of a secret. Well, not really a secret. We just hadn't gone public with it."

"What is the name of it?"

"The working title is *Cooking with Love: A Modern Take on Classic Tuscan Cuisine*. That's the English translation."

"It is a good name," said Beatrice.

"So all of the recipes we've been making will be in your cookbook?" said Julia.

Bridget nodded.

"You've all been guinea pigs."

"Guinea pigs?" said Beatrice, looking confused.

Domenico leaned over and whispered in her ear. Beatrice looked at him and laughed.

"You weren't worried about someone stealing them?" asked John.

"A good question."

Everyone turned to see Chief Inspector Manetti standing in the doorway.

CHAPTER 21

"What's he doing here?" Julia whispered.

"He probably tracked us here using that app," said John.

"Can we help you, Chief Inspector Manetti?" said Bridget.

Guin was impressed by how calm Bridget seemed.

"Is there someplace private we can speak?"

"Of course," said Bridget. "Shall we go to Dante's office?"

"What about the rest of us?" asked John.

"I will let you know if I need to speak with you." He then turned to Bridget and indicated for her to lead the way.

"Do you think she'll be okay?" Julia asked her husband. "Maybe she should have a lawyer with her?"

"You want me to go back there?"

"You cannot help her," said Domenico. "If she is in need of a lawyer, it must be someone who knows Italian law."

"But she's an American citizen," said Julia. "Isn't she?" she asked Glen.

"Pretty sure she still is," said Glen.

"Does the chief inspector think Bridget killed Signora van Leyden?" asked Beatrice. "It was her knife, yes? And I saw the two of them arguing."

"You did?" said Guin.

Beatrice nodded.

"I did not understand everything they were saying, but

Bridget, she was very angry."

"Did you tell the chief inspector?" asked Glen.

Beatrice nodded.

"I could not lie to him."

"When did you hear them arguing?" asked Guin.

"The day before she died."

"Did anyone else hear Bridget and Vera arguing?" John asked the group. Everyone shook their head no, and he turned back to Beatrice. "You sure they were arguing, and that it was Signora van Leyden and Signora O'Brien?"

"*Sì*," said Beatrice.

"What exactly did you say to the chief inspector?" asked Guin.

Beatrice frowned.

"I do not recall exactly, just that I heard them arguing."

No one said anything for several seconds, then the door to the kitchen opened. Everyone turned, expecting to see Bridget and the chief inspector. But it was Oliver.

"What?" he said.

"We thought you were the chief inspector," said Julia.

Oliver frowned.

"Why did you think that?"

"He's here," said Guin, "talking to Bridget."

That seemed to interest him.

"Is he here to arrest her?"

"What makes you say that?" asked Glen.

"Isn't it obvious?" Glen glared at him. "Signora O'Brien was clearly jealous of Vera. And she had threatened Vera the day before she died."

"She had?" said Guin.

Everyone looked over at Beatrice, who looked a bit smug.

"How did she threaten her?"

"She accused Vera of being here under false pretenses."

"False pretenses?"

"That she wasn't here to take her class but to steal her recipes, which was ludicrous."

Though Guin didn't think so.

"And you heard the two of them?"

Oliver hesitated.

"Did you or did you not hear them arguing?" said Glen.

"Yes, I would like to know that too."

Everyone turned to see the chief inspector. Bridget was standing just behind him. They were both looking at Oliver.

"I didn't actually hear them, but Vera told me everything. And why would she lie?"

The chief inspector was studying Oliver.

"I think perhaps the two of you should come with me to the police station."

"Why me?" said Oliver.

The chief inspector didn't answer. He just gave Oliver a look that brooked no argument.

Oliver scowled.

"Of course, Chief Inspector," said Bridget. "May I just let my husband know?"

He nodded.

"Where is Dante?" Guin asked Glen. He shrugged.

"He went to his other restaurant," said Domenico.

Guin hadn't realized. She turned and saw Bridget speaking into her phone away from the rest of the group. She wondered what Bridget was saying to her husband.

"I'm ready," Bridget said to the chief inspector a minute later.

"Signore Oliveira?"

"Fine," said Oliver, scowling.

The rest of the group followed them out of the restaurant.

"Do you need us to do anything?" Glen asked Bridget as he followed her to the chief inspector's car.

"Just wait here for Dante. He should be here soon."

"You were able to reach him?" asked Guin.

"I left him a message. You can fill him in when he gets here."

"Do you need a lawyer?" asked John.

Bridget glanced over at the chief inspector, then she looked back at John.

"I'll be okay."

A uniformed officer was standing by the car. He opened the back door, and Bridget and Oliver got in.

"So now what do we do, just wait?" said Julia. "What if he arrests Bridget?"

"Then we will make sure she gets a lawyer," said Domenico.

"Do you know someone?" asked Guin.

"Domenico knows everyone," said Beatrice.

They stood around the kitchen, not knowing what to do. Finally, Dante arrived, and they filled him in.

"Will she be okay?" Guin asked him.

"My wife is a very strong woman," he replied. Everyone was looking at him. "But she did not kill Signora van Leyden."

He sounded very sure.

"I do not mean to be rude," said Domenico. "But I need to make some calls. Will the van be returning? Otherwise, I will arrange for a taxi."

Guin had forgotten about the van.

"The van was to return at three-thirty," said Dante.

Several people looked at their watches or phones. It was three-forty.

"Maybe it's here?" said Guin.

"Only one way to find out," said John.

They poured out of the building. The van was there, waiting to take them back to the hotel.

When they got out, Domenico told Guin and Glen and the Adamses that he would make some inquiries—apparently he knew someone—and would let them know if he heard anything. They thanked him, then everyone went their separate ways.

Guin knew she should work, but she was too keyed up to sit in front of her computer.

"I'm going to go for a swim," said Glen as they headed toward their rooms. "Care to join me?"

"I should really get some work done. I'm way behind."

"Suit yourself," he said.

"Don't you need to edit photos?"

"I do, but I need to clear my head first."

"Fine. I'll join you. But just for a quick swim. Then I really do need to get some work done or Ginny will have my head."

Guin and Glen had just finished swimming and were drying off on the lounge chairs when Guin saw Domenico approaching. She tapped Glen, and they both sat up.

"Any news?" she asked him.

"They have assigned a *pubblico ministero*, a public prosecutor, to the case," he told them.

"What does that mean?"

"It means that there will be a criminal proceeding."

"Did they arrest Bridget?" Glen asked him.

"Not as yet."

"So they released her?" said Guin.

"For now," said Domenico. "But she cannot leave Greve."

"So what does this public minister do?" asked Glen. "Is he now in charge of the investigation?"

"*Sì*, that is correct."

"Does that mean no more Chief Inspector Manetti?"

asked Guin. "Do you know who this public minister is?"

"I do not. And as far as I know, the chief inspector is still in charge."

"I don't understand," said Glen. "I thought you said this public minister was in charge."

"*Mi scusi.* The chief inspector, he is still in charge of the investigation. But now he will report to the *pubblico ministero.*"

"Did your contact happen to say anything about Vera?" Guin asked him.

"No, I am sorry. And now I must go."

"Well, thank you for letting us know," said Guin.

"I am only sorry I could not be more helpful."

He left, and Guin turned to Glen.

"At least they haven't arrested her."

"Though no thanks to Oliver. If anyone should have been arrested, it should have been him," he grumbled.

Guin didn't disagree, but she didn't say anything. Instead, she got up.

"I'm going to head back to my room. You coming?"

"I think I'm going to swim a few more laps."

Guin opened her mouth to say something then shut it.

"Okay. I'll be across the hall if you need me."

"What are we doing about dinner?" he asked her.

"Dinner? After that big lunch?"

Just then they saw Matteo coming towards them.

"Is everything all right, Matteo?" Guin thought he seemed a bit nervous.

"Chief Inspector Manetti is here. And he would like to speak with everyone."

CHAPTER 22

Guin arrived at reception to find Domenico, Beatrice, and the Adamses already there, fully dressed, and felt a bit self-conscious being only attired in her bathing suit and a towel.

"Where's the chief inspector?"

"He is talking to Signora Lombardi," said Beatrice.

A few minutes later, the chief inspector and Rosa emerged from her office.

"Signora Lombardi has graciously lent me her office again so that I may speak with each of you one more time," said the chief inspector, his eyes taking in each of the guests.

"Signora Adams, if you would follow me?"

Julia made to follow him, but John stopped her.

"I should go with you. You don't know what he's going to ask."

She patted his arm.

"I'm sure I'll be fine. The chief inspector probably just has a few more questions about the body."

John looked over at the chief inspector and frowned.

"Okay, but if he starts pointing fingers, come get me."

"I'll do that," she said.

They started to walk to Rosa's office, but John stopped them again.

"So what are the rest of us supposed to do, just wait here?"

The chief inspector turned.

"*Sì, esattamente.*"

He had turned back towards Rosa's office when Guin spoke up.

"May I go change? I'll be quick."

He sighed.

"*Sì, Sì,* go," he said. "Any other questions?"

He gazed at the guests as if daring them to ask him a question.

Guin quietly asked Glen if he wanted to go change too. He nodded.

"Can Glen—"

"Yes, yes, he may also go change," said the chief inspector, clearly annoyed.

"*Grazie,*" said Guin. She then turned to Glen. "Let's go before he changes his mind."

They left the reception area and headed to their rooms.

"What do you think he wants?" Glen asked her.

"My guess? He wants to ask us about Bridget."

"It's because of Oliver, isn't it? I could strangle that man."

"Now, now. We don't want you accused of murder too."

Guin was trying to lighten the mood, but she had clearly failed to judging by the look on Glen's face.

They reached their rooms, and Guin said she'd just be a minute. She went inside and made her way to the bathroom. She looked longingly at the shower, but the last thing she wanted to do was annoy the chief inspector by taking too long.

Instead, she removed her wet swimsuit and quickly rubbed her body with a damp washcloth then dried off. She stared at herself in the mirror. Her hair was a mess. She again looked over at the shower. She would have to wash her hair later or first thing in the morning. For now, she would pull it back in a ponytail. That done, she went to get dressed.

She had pulled on a pair of nicer jeans and a shirt and

was about to put on a little makeup when there was a knock on the door. She froze.

Could it be the chief inspector coming to get her? She hadn't been gone that long, had she?

"I'll be right there!" she called.

She quickly made her way to the door and opened it to find Glen.

"Thank goodness it's you."

"You were expecting someone else?"

"I thought you were the chief inspector or Matteo."

"We haven't been gone that long. The chief inspector's probably still talking to Julia or speaking with one of the other guests."

"You're probably right."

"So, are you ready to go back up there?"

"As ready as one can be in ten minutes. Let me just get my phone and my card key."

They made their way back to the reception area. The Italians were still there, and Guin saw Julia.

"Where's John?" she asked her.

"In speaking with the chief inspector."

"How did your interview go?"

"Okay, I guess."

"What did he ask you?"

"I'm not supposed to say."

Guin frowned.

"He's probably making sure we don't try to coordinate our stories," Glen said.

"That was my thought too," said Julia. "Though maybe after he's interviewed the lot of us it will be okay."

They waited around until finally the door to Rosa's office opened and John came out, followed by the chief inspector.

"Ah, you are back," he said to Guin and Glen.

"Signore Anderson, would you come with me?"

Glen nodded and followed the chief inspector, Guin

watching them. Once the door had closed, she glanced around. Domenico was on his phone, and Beatrice was roaming around the room, idly examining the artwork and rugs.

Guin looked for the Adamses but didn't see them. Had they already left? As the chief inspector had now interviewed both of them, he probably told them it was okay to leave. And even though Julia had said they weren't supposed to discuss what the chief inspector had asked them with one another, Guin wanted to know how John's interview had gone. So she headed outside to see if she could find them.

She heard them before she saw them. They were just outside, arguing, or so it seemed. Guin quickly ducked behind the door so they wouldn't see her and listened.

"Did you tell him?" Julia said. "About you and Vera?"

Guin's eyebrows went up.

"All I told him was that I had done work for her husband."

"That's it?"

"Well, he did ask me how well I knew her."

"And what did you tell him?"

"That I had met her a few times, that we had had a coffee once or twice, and that she had asked me for help."

"Did he ask you what kind of help?"

"Yes, but I just told him legal help."

"Nothing else? You didn't tell him about…"

"I'm not an idiot, Julia."

"I didn't think you were. But what if he finds out?"

"And how's he going to do that? Vera can't say anything now that she's…"

Just then Guin's phone began to ring. She cursed inwardly. She had meant to silence it. She took it out and saw it was her mother calling and immediately sent the call to voicemail. She then put it on silent and was about to put it back in her pocket when her brother's number flashed up on the screen. Now she was worried. Had something happened?

As much as she wanted to continue eavesdropping, she moved away from the doorway and picked up.

"Lance? Is everything okay?" she asked in a hushed voice.

"Everything's fine," he replied. "Why are you whispering?"

Guin moved further away from the door.

"Sorry," she said in a normal voice. "Is this better?"

"Much."

"So why are you calling?"

"Do I need a reason?" Guin waited then heard him sigh. "Mom read about Vera van Leyden in the paper today."

Guin groaned.

"What did she read?"

"That Vera had died at the hotel you're staying at."

"Did the paper say anything about how she died?"

"I don't think so. Why? Did she choke on a meatball or something?" he said chuckling.

"No, she was murdered. Stabbed in the back with a kitchen knife."

"Whoa. For real?"

"For real."

There was silence for several seconds.

"Lance, you still there?"

"I'm still processing. You weren't the one who found her, were you?"

"Mercifully, no. It was Bridget's assistant, Leonardo."

"Any idea who did it?"

"I have some thoughts."

"What do the police say?"

"They're not talking. Though they've been interviewing us. I think they think that Bridget did it. A couple of the guests heard her threatening Vera just before Vera was killed."

Lance whistled.

"But I don't think she did it."

"Just promise me you won't investigate, that you'll let the Italian police handle it."

Guin didn't answer right away.

"Guinivere…"

"I promise," said Guin, though she had crossed both sets of fingers. "So, how's the South of France? You and Owen having a good time?"

Owen was Lance's husband. He owned an art gallery in Manhattan and was meeting with some artist who was based near Nice, seeing if he could represent him.

"It's hot," he replied. "And mostly."

"Yes, well, it is July. Did Owen sign that artist?"

"He's working on it."

Just then Guin spied the chief inspector coming towards her.

"Hey, Lance, I need to go."

"Okay. Just be careful."

"Aren't I always?"

Before he could answer, she ended the call and put away her phone.

"Chief inspector. Did you want to see me?"

His eyes were like two coals, the irises almost the same color as the pupils. And she felt them burning into her.

"If you are done with your call."

Was that sarcasm?

"I'm done," she said. "Let's go."

Guin followed the chief inspector to Rosa's office. He indicated for her to take a seat. She would have preferred to stand but she sat.

"I understand you are writing about the cooking class for your newspaper."

"That's right," said Guin. Though she hadn't done much writing, which she was feeling more than a bit guilty about.

"And as part of your series, you have interviewed some of the people taking the course as well as Signora O'Brien, yes?"

"*Sì.* I mean yes."

"Did you speak with Signora van Leyden?"

"I spoke with her but… Oh, you mean did I interview her?"

He nodded.

"I would have liked to, but she turned me down."

"And why was that?"

"She didn't seem to think very highly of my paper."

"Or could it have been because she thought you would bring up the accusations against her?"

"Accusations?" said Guin, playing dumb.

"The chefs accusing her of stealing their recipes."

"Ah, yes." The chief inspector waited for her to go on. "I did read about that."

"And did it ever cross your mind that perhaps Signora van Leyden was here to steal the recipes of Signora O'Brien and her husband?"

Guin opened her mouth to speak but quickly shut it. She needed to be careful.

"I did think it was a bit odd to have a famous cookbook author taking the course with us. But then again, Tuscan cuisine wasn't Vera's specialty. Maybe she wanted to learn from a pro."

"And when you learned she was working on a new cookbook, as were Signora O'Brien and Signore Moretti?"

Guin regarded him, wondering what Oliver had told him.

"Surely, you must have been concerned as a friend of Signora O'Brien's?"

"Glen and I both were. But Bridget—Signora O'Brien—said the recipes were protected, that everyone attending the course had signed an agreement that prevented them from sharing or publishing the recipes. So she wasn't concerned."

"Is that so?"

Guin nodded. She didn't want to tell the chief inspector that although everyone had signed the agreement, Vera could change a recipe ever so slightly and Bridget and Dante probably wouldn't be able to touch her.

"How well do you know Signora O'Brien?"

"I know she would never harm anyone."

The chief inspector's eyebrows rose slightly.

"Did you know her before attending her class?"

"No. But Glen did. They used to work together, as we told you."

"So you had not met her before."

"No."

"So how do you know she would never harm anyone?"

Guin thought on that.

"She's just not the type."

"So there is a type of person who harms other people?"

Guin was about to say yes, but she sensed this was a trap.

"What is it you want to know, Chief Inspector?"

"It was one of Signora O'Brien's knives that killed Signora van Leyden, and the two of them were heard arguing shortly before she died…"

"When was that exactly?" Guin asked him. "I mean, when did the medical examiner, or whoever is responsible for autopsies, say she died?"

"The time of death was placed between ten p.m. and two a.m."

So could one of the people she had heard in the kitchen have been the killer?

"Did you get the toxicology report?"

The chief inspector looked at her. Guin waited. When he didn't reply, she wondered if he had not understood her.

"Did they find any drugs in her system?"

"No, nothing other than alcohol."

"So it was the knife that killed her."

The chief inspector nodded.

"Bridget didn't do it."

"You seem quite sure."

"I am." Although she wasn't. "Surely, you must have another suspect. What about a burglar?"

"Nothing was taken."

"What about Oliver, Signore Oliveira?"

"What about him?"

Guin wasn't sure if the chief inspector genuinely wanted to know her thoughts. But she decided to answer him anyway.

"He had just as strong a motive to kill Vera as Bridget did."

"Oh?"

Was he playing dumb? Surely John must have said something. But she continued.

"They were constantly bickering. And Vera said she would fire him or ruin him if he didn't make some deal happen."

"Is that so? You heard this?"

Guin nodded.

"Very interesting," said the chief inspector, leaning back in Rosa's chair.

She waited for him to ask her another question. Instead, he surprised her.

"You are free to go, Signora Jones."

She stared at him.

"That's it? So when you say free to go, does that mean you'll give me back my passport?"

"I am afraid I cannot do that just yet."

Guin frowned.

"But as long as you use the app, you are free to move around Chianti."

"Thanks," she said sarcastically. She began to leave but stopped when she got to the door. "What about Vera's body?"

"What about it?" he asked her.

"Will you be releasing it to Signore Oliveira?"

"After they complete the autopsy report and we have heard from Signora van Leyden's sister."

"When will the autopsy report be completed?"

He shrugged.

"Now if you are done asking questions, please ask Signore Anderson to come see me."

CHAPTER 23

Guin waited as Glen spoke with the chief inspector. The interview didn't last long.

"So?" she asked him when he emerged from Rosa's office. "Did he ask you about Bridget?"

Glen nodded.

"What did you say?"

"Let's go get some food. We can discuss the chief inspector over dinner."

"You're hungry? After that big lunch we had?"

"It wasn't that big, and that was hours ago."

Guin marveled at Glen's appetite—and that he managed to stay so trim.

"How about we go into town and get pizza?"

Guin saw Beatrice looking over at them or rather at Glen.

"What about Beatrice?"

Glen looked confused.

"What about her?"

"Don't you want to invite her?"

"Do *you* want to invite her?"

"I just thought that since she invited you the other day and you two seemed so chummy…"

Glen frowned.

"I'd prefer it was just the two of us. That is if that's all right with you."

"Perfectly fine," Guin replied, relieved.

"So, pizza?"

"Sure. Why not?"

They drove into town in Glen's red convertible. The sky was beginning to turn light blue, or was it more lavender? Guin couldn't decide. She was enjoying the breeze and listening to the radio station Glen had found.

"If we weren't stuck here, I'd want to stay."

"That makes no sense," said Glen.

"You know what I mean." Guin gazed out the window. "It's really nice here. Nice scenery, good food, friendly people…"

"You just described Sanibel."

Guin laughed.

"True. Though Greve looks nothing like Sanibel. And there's no beach."

"Though there are plenty of beaches nearby. I hear Grosseto's very nice, and it's not that far. Less than two hours. We could drive there."

"And have the chief inspector come looking for us? Besides, I still need to write those articles for Ginny. I'm way behind."

"I'm sure she understands."

Guin doubted that.

They arrived at the restaurant. It was busy, but they managed to get a table for two outside.

Glen ordered a beer, and Guin ordered a glass of white wine, and they both ordered pizza.

"So, what did the chief inspector ask you?" Guin asked him after taking a sip of her wine.

"He mostly wanted to know about Bridget."

"What did he want to know?"

"How well I knew her, if I thought she was capable of killing anyone."

"And what did you tell him?"

He took a sip of his beer.

"I told him that I had known Bridget a long time, and that while she could be cutthroat when it came to trading stocks, she would never literally cut anyone's throat—or stab them in the back."

"How did he respond?"

"He asked how I could be so sure. And I said I just knew. I also told him that Bridget had changed since coming here."

"How so?"

"She's more relaxed, happier. Not someone I could ever picture plunging a knife into someone."

"Italy and being happily married can do that."

Glen nodded.

"But some of the old Bridget must still be in there," said Guin. "I mean, you can take the girl out of New York, but you can't take the New York out of the girl."

"What's that supposed to mean?"

"I mean, what if someone had provoked Bridget, made her really angry?"

"I just can't picture the new Bridget getting violent."

"What about the old Bridget?"

Glen looked thoughtful.

"What?" said Guin. "I see those wheels turning."

Glen sighed.

"There was this one trader, Chip."

"His name alone would make me angry," said Guin.

Glen smiled then continued.

"Chip was a bit of a prick."

"His parents should have named him Dick."

"Are you going to let me finish?"

"Sorry."

"Anyway, Chip was always saying stuff to Bridget, talking down to her, telling her to go find a husband or bake cookies or something whenever she got steamed."

"Total dick."

"Pretty much. And one day, Bridget had enough."

"What did she do?"

"She made him brownies."

"She made him brownies?"

"And laced them with a laxative. A lot of laxative. Chip spent the whole day in the bathroom and went home early."

Guin burst out laughing.

"Did he retaliate?"

"Bridget left for Italy soon after, so he didn't have a chance."

"Good for her!" said Guin, still smiling. "So are you saying that if Bridget wanted to teach Vera a lesson, she would have slipped her some extra-strength Ex-Lax?"

Glen smiled.

"Possibly. But that would be the extent of it. She would never have stabbed Vera, even if Vera had provoked her."

Their pizzas arrived, and they dug in.

"So what did the chief inspector ask you?" asked Glen.

"The same as you: how well I knew Bridget and what I thought of her."

"And what did you tell him?"

"I told him that I didn't know her that well. That she was your friend. But that I didn't believe she killed Vera."

"Do you think he believed you?"

"I don't know. I also told him he should look into Oliver's whereabouts that evening, that I had heard the two of them arguing, and that he had just as good a motive to kill Vera as Bridget did."

"You really think Oliver could have plunged that knife into Vera's back? As much as I want to believe Bridget is innocent, and that Oliver did it, I just don't see him doing it."

Guin had to admit, she also had a hard time picturing Oliver wielding a knife, other than to slice vegetables.

"Well, someone put that knife in Vera's back. And he had motive and opportunity. Also, the chief inspector said that Vera died between ten p.m. and two a.m., and Bridget said she was at home with Dante then. Though she could be lying." She looked thoughtful. "Maybe you should have a word with her."

"And what am I supposed to say? Did you lie about being home with Dante when Vera was killed? I still say it could have been a burglar."

"But the chief inspector said nothing was stolen."

But what if something had been stolen, something small but important? Though she had no idea what that could be. Still, she made a mental note to speak with the kitchen staff and ask them. Maybe there was something they had overlooked.

"Eat," said Glen. "Your pizza's getting cold."

"Fine," said Guin, cutting off a piece and popping it into her mouth. "You happy now?"

Glen smiled at her. It was a smile that made her feel warm inside.

"Very," he said.

"So, shall we go get some gelato?"

They had paid for dinner and left the restaurant.

Guin stared at him.

"How can you eat more after that?"

"The pizza wasn't that big, and I always have room for gelato."

Guin shook her head.

"I don't know where you put it. I can't eat another bite, but I'll keep you company."

"Okay," he said. "But if you change your mind…"

They walked to a nearby gelateria, and Glen ordered a cup of *stracciatella*, which was similar to chocolate chip.

"You sure you don't want some?"

Guin had been eyeing the flavors.

"Maybe just a little cup," she said, unable to resist.

She ordered a small cup of tiramisu, and they went outside.

It was getting dark, but the moon was out, and the streetlamps had just come on, and Guin didn't feel like going back to the hotel. So they strolled through town, watching couples holding hands and families eating at the outdoor cafés.

"Do you ever regret not having children?" Guin asked Glen, looking at a couple with two children, a boy and a girl, who were chasing each other.

"Sometimes, but not really."

"Though you could still have children," she said.

"I guess," he said. "What about you?"

"I told you. We tried, but it wasn't meant to be."

"You're still young."

Guin looked up at him.

"Not that young."

"Plenty of women have kids well into their forties. Maybe you just weren't with the right man."

He was looking at her again, and Guin felt that same flutter.

"Let's change the subject. Do you think we'll have class tomorrow? It was supposed to have been our last day."

"I don't know. Maybe Bridget sent out a group message?"

They took out their phones.

"I don't see anything," said Guin. "You want to ask her?"

"Why me?"

"You're her friend."

"So? If you want to know if there's class tomorrow, message her."

"Fine."

A few minutes later, Guin felt her phone vibrating. She plucked it out of her back pocket.

"Is it Bridget?"

"No, it's Ginny."

"What does she want?"

Guin read the email.

"She wants to know when we're going to send her more stuff."

"You told her about Vera and the investigation and that we've been busy?"

Guin nodded.

"But she has space to fill."

"Tell her we'll get her something as soon as we can."

"Maybe I should just call her."

"Do you really want to do that?"

"Not really, but it'll be faster."

Guin had Ginny's number on speed dial and called it. Ginny picked up after two rings.

"Buttercup! How the heck are you? Are you with Glen?"

It always amazed Guin how Ginny knew things.

"As a matter of fact, I am."

"Tell him to send me more pictures."

Guin smiled, and Glen looked at her. She covered the phone.

"She wants to know when you're going to send her more pictures."

"Tell her I'll send her some later."

She uncovered her phone.

"He says he'll send you some later."

"And when will I see those articles you've been promising me?"

"Soon. This whole Vera thing kind of put a dent in our plans."

"What's the latest? Did they figure out who did it yet?"

"Not yet," said Guin, not wanting to mention Bridget. "They haven't even completed the autopsy."

"Didn't you say she was stabbed in the back?"

"Yes, but…"

Ginny cut her off.

"I need to go. Just send me something I can post. And get your tails back here."

"We're trying."

"Try harder," she said. Then she ended the call.

Guin sighed.

"What'd she say?" asked Glen.

"She wants more pictures and articles. And she told us to get our tails back there."

"Did you tell her the police still have our passports?"

"I don't think that matters. Come, we should get back. I need to try to get some work done."

CHAPTER 24

Glen parked the car in the lot and turned to Guin.

"Any word from Bridget?"

Guin took out her phone and shook her head.

"Nothing."

Glen frowned.

"Do you think they've arrested her?"

"We'd have heard something," Guin assured him. "But if you're concerned, message Dante."

"I'm sure he's working."

"Not if Bridget was arrested. Send him a message."

"Okay."

He took out his phone and began to type.

"Though we could also ask Rosa," said Guin. "She'd probably know."

"You think she's around? It's pretty late."

"Only one way to find out."

They made their way to reception, but Rosa wasn't at her desk.

"Maybe she's in her office."

Guin walked over and knocked on the door.

"*Sì?*" came a voice.

"Rosa, it's Signora Jones and Signore Anderson. May we come in?"

"*Sì,*" came the reply.

Guin opened the door to see Rosa seated at her desk in

front of a computer, a stack of paperwork beside her.

"You're working late."

Rosa sighed.

"I did not think the chief inspector would be here for so long. And it is our busy season."

Though Guin wondered if it would still be busy once word of the murder got out. Word had already spread. And it was only a matter of time until others outside of Greve learned what had happened at the Albergo Dell'Incanto.

"So no one has canceled their reservation?"

"Not yet. Though the chief inspector will not allow anyone else to stay here until they are done with the investigation."

"But that could take weeks."

"*Sì.* Though he told me he would not hold the hotel hostage for that long, just a few more days."

"Well, that's good. So you won't be kicking us out?"

Rosa smiled.

"No. You may stay here until the chief inspector returns your passports."

"Thank you," said Guin.

"What about the guests who were supposed to be checking in?" said Glen.

Rosa's smile went away.

"We offered to find them other accommodations or refund their money."

"That's very good of you, but won't that hurt the hotel?" asked Guin.

"What else can we do?" She paused. "So, what is it you wanted to ask me?"

Guin saw the stack of papers on Rosa's desk.

"If you're busy, we can come back in the morning."

"You are here now. What can I do for you?"

"We were wondering if you had heard from Bridget, if she was okay."

"We're worried that the police might have arrested her," added Glen.

"I have not heard from her or the police. Did you try messaging her?"

"I sent her a message," said Guin. "But she hasn't gotten back to me."

"And I messaged Dante," said Glen.

"And you did not hear from either of them?"

They shook their heads.

"If you don't mind me asking," said Guin, "what did you tell the chief inspector about her?"

"I told him that Signora O'Brien had brought many new customers to our hotel and that everyone loved her."

"Did he ask you anything else?"

"He asked me if anything had been stolen."

"From the hotel?"

Rosa nodded.

"And?"

"We are still checking, but I do not think so."

Guin was about to ask her another question when Rosa's phone began to ring. Rosa looked down at it.

"Please, get that," said Guin. "We'll see ourselves out."

"*Grazie*," said Rosa.

They left the office, closing the door behind them.

"Now what?" said Glen.

"I don't know. We should probably speak with Leo and Francesca."

"I don't feel right bothering them at home."

"Sorry. I didn't mean now. I meant in the morning."

"Okay. So what's our next move?"

Guin smiled at him. She liked that he now felt vested in finding out who had killed Vera, or at least in proving that Bridget hadn't done it.

"We go back to our rooms, and you send Ginny some photos while I stay up late and get Ginny another article."

"You sure?"

"Not much else we can do tonight."

They were walking to their rooms when Guin stopped.

"Oh, I forgot to tell you. I heard a strange conversation between John and Julia after they had been interviewed by the chief inspector."

"Strange how?"

"Julia was asking him what he had said to the chief inspector. She sounded worried."

"Why would she be worried?"

"I don't know. She asked John if he had told the chief inspector about him and Vera."

"Him and Vera?"

Guin nodded.

"You make it sound like they were having an affair," he said jokingly.

"Maybe they were."

"What? I know John did work for Vera's husband. But do you honestly believe he could have had an affair with Vera? And if he did, do you think he would have told his wife?"

He had a point.

"I don't know. You wouldn't think so. But maybe Julia found out, and she was worried John might have said something. Though he made it clear he had said very little to the chief inspector, just told him he had done some work for Vera's husband and had met her a few times.

"Though if they had had an affair…"

"Sorry, I just can't picture it," said Glen.

Guin sighed.

"I know. I'm probably imagining things. Still, Julia was clearly worried that John might have said something that could have incriminated him."

"Or her," said Glen.

Guin looked at him.

"Or her?"

"Well, if you happened to run into the woman your husband had had an affair with while you were on vacation, would you be happy about it?"

Unbidden, Guin pictured her former hairdresser, Debbie, the woman her husband had had an affair with. Assuming she and Art had reconciled after he had betrayed her, and they ran into Debbie on vacation, Guin would certainly not have been happy to see her. But would she have stuck a knife in Debbie's back? She would like to have thought not. Even though she felt that Debbie had certainly stabbed her in the back.

"Guin?" he said.

"Hm?" He was looking at her. "Sorry. I was lost in thought. To answer your question, no, I would not be happy about it. But I'd like to think I wouldn't have tried to kill her." *Maybe just baked her Ex-Lax brownies.* The thought made her smile.

They arrived at their rooms.

"Well, good night," said Glen.

"Good night," said Guin. "See you in the morning. Let me know if you hear from Dante—or Bridget."

"I will."

They stood there awkwardly for a few minutes, then they went into their respective rooms.

Guin had planned on working, but she kept thinking about Vera. She entered Vera's name in her search engine then clicked on "News." There were dozens of results, including an article just published in the *Boston Globe*. She clicked on it and began to read.

The article, a partial obituary with more to come per the editorial note, mentioned Vera's humble upbringing; her marriage to Nicholas van Leyden; the tragic death of her son

Christian when he was only twenty-four; her divorce; her rise as a successful private chef then cookbook author; the allegations against her, which were never proven; and that she had been working on a new cookbook in Italy when her life had been tragically cut short.

The piece wasn't very long, and Guin re-read it a couple of times, even though most of the information wasn't new. It struck her that both Vera and her son had died in Italy, an odd coincidence. Could there possibly be a connection? She typed his name into her search engine.

The screen immediately populated, and Guin was surprised by the number of results. But apparently Christian van Leyden's death had been big news. She started to read. Christian had been an up-and-coming artist who had been studying in Florence when he died of a drug overdose.

She searched for images of his artwork and found plenty of examples. Christian's style, for lack of a better word, was taking classic Renaissance images and updating them, giving them a Modern or Contemporary look. Kind of like if David Hockney had painted the Mona Lisa. His work wasn't her cup of tea. (Guin wasn't a huge fan of Contemporary art.) But she could see that Christian had talent. Certainly the art critics thought he did.

She continued to read about him.

He had gone to Italy on a grant and had been happy there, working on his art and making a name for himself. He was supposed to have returned to the States after two years, but he had decided to extend his stay. Some suspected it had to do with a woman, the muse who had inspired many of his paintings.

Then something had happened. It was rumored that he and his muse had parted ways. And soon after Christian had been found in his studio, dead from a drug overdose. There was a brief investigation, and his death had been ruled an accident. His parents and the art world had been devastated.

"Poor Vera," said Guin.

She took another look at Christian's artwork, to see if she could find this muse the articles spoke of. There was one woman in particular who appeared in several of his more well-known paintings. But her face was always somewhat obscured. The same could not be said of her body, which was often naked and lush. Something about her felt familiar. But Guin couldn't place her. Then again, all the women in Renaissance paintings looked pretty much the same to her.

As she was staring at her computer, her phone began to vibrate across her desk. She picked it up and saw that she had a message from Bridget. There would be class tomorrow, in the afternoon. They would be making a four-course Italian dinner to celebrate the end of the course.

Well, that was good news. Clearly, Bridget had not been arrested if she was able to teach a class. And now Guin would have the entire morning to work. She let out a yawn and looked at the clock on her laptop. She thought about blowing off work until the morning. Instead, she closed her browser and opened a new document. Sleep would have to wait.

CHAPTER 25

Guin wound up not going to bed until nearly midnight. But she had been productive, finishing the first draft of her article. She set her alarm for seven the next morning. That way she could go for a walk and have breakfast before getting back to work.

She had slept soundly, so soundly she almost didn't hear the alarm go off. She had thought about staying in bed, but there was sunlight streaming in through the window. No doubt it was another beautiful day. So she got up.

She was about to leave for her walk when she remembered to message Glen. She was surprised when he messaged her right back, saying he would meet her outside. She smiled and put away her phone. He was waiting for her when she walked through the door.

"Good morning," she said. "You're up bright and early."

"It's the best time to take photos."

"Right. Speaking of photos, did you send some to Ginny?"

"I did. What about you? You work on that article?"

"Finished the first draft last night, though I'll need to review it before sending it to her. Who knows? I may even write another one before we have to go to class."

"Well, look at you. Aren't you the productive one?"

"I was inspired. And I finally got a good night's sleep."

"So, where were you planning on walking?"

"I hadn't decided. I don't really want to walk into town or to the vineyard."

"Have you done the trail to the old villa?"

"What trail to the old villa?"

"Come. I'll show you."

Guin followed him to the back of the hotel, where he showed her a barely visible trail.

"Is this it?"

He nodded.

Guin followed him. The trail was hard to see, marked only by crushed grass and exposed dirt. She wondered how Glen had found it. They walked in silence until they came to a top of a small hill with an old stone villa perched atop it. It looked deserted.

"What is this place?"

"An abandoned estate."

"No one lives here?"

He shook his head.

Guin looked around. The view was amazing.

"I'm surprised. You would think someone would have scooped this place up, if only for the view."

"Bridget said the family who owns the property can't decide what to do with it."

"Ah. Well, if they don't want it, they should sell it."

"You want to buy it?"

"I wish. But it looks like it needs a lot of work. And considering my track record with renovation, probably not a good idea. Also, I'm sure it's not cheap."

"I could help you."

Guin smiled at him, and Glen smiled back at her. He was intimately familiar with Guin's home renovation woes, having helped her finish her home renovation project after her contractor died mid-renovation. Not that the contractor had been doing a great job when he was alive.

"Thanks. I appreciate the offer." She took out her phone.

"We should head back. I need to work. And I could use some coffee."

"Okay," he said. "Shall we take a selfie first though?"

Guin was not a fan of selfies, probably because her arms were too short to get a good one.

"Only if you take it."

"Of course."

She went over to him, and Glen put his arm around her. It felt good.

"Okay, ready?"

She nodded.

"Smile!"

She complied.

"Got it."

He took a look.

"Let me see."

He showed her the picture.

"Not bad."

"Not bad? We look great!"

"We do look pretty good," Guin admitted, not able to hide her smile.

"Okay, let's head back," he said.

John and Julia were helping themselves to food as Guin and Glen arrived on the dining terrace.

They sat at an empty table, and Francesca came over and asked if they'd like coffee.

"*Prego,*" said Guin, smiling up at Francesca. "*Due cappuccini, per favore.*"

"*Qualunque altra cosa?*"

Guin looked confused.

"Anything else?" Francesca translated.

"Some water, please."

Francesca nodded and left.

"Shall we get some food?" said Glen.

"Sure."

On the way to the buffet, they passed John and Julia and said good morning to them.

"Hard to believe it's the last day of class, eh?" said John.

"I know," said Guin. "Well, enjoy your breakfast."

When they returned to their table, their cappuccinos were waiting for them, and Guin immediately took a sip. She could have downed the whole bowl in one gulp. But she didn't.

"So I was doing some research last night, into Vera," Guin told Glen after eating a mini *pain au chocolat.* "Did you know Vera's son was an up-and-coming artist?"

"I did not."

"He was considered something of a prodigy and had received a grant to study in Italy. He died here unexpectedly, just before he was supposed to go back to the States."

"How awful. What happened?"

"Drug overdose."

"When was this?"

"Around nine or ten years ago. He was only twenty-four. It made headlines in the art world. His work was to be featured in some big exhibit in Florence, and he was being touted as the next Andy Warhol or something."

"Did he have a drug problem?"

"His roommates said he didn't. But he could have hidden it from them. They thought it must have had something to do with a recent breakup. The girlfriend was supposedly his muse."

"Ah."

"Ah?"

"Muses are very important to artists. And if he was in love with her and she broke his heart…"

"We don't know that. The article didn't say."

"Still, my money is on a broken heart."

"You speak from experience?"

Glen looked at her, and Guin felt her face grow warm.

"Anyway, it made me feel bad for Vera. No one should lose a child."

"I'm sorry, but I couldn't help hear you mention Christian van Leyden." Guin turned to see John leaning over. "Terrible tragedy."

"Did you know him?"

"I met him a couple of times. His father introduced me. He was very proud of Christian. Hoped he would take over the business one day. I don't think Christian was interested though. He was more interested in being an artist than dealing art."

"And how did his parents feel about that?"

"They didn't discuss personal matters with me. I was Nicholas's attorney, not his friend."

"What about Vera? Were you her friend?"

John looked like he was going to reply. Then Guin saw Julia give a slight shake of her head.

"I worked for Nicholas."

That didn't answer the question.

"You didn't do any work for Vera or become friendly with her?"

Guin glanced at Julia. She was giving John a look.

"No," said John.

"Did you ever meet Christian's girlfriend, the one he had in Italy?"

"No. He never brought her home. They wouldn't allow it."

"Why wouldn't they allow him to bring home his girlfriend?"

"They didn't approve of her," said Julia. "She was a model. Posed nude for some of the art students."

"So? Mr. van Leyden must have known plenty of artist's models, having been in the business."

"No doubt. But there's a big difference between one of your clients sleeping with his model and your son bringing his nude model home to meet mother."

Guin thought that rather snobby of the van Leydens, but she didn't comment.

"So did Christian's death precipitate their divorce?"

John nodded.

"I don't think things had been good between them for a while, and Christian's death... Well, that was the final nail in the coffin."

"Really, John," said Julia.

"Sorry. Poor choice of words."

"So, do you still do work for Mr. van Leyden?" Guin asked him.

"No, we parted ways."

"Oh? How come?"

Just then Julia got up.

"Come, John. We need to go. We don't want to be late."

"Where are you going?"

"To Siena. We have a private tour booked."

John put his napkin on the table and got up.

"Will we see you in class later?" Guin asked them.

"We were planning on it," said Julia.

"Enjoy your morning," said John.

Guin watched them go.

"Speaking of private tours," said Glen.

"Yes?" said Guin, turning to face him.

"Beatrice invited me to go with her to San Gimignano this morning."

"Oh? And when did she do that?"

"Last night."

Had he gone to see Beatrice after they had said good night? Guin was about to ask him but was afraid of the answer so didn't.

"Well, have fun!"

"Thanks. Is everything all right?"

"Everything's fine. Why?"

"You look a bit annoyed."

Guin thought she had hidden it.

"I'm fine. Just thinking about all the work I need to do," she lied. "Also, did you notice the way Julia was looking at John as we talked about the van Leydens?"

"I did notice something."

"Maybe something was going on between him and Vera, something Julia doesn't want people to know about."

"It's possible," said Glen.

"I wonder if she could have killed Vera."

"You don't really think Julia killed Vera, do you? She's a doctor."

"And as a doctor, she'd know just where to stick the knife."

"I don't buy it."

"I know it sounds crazy, but I've seen crazier things."

"What happened to Oliver? Do you no longer suspect him?"

"Oh, he's still a suspect."

"And didn't you say you heard Domenico threaten Vera?"

"Oh, right. I forgot about him. And isn't his family in the hotel business? He's their director of business development or something like that. Maybe he came here to buy the hotel and Signore Cassini said no, and he killed Vera to cast a pall on the hotel, so Cassini would change his mind about selling it."

Glen was shaking his head.

"What?"

"Has anyone ever told you that you have an active imagination?"

"Now you sound like Detective O'Loughlin. Forget I said anything. Though someone stuck that knife in Vera.

And we both agree it wasn't Bridget. Though you should still talk to her and Dante and verify that Bridget was really at home all evening."

Glen sighed.

"I will, but I don't like it. Also, I should go."

He got up. Guin remained at the table.

"Take lots of pictures."

"I will."

"So will I see you in class later?"

"I'll be there."

Though Guin wasn't so sure.

"Okay. Ciao for now then!" she said cheerily. Though inside she was fuming.

CHAPTER 26

Guin was heading back to her room when she saw Domenico speaking on his phone. She unconsciously headed toward him. He saw her approach and quickly ended his conversation and put his phone away.

"*Buon giorno!*" she said.

"*Buon giorno,*" he replied.

"Beautiful day!"

"*Sì.*"

"How do you say that in Italian, *it's a beautiful day*?"

"*È una bella giornata.*"

"It sounds so nice when you say it. You going to class this afternoon?"

"*Sì.*"

Guin could tell he wasn't in a chatty mood but kept going.

"Did you have breakfast?"

"I do not eat breakfast."

"How come?"

He shrugged.

"I am not hungry in the morning."

"Do you drink coffee?"

He looked at her as though that was a ridiculous question.

"I'll take that as a yes. So, what will you be doing with your free morning?"

"Working."

"Sorry to hear that."

He shrugged as if to say, *such is life.*

"And you?"

"Actually, I'm working too. I understand your family owns a lot of hotels, yes?"

"That is correct."

"And you're in charge of new business."

He nodded.

"Are they thinking of buying this hotel?"

"I do not believe the Incanto is for sale."

"So you didn't discuss the hotel with Signore Cassini?"

"We talked. But as I said, the hotel is not for sale."

"I see. But your family would buy it if it was for sale?"

He was looking at her suspiciously, or so Guin thought. But she ignored it and plowed ahead.

"So I couldn't help overhearing you the other day, talking to Vera. It sounded like the two of you were arguing."

He didn't say anything.

"I'm pretty sure I heard her threatening you."

"I do not remember this. Are you sure it was me you heard speaking to Signora van Leyden?"

"Oh, yes. It was definitely you. And I recall you telling her to 'leave her out of it.' Though I have no idea who she was referring to."

Domenico looked annoyed.

"You must be mistaken. I barely spoke with Signora van Leyden. And I do not remember such a conversation."

"Oh, it seemed like you two knew each other."

Domenico didn't say anything.

"So you never met her, I mean, before here?"

He hesitated, then spoke.

"We met once, a long time ago."

"Here or in the States?"

"Here."

"Was she doing a book signing?"

He didn't reply.

Guin was getting frustrated, but she wasn't ready to give up.

"I'm sure I saw the two of you talking about something. Did it have something to do with your hotels?"

Domenico sighed.

"If you must know, she wanted me to hire her to teach cooking classes."

"At one of your hotels."

He nodded.

Guin wondered if that was the deal Vera and Oliver had been talking about.

"And what did you tell her?"

"I told her I would think about it."

"And where were you Saturday evening between ten p.m. and two a.m.?"

Domenico frowned, clearly annoyed.

"You cannot think I had anything to do with Signora van Leyden's death."

Guin didn't say anything, just waited for him to reply.

"I was in my room."

"Can anyone vouch for you?"

"You can ask Beatrice. She will tell you."

Guin had no doubt Beatrice would corroborate his story, even if it was a lie.

"Now I am afraid I must go, Signora Jones. See you in class."

Before she could say another word, Domenico turned and left.

Beatrice was grinning.

"Did I not tell you?" she said.

They were in San Gimignano. Beatrice was playing tour

guide. She was dressed like a movie star—or a Kardashian— wearing a form-fitting dress, high heels, a big hat, and sunglasses. And Glen noticed several people staring at them, or really her.

"You were right," he said. "It's beautiful."

She squeezed his arm.

"I am so glad I could share this with you."

San Gimignano was located on a hill, around an hour southwest of Greve. It was a UNESCO World Heritage Site, known for its 13th-century walls, medieval stone houses, and 12th-century church that contained frescoes by Ghirlandaio.

Beatrice said it was one of her favorite places in Tuscany and had insisted on taking Glen there.

They had taken the scenic route, passing through olive groves, vineyards, and farms. Beatrice seemed to know the area well, though she had been away for many years.

The scenery reminded Glen a bit of the Hamptons or the North Fork of Long Island. Probably because of the farms and vineyards. Though the two places weren't at all alike.

"Let us go get a *caffè*," she said. "I know just the spot."

She led him to a small café where the proprietor greeted her with two kisses, one on the left cheek, then one on the right, and embraced her as though she were an old friend.

"Andrea, *come stai?*" she asked him.

"*Molto bene e tu?*"

They spoke in rapid Italian as Glen looked on. Then Andrea looked at him and said something to Beatrice in Italian.

"This is my friend, Glen," she said. "He is a famous American photographer."

Glen opened his mouth to correct her, but she smiled and winked at him and he shut it.

"He has never been to San Gimignano," she continued.

"What?" said Andrea. "You have never been to San Gimignano?!"

"This is actually my first trip to Italy."

"He is taking a cooking class with me in Greve," Beatrice informed Andrea.

"A cooking class? But your *nonna*, she was the best cook in Tuscany. Did she not teach you her recipes?"

"She tried. But I fear I was not a very good student. Now I am ready to learn."

They chatted again in Italian, Glen having only a vague idea of what they were saying. He guessed they were catching up.

"But I am being rude," said Andrea, switching back to English. "Please, come with me."

He led them to a table and asked what he could bring them. They ordered coffee, and Andrea returned a few minutes later with their drinks and a plate of biscotti.

"My wife, she just made these," he said, full of pride.

He waited while Glen and Beatrice tried the biscotti.

"They're delicious," Glen said.

Andrea beamed.

"Maria's biscotti *sono i migliori*," said Beatrice. "They are the best." She then dunked her biscotti in her coffee.

"It's okay to dunk them?"

"*Assolutamente!*" said Beatrice. "Biscotti are made to be dunked."

Glen then dunked his and took a bite. Beatrice waited.

"Mm," he said, his mouth full of biscotti.

"Good, eh?"

Glen nodded.

"I should get some of these to bring to Guin. She loves biscotti."

Beatrice pouted.

"What?" he said.

"You are always talking about Guin."

"Am I?"

"*Sì*," said Beatrice, folding her arms over her ample chest.

"I wasn't aware."

"You like her."

"Of course I like her. We're friends."

"Perhaps you like her a bit more than as friends."

Glen looked down at his coffee.

Beatrice leaned across the table, her cleavage on display, and placed a finger under his chin, forcing him to look at her.

"I would like to be your friend."

Though the way she said it made Glen think she wanted to be more than friends.

"I thought we were friends."

"Very good friends."

He felt her foot rub against his leg and moved his leg away.

"Let's go for a walk."

"But you have not finished your coffee and biscotti."

Glen drained his coffee and took another bite of biscotti. Then he signaled to Andrea.

"Yes?" said the proprietor.

"The check, please," said Glen.

"You are my guests. It is on me."

"But I would like some of Maria's biscotti to go. May I at least pay for that?"

Andrea reluctantly agreed and returned a minute later with a box of biscotti.

"*Grazie*," said Glen.

"*Prego*," said Andrea.

Beatrice kissed Andrea goodbye, then she led Glen over to City Hall.

"From the tower, you get the best view of the city," she informed him.

Glen looked up. The City Hall tower rose 200 feet, and you could see all of the terracotta roofs and the surrounding countryside from the top. He immediately began taking photos.

"Take one of me!" said Beatrice posing for him.

She laughed and smiled as the camera clicked, as though she had done this a thousand times. People were looking at them and pointing, and Beatrice drank it up. She was a natural.

"You ever think about modeling professionally?" Glen asked her.

"No," said Beatrice. "My modeling days are over. Now come, we have more to see."

She led him down the steps of the tower and they spent the next hour roaming the streets of San Gimignano.

"This has been great," said Glen as the clock struck noon. "But we should head back. We don't want to be late for class. Do you know someplace along the way where we can get a bite to eat?"

"I know just the place!" she said, a twinkle in her eye.

They arrived back at the hotel just as class was to begin. Lunch had taken longer than he had expected. But what had he expected? This was Italy.

Beatrice said she would be right there. She needed to freshen up first. So Glen went into the kitchen on his own and took his place next to Guin.

"Nice of you to join us."

Glen looked at her. Was she pissed at him?

"You and Beatrice have a good time in San Gimignano?"

Yep, she was definitely pissed. He couldn't help smiling at the thought. Though that only made her look more pissed off.

"We did. You'd love San Gimignano. I got you a little something."

He held out the box.

"What is it?" she asked, examining the white pastry box.

"Open it and see."

She opened the box.

"It looks like biscotti."

"Not just any biscotti. They're Maria's biscotti."

"Who's Maria?"

"The wife of the man who runs the little café Bea took me to, and the best biscotti maker in Tuscany. At least according to her husband."

Glen saw her smile, though she quickly covered it up, along with the box.

"You're not going to have one?"

"I'll have one later. Class is about to begin."

CHAPTER 27

Guin didn't know why she was in a bad mood. Well, she did. She just didn't want to admit it. Glen was a grown man and single. What right did she have to say who he could or couldn't date? Though the thought of him dating Beatrice annoyed her. She had to be at least ten years younger than Glen. Though men dated younger women all the time. Something else that annoyed her.

But why did Beatrice have to go after Glen? She could have her pick of men. Domenico clearly wanted her, but she didn't seem interested in him that way. Maybe she was the type of woman who went after other women's men. Not that Glen was her man.

She told herself to stop thinking about Beatrice—and Glen. But it was hard, especially with him standing right next to her.

"Guin?" It was Glen.

"Hm?" she said. She hadn't realized Glen had said something to her.

"I asked if you sent your article to Ginny."

"Oh, yeah, and I finished the first draft of the next one."

"That's great. So you're all caught up?"

"Hardly."

Guin glanced around but didn't see Beatrice.

"Where's Bea?"

"She said she was going to change, but she should be here soon."

"Can we start now?" said Oliver, sounding whiny.

"Let's give Beatrice another minute," said Bridget.

Oliver frowned.

A few seconds later, Beatrice waltzed in, apologizing to everyone for being late. Though Oliver continued to frown. Guin stared at her. Her dress left little to the imagination, and Guin wondered how she could breathe, let alone cook, in it. She turned to Glen.

"I hate to think what she was wearing before."

Glen looked sheepish.

"Okay, now that we're all here," said Bridget, "let's begin." She glanced around the room, making sure she had everyone's attention. "Today we will be making a traditional four-course Tuscan meal using the recipes we made earlier this week. Though you may use any of the recipes in the binder, provided your partner is game.

"We will be dividing up the class, with one or two of you responsible for each course—*antipasto*, *primo*, *secondo*, and *dolce*. I will say the name of the course, then raise your hand if you are interested. Got it?"

Everyone nodded.

"Very good. Now, who would like to be in charge of the *antipasti*?"

After some negotiating, Oliver and John were put in charge of the antipasti. Domenico was given the first course. Glen would prepare the second course. Julia would make the side dishes. And Guin and Beatrice were put in charge of dessert.

Guin was not thrilled to be working with Beatrice. And Beatrice didn't look happy about being paired with Guin. But neither said anything when Bridget assigned the two of them dessert. Fortunately, they didn't actually have to work together as Bridget said they could each make a dessert. But they would have to work next to each other.

"So, what are you going to make?" Guin asked Beatrice.

"I will make a tiramisu," Beatrice stated.

Guin frowned. She had wanted to make a tiramisu. *Could they both make tiramisu?* Probably not.

"Why don't you make the *torta*?" Beatrice suggested. "The recipe is quite easy."

"Thank you," said Guin, forcing a smile. "I think I will."

Bridget came over.

"So, have you two decided which desserts you're going to make?"

"*Sì*," said Beatrice. "I am going to make a tiramisu, and Guin will make *torta della nonna*."

"Sounds good. Now get your ingredients and let me or Leo know if you need any help."

"I am sure I will be fine," said Beatrice. "Though I am not so sure about Guin."

"I'm sure I can handle it," said Guin, seething inwardly.

Bridget eyed the two of them then moved on.

Guin placed everything she would need for the *torta della nonna* in front of her. Then she read through the directions one more time and began warming the milk in a pot. As soon as the milk was the right temperature, she moved the pot to the side. Then she began to crack the eggs, separating the white from the yolk and saving the yolks.

"I heard you took Glen to San Gimignano," she said casually.

"*Sì*," said Beatrice, who was also separating eggs. "He told me he had never been, and it is one of my favorite places in Tuscany."

"I heard San Gimignano is very beautiful."

"It is. And Glen is such a charming companion. He took my picture and told me I could be a model."

"Is that so?" said Guin, feeling her body stiffen.

Beatrice nodded.

"You know, I used to model when I was younger… in the nude, for the art students at university," she said in a low, sultry voice. Guin cracked her egg too hard against the bowl, causing pieces of the shell to fall in. Beatrice tsked.

Guin scowled and picked out the pieces of eggshell. Then she began beating the eggs and sugar together, attempting to ignore Beatrice.

"I told Glen I would show him Firenze next."

"You did?" said Guin, nearly scalding herself on the milk she had been warming.

"*Sì*. I suggested we go this weekend if we are all still here."

Guin frowned. Glen hadn't said anything about going to Florence with Beatrice.

She turned and looked down at the recipe. *Ignore her*, Guin told herself. She looked over at Glen and noticed Domenico looking their way.

"How does Domenico feel about you spending so much time with Glen?"

"Domenico is not my keeper," Beatrice retorted.

Guin looked over at him. He was busy working on his pasta. She watched him for a few seconds then returned to her *torta della nonna*, stirring the egg and milk mixture over low heat until it got thick and blocking out all other thoughts.

Glen had wanted to make *Bistecca alla Fiorentina*. But Bridget had nixed that idea. Instead, she had suggested he make *arista*, a roasted pork loin seasoned with rosemary, thyme, garlic, and salt.

"Shouldn't I make the porchetta or the *peposo*?" he had asked her.

"You're welcome to make either," Bridget had told him. "Though we don't really have enough time for the porchetta. The *arista* is similar. It just takes less time. And I thought you'd enjoy trying something new."

"Usually. But not when it comes to cooking."

"Come on. You've got this," she assured him.

But Glen wasn't so sure. He looked over at Domenico. "What's he making?"

"Pappardelle with a wild boar ragu."

"Is he making the pasta from scratch?"

"He is."

Glen scowled.

"Fine, show me the recipe for this *aristo*."

"It's *arista*," said Bridget, putting the emphasis on the *a*. "And the recipe's in your binder."

She flipped to the page and showed him.

"See, nothing to it."

Glen looked at the recipe then back over at Domenico.

"Do you have something a bit more difficult?"

"More difficult?"

Bridget caught him glancing at Domenico.

"Ah," she said. "You know, *arista* may look simple, but it requires a lot of finesse."

"It does?"

Bridget nodded.

"You need to season the pork just right. And make sure not to overcook it. And the sauce can be quite tricky."

"Hm," said Glen, mulling it over.

"Of course, you could always just make *peposo*…"

Glen looked over at Domenico again. He was completely absorbed in what he was doing.

"I'll make the *arista*."

"Good man," said Bridget, patting him on the back. "Let me know if you need any help."

"I'll be fine," he informed her.

Guin had finished making her pastry cream and had put it in the refrigerator to chill. Now she was working on the pastry crust. She sifted the flour and the other dry ingredients in a large bowl then added the egg and butter. She used her hands to bring the mixture together, kneading it until all of the flour was absorbed and then forming the mixture into a smooth ball. Then she wrapped the dough in plastic wrap and placed it in the refrigerator.

She closed the refrigerator door and exhaled. Was this what it felt like to be on the *Great British Baking Show*? Though they weren't being timed. Still, she felt an unspoken pressure.

The recipe had called for the dough to chill for at least 30 minutes, an hour being preferable. Rather than waiting around in the warm kitchen, Guin picked up her water bottle and went outside. The fresh air felt good.

She noticed Oliver standing a short way away. Was he smoking a cigarette? She went over to him. Upon seeing her, he removed the cigarette from his mouth and stubbed it out.

"I didn't know you smoked," she said.

"I don't," he said. Though clearly he did.

"Any luck regarding Vera?"

"No. And I frankly don't know what the delay is," he said, sounding annoyed. "I even offered them money to speed things along, but the chief inspector said that was not the way things were done here. He actually looked insulted."

Good for him, thought Guin.

"He went on about the autopsy and the investigation," Oliver continued. "But I don't understand what's taking so long. It's obvious who killed Vera."

"It is?" said Guin.

He nodded.

"It was Bridget. She had motive and opportunity. And it was her knife."

"Though anyone could have taken that knife and used

it," Guin pointed out. "It wasn't locked in some drawer. And Bridget was at home."

"So she says."

"As does her husband."

"Oh really? I would have thought he'd have been working in that restaurant of his."

Guin frowned. He had a point.

"I need to go finish my crostini," said Oliver. Then he turned and headed back to the kitchen.

"He is a most disagreeable man."

Guin turned to see Domenico.

"I don't disagree with you." She paused. "Do you think Bridget killed Vera?"

He shook his head.

"So, who do you think did?"

She saw him watching Oliver.

"You think it was Oliver?"

"There is only so much a man will put up with."

"Oh?" said Guin.

"I saw the way Signora van Leyden picked on him. Nothing was ever good enough for her. She told him if I did not hire her, she would fire him."

"How do you know that?"

"He told me."

"And did Signora van Leyden also pick on you?"

He smiled. Though it wasn't a friendly smile.

"I should return to the kitchen."

Guin followed him with her eyes. Could he have killed Vera? She felt her phone vibrating in her back pocket and took it out. She had a new email. She looked at the time. Her dough needed to chill some more. She thought about heading back into the kitchen but decided to remain outside a little bit longer.

CHAPTER 28

Guin admired her *torta della nonna* as she placed it in the refrigerator. It was a little lopsided, but Glen assured her that she was the only one who would notice. Though Guin doubted that. Of course, Beatrice's tiramisu looked perfect.

She shut the refrigerator and went over to Glen's station. As his *arista* didn't require as much time to prepare as some of the other dishes, Glen had spent most of the afternoon taking photos of the other students as they prepared their dishes. But he had spent the last fifteen minutes or so working on his pork roast.

"It looks good," said Guin. "I bet it'll be yummy."

"I hope so."

He lifted the roasting pan and took it over to the oven, which had been preheated.

"Okay," he said. "Here goes."

He placed his *arista* in the oven then stepped back.

"Now what?" asked Guin.

"Now I keep an eye on it."

"Literally?"

He smiled.

"No, not literally. I figured I'd have a word with Bridget while it roasted."

"Ah."

She looked over and saw Bridget talking with Leo.

"Shall I hang out with you?"

"You worried I might overcook the roast?"

Guin smiled.

"Not at all. I just thought you might like some company."
He gave her a look. "And, okay, I want to hear what Bridget
has to say."

"I thought you wanted me to talk to her, alone."

"I..."

They were interrupted by Bridget.

"You put the pork in the oven?" she asked Glen.

"Just did."

"Okay. Just remember to turn the oven down to two-oh-
five after twenty minutes. Then you'll need to let it cook for
another forty-five to fifty minutes, until the meat registers
sixty degrees Celsius."

"Got it," said Glen.

"And don't forget about the sauce."

Glen smiled at her.

"Worried I'll screw it up?"

Bridget looked bashful.

"I'm sure it'll be perfect. Though if you have any
questions, Leo and I will be here tidying up."

"Duly noted."

Guin nudged Glen.

"Actually, I do have a question," he said.

"Yes?" said Bridget.

"It's about Vera." Bridget waited for him to go on, as did
Guin. "What did the chief inspector want to know?"

"What you would expect. Where was I when Vera was
killed? Who had access to the kitchen and the knives? Did I
think Vera was stealing my recipes?"

"And what did you tell him?"

"I told him I was at home all evening. That anyone could
have gone into the kitchen. It wasn't locked. And anyone
could have taken that knife. And yes, I was worried about
Vera using my recipes. But there was nothing I could really

do about that. And I certainly wouldn't have stuck that knife in her back. It was one of my best knives."

"Was Dante at home with you?" asked Guin.

"Yes," said Bridget.

"All evening?"

Bridget eyed her.

"You don't believe me?"

"It's just that I know Dante works late. And the chief inspector said Vera was killed between ten and two."

Bridget continued to look at Guin.

"You're right. Dante didn't get home until nearly midnight. But I was at home the whole time."

"So you weren't arguing with Vera in the kitchen around ten-thirty? Glen and I were on our way home from dinner, and I heard two people arguing in the kitchen. I'm pretty sure one of the voices I heard belonged to Vera and the other belonged to a woman."

Guin hadn't been sure it was Vera she had heard. At least at first. But the more she had thought about it, the more she was convinced it had been. And she was pretty sure the other voice had belonged to a woman. Though she couldn't say who.

Guin was looking up at Bridget and noticed Bridget's right eye twitch.

"Tell us the truth, Bridget. Were you in the kitchen with Vera that night?" Glen asked her.

She looked at him and sighed.

"I had gone home, but Dante was at work, and I was restless. So I decided to test a recipe. But when I went to get my recipe book, the one with all of my notes, I realized I must have left it here. So I got in my car and came back here."

"What time was that?" asked Guin.

"I'm not sure. Maybe ten? I got to the hotel and headed straight to the kitchen. There was a light on, which I thought odd. Though guests are welcome to go in and grab a snack or a bottle of water. I peered inside and saw Vera. She was going through my notebook."

"Did you go in and confront her?" asked Guin.

"I was about to, but Mrs. Adams showed up."

"What did she want?"

"I have no idea. Perhaps a bottle of water?"

"Did she see you?" asked Glen.

"I don't think so."

"Then what happened?" asked Guin. "Did you go into the kitchen?"

Bridget shook her head.

"Mrs. Adams and Mrs. van Leyden had started to argue. So I waited outside."

"Did you hear what they were arguing about?"

"I didn't want to eavesdrop. But I think it had something to do with Mr. Adams."

Guin and Glen exchanged a look.

"Then what happened?" asked Guin.

"Mrs. Adams left with a bottle of water."

"And what did you do? Did you get your recipe book?"

Bridget nodded.

"Did Vera say anything to you?"

"No."

"Did you say anything to her?"

"No. I just took my recipe book and left."

"You didn't ask her what she was doing with it?"

"I thought it rather obvious."

"And you still didn't say anything?" said Glen.

Bridget looked at him.

"There's no law stating she couldn't look at my recipe book, especially when I had left it lying there."

"So you just took the recipe book and left?" said Guin.

Bridget nodded.

"What time was that?"

"I don't know. Around ten-thirty? I wasn't wearing a watch and I'd left my phone in the car."

"Did you see anyone as you were leaving the kitchen?"

"No, though I was too absorbed in my thoughts to notice."

"When did Dante get home?" asked Glen.

"Around midnight."

"But Dante told the police you had been home all evening."

"I was home when Dante got there. He just assumed that I had been there the whole time."

"And you didn't correct him."

"No."

"What about Vera? Did she leave the kitchen when you did?"

"No. She was there when I left."

"And you're sure you didn't see anyone go into the kitchen after you left?"

"As I said, I was a bit preoccupied. And it was dark. I suppose someone could have been lurking outside, waiting for me to leave, but I didn't see anyone."

Guin and Glen exchanged a look.

"I swear to you both on my grandmother's grave, I did not kill Mrs. van Leyden."

"I believe you," said Glen.

"I do too," said Guin. "But you should tell the police what you just told us."

"They'll arrest me."

"They won't arrest you," said Glen.

"You don't know that," said Bridget.

Just then something started beeping. They looked around.

"Sorry, it's my reminder to turn down the oven," said Glen, pressing a button on his smartwatch.

CHAPTER 29

Glen announced that he was going to stretch his legs while his pork finished cooking. Did Guin care to join him? She thanked him for the invitation but said that she should probably go back to her room and do a little work before dinner.

She was halfway there when she saw the pool out of the corner of her eye. She wandered over. There was no one there. And the water looked inviting. Now that she thought about it, she could do with a little exercise. Especially as she would be eating another big meal.

She looked up at the sky. It was still light out and warm. And she wasn't really in the mood to work. She made her decision and hurried to her room to get changed.

Guin felt her phone vibrating as she unlocked her door. She took it out and saw that she had several messages. She thought about ignoring them and went to put her phone down. Then changed her mind.

She opened her email and clicked on the first message, quickly reading it. She started to type a reply but decided it would be faster to do it from her computer. She sat down and finished. Then she wound up reading another message. Before she knew it, twenty minutes had gone by. She frowned and looked out the window. She had wanted to go swimming. But now that she was seated in front of her computer, she should probably work.

She glanced out the window again, debating what to do. Maybe just a quick swim, a few laps. It would probably help her to concentrate better, she told herself. Her decision made, she got up and went to put on her swimsuit.

Guin was humming to herself as she walked to the pool, a towel wrapped around her waist. But when she got there, the pool was no longer empty. Beatrice was floating on her back, her blonde hair forming a kind of halo around her. Guin stared at her, thinking she looked like someone from a painting by Botticelli. Venus in a bathing suit.

She thought about turning around but decided she was being silly. She had come to swim. Why let the sight of Beatrice scare her away?

"Are you coming in?" called Beatrice. "The water is very nice."

Guin wondered how Beatrice knew she was there. Maybe she was a witch. She certainly seemed to have bewitched Glen.

"I was planning on it," said Guin.

Beatrice gracefully rolled over and swam to the side of the pool. She slowly got out, her swimsuit clinging to her as water shimmied down her body.

Guin watched as Beatrice picked up her towel and began to dry herself off. Finally, she tore her gaze away from the Italian goddess and looked down at the pool. She dipped her right foot in and quickly pulled it out. The water was cold. Though what had she been expecting?

"You must jump."

Guin looked over to see Beatrice watching her.

"Or are you afraid?"

"I'm not afraid. It's just cold."

"What would your friend Glen say?"

"He'd tell me to jump. But he's a guy, so…"

Beatrice smiled.

"He is a guy, and a very good-looking one." Beatrice sighed. "I envy you."

"You envy *me*?" Guin found that hard to believe.

Beatrice nodded.

"Glen is—how you say?—one of the good ones. He reminds me of someone I knew a long time ago. He was good-looking and kind too, just like your Glen."

Guin was going to say he wasn't her Glen, but she held her tongue.

"Was he a friend of yours, this good-looking, kind person?"

"*Sì*. He was the love of my life."

"Not Klaus?"

"I loved Klaus very much but…"

"What happened to him, the man Glen reminds you of?"

"He died."

"Oh," said Guin. "I'm sorry. What happened?"

"It is a sad story." Guin waited for her to go on. "His parents, they did not approve of our love."

"How come?"

"They did not think I was good enough for their son. We were to be married, but when his mother found out, she became angry."

Guin pictured a big, dark-haired Italian woman scowling at Beatrice, telling her to leave her son alone.

"She told him I would ruin his life. But he said he did not care."

"So he still planned on marrying you?"

"*Sì*. At first. Then his mother sent his father to talk to him, and he changed his mind."

"About marrying you?"

Beatrice nodded.

"He told me that he still loved me, but that we were too young. That he had to think of his career."

"What did he do?"

"He was an artist."

"So he broke things off?"

She nodded again.

"He told me he was going back to the States. I begged him to take me with him. I said we did not need to get married. I just wanted to be with him. But he said no."

Beatrice's story made Guin think of the detective. But she quickly pushed the thought away.

"That must have hurt."

"*Sì.* I was—what is the English word?—devastated. I could not imagine my life without him."

Guin could feel Beatrice's heartache.

"When did he die, after he returned to the States?"

"No. It was before he was to leave."

"What happened?"

"He took his life."

"How awful! Why?"

"His friends say he could no longer paint without me."

Guin thought Beatrice had to be exaggerating. Though looking at her, she could imagine an artist falling madly in love with her and being devastated by her absence.

"He never reached out to you, asked you to take him back?"

"Once. But he was drunk. And I was still hurt. So I did not reply. The next day, his roommates found him. Dead."

Guin thought Beatrice would have made a good actress. She certainly knew how to play up the drama.

"At first, I blamed myself," Beatrice continued. "But his mother was truly the one to blame. If she had not interfered, Cristiano would still be alive."

"Did you ever meet his parents?"

"*Sì.* When they came to visit him. But they refused to see me afterward. They blamed his death on me."

"On you?"

Beatrice nodded.

"They said I had cast a spell on him."

"That's ridiculous." Or maybe it wasn't. Just a few minutes ago she had thought Beatrice a witch.

"But that was long ago."

"And then you met Klaus."

"*Sì*. Though he died too." She looked sad as she said it. "I guess I do not have good luck with men."

"What about Domenico? He seems healthy. And he clearly cares for you."

"Nico?" she said. "He is like a brother to me." She looked at something off in the distance then turned back to Guin. "I must get ready for dinner. Enjoy your swim."

Guin watched as Beatrice headed back to the hotel, her hips swaying to some silent beat. She shook her head then looked down at the pool. She could see her reflection rippling in the water. She stared at it for several seconds. Then she turned around and headed back to her room, no longer in the mood for a swim.

Guin had been sitting in front of her computer, working on another article, when she thought she heard her phone. She had placed it in a drawer and had been ignoring it. But the buzzing had grown louder.

She pulled it out and saw that she had several messages from Glen. She looked at the clock on her laptop. She was late for cocktails. She had been so busy typing away, she had lost track of the time. Again.

She saved her document and went to get changed.

The dining terrace was strung with fairy lights, giving it a magical feel, and there was jazz music playing softly in the background.

"Would you like some prosecco?" Matteo asked her.

"Thank you," said Guin, taking a glass.

She glanced around and saw Glen talking with Beatrice. They were standing so close, it looked as though they were touching, and Guin felt her nails dig into her palms.

"They make a rather good-looking couple, don't you think?"

Guin turned to see Julia standing next to her.

"He's quite handsome in a Brad Pitt kind of way. And she looks a bit like a blonde Angelina Jolie."

Guin regarded them. She didn't think that either of them looked like the movie stars Julia had cited. Though they were both attractive in a movie star kind of way.

"As I recall," said Guin, still looking at Glen and Beatrice, "things didn't work out for Brad and Angelina."

"Though they did have six children."

"Several of them adopted."

"Still, they were together a while. And madly in love, at least part of the time."

Guin frowned.

"You like him, don't you?" said Julia.

"Of course I like him," said Guin. "He's been a good friend."

"I meant as more than a friend. John and I saw the way you two looked at each other over dinner the other night."

"Even if I did like him as more than a friend, we work together."

"So?"

It was time to change the subject.

"How did your *contorni* turn out?"

"Good. At least I think so. You'll have to let me know."

"What did you make again?"

"An arugula, pine nut, pecorino, and pear salad with a balsamic drizzle; stuffed tomatoes with parsley, capers, breadcrumbs, garlic, and oregano; and some roasted vegetables."

"Wow. I'm impressed! You made all that in just a few hours?"

"You're giving me way too much credit," said Julia. "None of it was very hard. Not like making dessert."

Guin saw John speaking with Domenico out of the corner of her eye.

"How did John do with the *antipasti*?"

"Good! I think he was very pleased with himself."

They watched the men for several seconds. Guin wanted to ask Julia about her argument with Vera, the one Bridget had overheard. But she wasn't sure how. *Just ask her,* said the voice in her head.

"Speaking of John..." Guin began. "Bridget mentioned she overheard you arguing with Vera about him... the evening she died."

"She must have been mistaken," Julia cooly replied, still looking at her husband.

"Why would she lie?"

Julia turned to face her, and Guin could suddenly picture her stabbing someone.

"Isn't it obvious? She was trying to divert attention away from herself. She said she had been at home all evening. But if she had been, how could she have heard me arguing with Vera? Clearly, she was there and lied."

Guin didn't know what to say.

"Would you excuse me? I should go be with my husband."

Before Guin could say anything, Julia moved away. Guin watched as she went over to her husband and whispered something in his ear. That certainly looked suspicious. They were hiding something. Guin was sure of it. But what?

CHAPTER 30

Guin was relieved when it was time to sit down to dinner. Though she wasn't that hungry. She took a seat, and Glen sat down next to her. Oliver took a seat across from them, and Beatrice took the seat on the other side of Glen, Domenico on her other side. Julia and John sat opposite them.

"Do you think Bridget will join us?" asked John.

"I don't think so," said Glen. "When I saw her before, she planned on supervising things in the kitchen."

"Surely that assistant of hers can do that. We should get her."

He made to get up, but Julia pulled him back down.

"I'm sure she'd join us if she could," she said.

"We can always ask her to join us later," said Glen.

A few minutes later, Bridget appeared. She was dressed in her chef's whites. She welcomed them and told them what a wonderful group they had been and how she would miss them. Then she recited the menu for the evening, acknowledging each chef. When she was done, John told her she should join them. The rest of the guests nodded in agreement, except for Oliver.

"Thank you," said Bridget. "But I want to make sure all of your hard work doesn't go to waste."

"Can't that young fellow do that?" said John.

"Leo had to leave."

"Oh, is everything all right?" asked Julia.

"Everything's fine. He just had a family commitment. Now if you will excuse me, I will go get the antipasti that John and Oliver made."

Dinner lasted two hours. Everything had been delicious, even her *torta della nonna*, but Guin was glad when it was over.

Beatrice had coopted Glen, so Guin wound up spending most of the evening talking to Oliver or trying to. He wasn't in a particularly chatty mood. She had asked him again about Vera, and he had grumbled about Italian bureaucracy and said no wonder the country was in such bad shape when they couldn't manage to complete an autopsy or process a death certificate in a timely fashion. And Guin had wound up listening to Glen and Beatrice talk about art.

After dessert, Glen had gone to the kitchen to speak with Bridget, so Guin had headed back to her room alone. There was an email from Ginny waiting for her, asking for an update on the Vera investigation and their passports. Guin wrote her back, saying she didn't have anything new to share. They would likely be there for a few more days. But, hopefully, the chief inspector would return their passports soon and they'd be able to fly back to Florida.

That reminded her, she still hadn't heard from her neighbor, Sadie. She sent her another email, asking if Fauna was okay, cc'ing her husband Sam. Hopefully, he would read it and pass along the message. Though, of course, she could just pick up the phone and call them. It was six hours earlier there.

Guin stared at her laptop, wondering if she should do some work as she wasn't tired. Which was unusual. She normally was in bed by ten. Then again, she normally didn't have dinner at eight and drink espresso afterward. But nothing had been normal since coming to Italy.

She pulled up the document she had been working on earlier and began to read. She hadn't gotten far when her eyelids began to feel heavy, and she let out a yawn. She shook her head and began to read again, but she could tell she would not be doing any more work tonight. She closed the document and shut down her computer. Then she went to change into her nightshirt and brush her teeth. She was about to get into bed when there was a knock on her door.

For a moment she worried that someone else had been murdered. Or maybe the police had discovered something and wanted to speak with everyone again. Then she told herself she was being silly.

"Who is it?" she called.

"It's Glen."

She opened the door. He was still dressed for dinner. He looked at her, taking in her nightshirt, and Guin suddenly felt exposed.

"Hey," she said. "Everything okay?"

"Everything's fine. I just wondered where you went."

"You went to speak with Bridget, so I went back to my room."

"I thought you'd wait for me."

"I didn't know you wanted me to wait for you."

They stood there regarding each other.

"Besides, you were so busy chatting with Beatrice all evening, I didn't think you'd miss me."

Glen gave her a funny look.

"What?"

"Are you jealous?"

"I am not jealous," said Guin.

"Then why is your face turning pink?"

Guin frowned. Curse her fair complexion.

"I'm just warm."

Glen looked down at her nightshirt then back at her face.

"Yes, well."

He smiled.

"Stop smiling!" she commanded.

"You *are* jealous."

"Okay, maybe a teensy tiny bit. I mean, look at her! She's a freaking goddess. And you're…" She waved her arm. "You!"

His smile grew broader.

"Stop that!" she said, whacking him on the arm. "It's not funny!"

She went to hit him again, but he took hold of her arm. His hand felt warm, and she felt her whole body heat up. She looked up at him. He was no longer smiling.

"Guin," he said, closing the distance between them. His breath smelled of red wine and espresso, a combination she found intoxicating.

"Yes?" she said.

His face was now just inches away, and before she knew it, his lips were softly kissing hers. She kissed him back, closing her eyes. The kisses became deeper, hungrier, and she felt herself pressing up against him.

Glen lifted her, so their faces met. Guin wrapped her legs around his waist as they continued to kiss. He carried her to the bedroom, murmuring her name, his voice filled with longing, and gently placed her on the bed. She looked up at him as if in a trance. He looked like a Greek god with his wavy, ash-blond hair, strong jaw, and athletic build. How could she not have noticed before?

"Take off your shirt," she commanded.

He immediately began to unbutton it.

She had seen his chest before, of course, but this time it was different. He leaned down and began to kiss her again. He whispered in her ear, then darted his tongue in and out as Guin let out a soft moan. Then he worked his way down her neck, onto her collarbone, then to her breasts.

He pulled up her nightshirt and Guin didn't stop him.

Then he moved his tongue lower. Guin heard herself moan. Every nerve ending in her body was on fire. He had reached the sensitive area between her legs and had begun to remove her underwear when Guin told him to stop.

He looked up at her, his face a question mark.

"I'm sorry," she said, moving away from him. "I can't do this." She reached for her nightshirt.

"Did I do something wrong?"

Guin noted the hurt and confusion in his voice and on his face.

"No. You did everything right. It's me."

Again, there was that look. And a part of her wanted to say, *Ignore me, just keep going.* But she held firm.

"I don't understand."

"It's simple. We're friends. And we work together."

"So?"

"I don't want to mess that up."

"You really believe this will mess up our friendship?"

"You don't?"

"No! Guin, you know I've wanted you since the day I met you. But I held back because you were seeing someone."

"Wait, you've wanted me since the day you met me? Weren't you seeing someone?"

"Well, maybe not that first day but soon after," he said, smiling at her.

"Why didn't you say something?"

"I thought it was obvious."

"Well, it wasn't."

"Maybe that was because you were so focused on winning over Detective O'Loughlin, a man who made Mr. Spock look like an emotional basket case."

"I was not trying to win over the detective." Though now that she thought about it, maybe she had been. And she couldn't deny that the detective was a cold fish emotionally.

She glanced up at Glen's bare chest. She wanted to touch

it. Actually, she wanted to do a lot more than touch it. But she held herself in check.

"What about Beatrice?"

Glen looked confused.

"What about her?"

"She's gorgeous, and Italian, and she totally wants you. And from the looks of it, you want her too."

Glen scowled.

"That's not true."

"Oh? You two looked pretty cozy during dinner. And she took you to her cousin's restaurant and to San Gimignano. If you weren't interested in her, why did you go?"

"Get up," he commanded.

"Why?"

"Just get up."

Guin got up off the bed, her nightshirt once again covering her.

He looked down at her.

"You are the only person I am interested in that way, Guinivere Jones, not Beatrice nor anyone else."

"Oh," said Guin, feeling her heart hammer against her chest. Speaking of chests, she was unable to stop looking at Glen's and placed a hand on it. It felt solid and warm. She wanted to caress it. Instead, she placed her hand on his face. The way he was looking at her...

"Guin..."

Then they were kissing again, and she didn't want it to stop. However, this time Glen was the one who pulled away.

"Why did you stop?"

"If I didn't stop, I... And you said you didn't want this."

Guin bit her lip.

"I don't know what I want."

"Did it ever occur to you that this could make our friendship stronger, better?"

"Do you honestly believe that?"

"I do."

"But what if things don't work out? I'd hate to lose you as a friend. And we work together." Though Glen was technically freelance and could probably find loads of photography work elsewhere.

Glen sighed.

"I will always be your friend, Guin. And if you don't want this to happen, I won't force you. But if you change your mind…"

"And you really aren't interested in Beatrice? You know she wants you. She told me you reminded her of her ex-boyfriend, who died tragically."

"Cristiano."

"So she told you."

He nodded.

"Just promise me you won't fall in love with her and kill yourself."

Glen looked exasperated.

"The only person I'm in love with is you."

Guin stared at him.

"I'm sorry. I don't think I heard you correctly."

"You heard me," said Glen, putting his shirt back on. He headed to the door.

"Wait," Guin called, following him.

He stopped and turned to look at her.

"Yes?"

She wanted to tell him not to go, to stay there with her. Instead she said, "Will I see you in the morning?"

He nodded. Then he left, not bothering to say good night.

She locked the door behind him, leaning against it. Had she made a mistake?

Guin slept restlessly that evening and woke up feeling tired and anxious. She checked the time. It was nearly eight o'clock. She had no idea she had slept that late. Probably because she had kept waking up.

She went into the bathroom, got changed, then headed to breakfast, not bothering to message Glen or knock on his door.

As she stepped onto the dining terrace she was surprised to see Glen and Beatrice having breakfast together. Beatrice never ate breakfast. And Guin felt as though someone had kicked her in the stomach. She took a seat at a table on the other side of the terrace, hoping they wouldn't notice her.

"Would you like a cappuccino?" Francesca asked her.

"*Prego*," said Guin. "Could I possibly get it to go?"

Francesca bobbed her head and made to leave. But before she did, Guin asked if she had seen Rosa.

"She is in her office," Francesca told her.

"Great," said Guin.

Francesca returned with her cappuccino a few minutes later. Guin thanked her then went to seek out the hotel manager.

CHAPTER 31

Guin knocked on Rosa's door then poked her head inside. Rosa was seated at her desk, a pile of paper next to her. Guin wondered if it was the same pile or a new one.

Rosa looked up as Guin entered.

"You're working early."

Rosa sighed.

"There is much to do this time of year. And now with…" She trailed off, waving her hand in the air.

"Should I come back later?"

"You are here now. How can I help you?"

"I wanted to get in touch with the chief inspector. Do you know how I can reach him?"

"What do you want with the chief inspector?"

"I just wanted to see how the investigation was going and when he might return our passports. Has he said anything to you?"

"Chief Inspector Manetti does not share such information with me."

"Though he will tell you when you can have guests check in again, yes?"

"*Sì*. Though it has only been a few days. We must be patient."

Patience was not a virtue Guin possessed.

"I see," said Guin. "Though surely they've made some progress?"

"I will give you the chief inspector's information, and you can ask him."

"*Grazie*," said Guin.

Rosa reached into her desk and pulled out a card. Then she began to write. When she was done, she handed the piece of paper to Guin.

"Thank you," she said, taking it. Guin glanced down the piece of paper. "What's the best way to reach him?"

"Try his mobile number."

"Okay." She slipped the paper into her pocket and looked back up at Rosa. "So I'm guessing he hasn't arrested anyone yet or you would have heard."

"As I said, the chief inspector has not confided in me."

"But you don't think Bridget could have done it, killed Vera, that is?"

"*Assolutamente no.*"

Guin was relieved to hear it.

Rosa continued to look at her.

"Is there something else I can help you with?"

"Where were you the evening Vera was killed?"

She hadn't planned on asking Rosa. Or making it sound like an accusation. It just sort of came out that way.

"At home, in bed," said Rosa, frowning. "Now if you would excuse me, Signora Jones? I have work to do."

"Of course," said Guin. "Thank you for the chief inspector's information."

Rosa nodded, then turned her attention back to her computer.

Guin saw herself out, pausing outside Rosa's door. Was Rosa angry with her? Surely the police had asked her the same question. Though she probably didn't expect a guest to interrogate her. Not that Guin was interrogating her. She had just been curious to know where Rosa had been that evening.

She had started to move away, lost in thought, when she bumped into Matteo.

"Sorry," said Guin. "I should have watched where I was going."

"No, no. It is my fault," said Matteo.

"Were you going to see Rosa, I mean Signora Lombardi?"

He nodded.

"*Sì*."

That reminded Guin.

"Matteo, do you happen to know if anything went missing the night Signora van Leyden was killed?"

He looked thoughtful.

"Not that I know of."

"So nothing in the kitchen or the main hotel?"

"I do not believe so. Why?"

"I was just wondering if a burglar could have been responsible for taking Signora van Leyden's life."

"Ah," he said. "It is true there have been some burglaries nearby. But I do not think it was a burglar who killed the signora."

"Who do you think did it?"

He glanced around.

"I think it was that agent of hers. I heard them fighting. I do not think they liked each other."

"I have to agree with you. At least about them not seeming to like each other."

Matteo asked if there was something else he could help her with, and Guin said no. Then he went to knock on Rosa's door. Just as he raised his fist, however, they heard Rosa. It sounded as though she was yelling at someone. Guin couldn't make out what Rosa was saying, but something about her voice sounded familiar. Though, of course, she had heard Rosa speak before. But something about the tone reminded her of another angry conversation.

Then it came to her. The voice sounded like one of the ones she had heard the night Vera had died. Could Rosa have been in the kitchen with Vera that evening? But she said she had been home. Then again, so had Bridget. And she knew Bridget had lied.

Guin took a sip of her cappuccino and made a face. It had grown cold. She sighed. Should she try to get a fresh cup? She really didn't want to go back out onto the dining terrace, not with Glen and Beatrice there. Though maybe they had finished eating. Then she had a better idea. She would go to the kitchen.

"Hello?" said Guin.

There didn't appear to be anyone in the kitchen, which seemed odd. It was technically still breakfast time. A minute later, Leo appeared. He looked a bit flustered.

"Can I help you?" he asked.

"I was hoping I could get a cup of coffee."

"Did you want a cappuccino?"

"Whatever you have is fine. I just need something warm with caffeine, a lot of caffeine."

Leo smiled at her.

"Coming right up."

He went over to the espresso machine and made her a double espresso. Guin smiled and thanked him as he handed it to her.

She took a sip, closing her eyes.

"*Mille grazie*," she said. She immediately took another sip. The coffee was strong and a bit bitter, just the way she normally liked it.

She looked over at Leo. He was glancing around the kitchen and frowning.

"Is everything all right?" she asked him.

"Everything is fine," he replied. "It is just... a delivery did not show up. And we are a bit shorthanded."

"Can I help with anything?"

"No, no. We will be fine. It is just that Bridget said she would be here and..."

"She's not here?"

He shook his head.

"Did you try messaging her?"

He nodded his head.

"I did. But she did not answer."

Now Guin was worried. Had something happened to Bridget between last night and this morning?

"Did you call Dante?"

"I did not want to bother him."

"Is she usually late?" she asked, remembering that Bridget had arrived late the morning Vera's body was found.

"No, though…" Guin waited. "Recently, she has been late a few times. But I believe that is because she has been up late testing recipes."

"Is that why you were the one who found Signora van Leyden's body that morning?"

He nodded his head.

"I did not see her at first. Then…"

It was as though he was seeing her body all over again.

"Where was Francesca?"

"In the pantry. She arrived just after me."

"And you went to tell Signora Lombardi?"

He nodded.

"*Sì.*"

"And Signora Lombardi, she notified the police?"

Another nod.

"Did you notice if anything was missing?"

"The police asked us that. But we did not find anything missing, other than a bottle of water and some food."

Guin immediately thought of Julia but didn't say anything.

"I know guests are welcome in the kitchen when you are not preparing food. Did you ever see Signora van Leyden here?"

Leo hesitated then nodded.

"What was she doing here? Did she ever speak with you?"

He nodded again.

"What did she say?"

"She asked me about Tuscan food."

"Anything in particular?"

"She wanted to know if I had any family recipes I would be willing to share with her. She said she would pay me for them."

Guin stared at him.

"She did?"

Again he nodded.

"What did you tell her?"

"I told her my family's recipes were not for sale."

"She asked me too," said Francesca. Guin hadn't seen her come in. "And I also tell her no."

Guin regarded the two of them.

"Do you know if she asked Bridget?"

They looked at each other, and Guin saw Francesca nod to Leo. He looked at Guin.

"We overheard her. She tell Bridget she will pay her a lot of money if she allows Signora van Leyden to use her recipes in her new cookbook. But Bridget said no, her recipes were not for sale."

"Was Signora van Leyden angry?"

"I do not think she was happy," said Leo.

"We hear her say to Bridget that she was making a big mistake," said Francesca.

Guin wondered if that was why Vera had snuck into the kitchen that evening, to steal Bridget's recipe book. Though she already had the recipe binder from class. But that only contained a handful of recipes.

"Sorry I'm so late!" called a familiar voice.

They all turned to see Bridget. Guin sensed their relief and felt relieved too.

"You would not believe the morning I had! First, the battery in my car died, then the battery in my phone!" She came over to them and saw their faces. "Is everything okay? Did something happen? No one died, did they?"

Leo and Francesca shook their heads.

"They were just worried about you. I was too," said Guin.

"I'm sorry," said Bridget. "I should have had Dante call or message you. But I'm here now. Did breakfast go okay?"

"The bakery did not deliver the bread. But we had some left over from yesterday," said Leo.

Bridget sighed.

"I'll call them and see what's up. Anything else?"

Leo said something to her in Italian.

"Okay," she said in English. "I'll go talk to Rosa." Then she turned to Guin. "How would you feel about a class on Italian pastry this afternoon?"

"Is that a trick question?" said Guin.

Bridget smiled.

"No. I want to test a couple of recipes and figured since you all were stuck here, might as well see if you could make them."

"I'm game," said Guin. "And I'm sure the others would be too. Just send them a message."

"I'll do that."

"Great." She turned to Leo. "Thanks again for the coffee."

"You are welcome," he said.

Then Guin turned and left the kitchen.

CHAPTER 32

It was another beautiful day. The temperature was in the low seventies, and the scenery along with the puffy white clouds against the blue sky made Guin feel as though she were inside a painting. Did she really want to spend the morning in her room, in front of her computer? No, she did not. Though she risked Ginny's wrath if she didn't send her another article. Hopefully, Glen had sent her some more photos and that would tide her over.

She took out her phone to ask him. Then she put it back in her pocket. She wasn't yet ready to talk about last night. Instead, she headed to the trails that led to the vineyard and into town. She stood looking at them, deciding which one to take. Then she remembered the piece of paper in her pocket and decided to take the latter. While she was in town, she would visit the police station and see if the chief inspector was in.

That decided, she headed off.

As she made her way along the trail, her mind wandered. She thought of Glen and what he had said and the way he had kissed her. Immediately, she began to feel warm, and a part of her regretted sending him away. But she knew it had been the right decision, especially after seeing him with Beatrice at breakfast this morning. Had he gone to Beatrice's room after he had left her?

An image of Glen and Beatrice in bed came unbidden.

Guin did her best to snuff it out. She focused on Vera instead. Who had killed her?

Guin wanted to believe that it wasn't anyone who worked at the hotel or one of the guests. But who did that leave? It didn't seem as though a burglar had done it.

She recalled what she knew about each of the guests and what she had overheard. Both Oliver and Domenico had argued with Vera and potentially had reason to want her gone. And something had happened between Vera and John and Julia. And hearing Rosa argue with someone in Italian had made Guin wonder if it had been Rosa she had heard in the kitchen that evening. But what reason did the hotel manager have to kill Vera?

Before she knew it, Guin had arrived in town.

"Now which way is the police station?" she said aloud.

She was about to ask a passerby but as her Italian was nearly nonexistent she decided to look it up on her phone instead. Fortunately, it wasn't far.

As she made her way there, she passed by a bakery. The smell of fresh bread wafted out. She hadn't eaten anything since dinner the night before and was tempted to go in. No, *business first*, she told herself, tearing herself away from the window.

The police station was housed in an old-looking building. Guin entered and didn't see anyone at first. Then she spied a policeman making his way across the floor.

"*Mi scusi*," she said, flagging him down. "Is Chief Inspector Manetti here?"

The officer stopped and looked at her.

"*Parla inglese*?" Guin asked him.

"*Un po*. A little. *L'ispettore capo Manetti non c'è*, not here," he told her.

"Do you know when he will be back?"

The man shrugged.

"May I leave a message for him?"

She mimed writing on a piece of paper.

The officer nodded, and Guin quickly searched her bag for a pen and paper. The pen she found, but the only paper she had was a crumpled piece of notepaper taken from a hotel notepad. But it would have to do.

She hastily scribbled a note, asking the chief inspector to contact her. Then she handed the piece of paper back to the officer along with her business card.

The policeman glanced at it.

"Will you give my note and my card to Chief Inspector Manetti when you see him?"

He looked at her and nodded.

"*Grazie*," she said. Then she left the police station.

She took a few steps then stopped. Should she have tried to find someone who spoke English? But there didn't seem to be anyone else around. No doubt the local police were out patrolling the streets or busy working elsewhere in the station. She would just have to trust that the police officer would deliver her note to Chief Inspector Manetti.

She resumed her walk and was about to pass by the bakery again when the door opened. Again there was the smell of freshly baked bread. Unable to resist, Guin went in.

The bakery was busy, even though it was mid-morning. Clearly, it was a popular spot. She glanced around and saw loaves of rustic-looking bread lining the shelves. And in the cases were various Italian pastries, some of which she was familiar with and others she wasn't. She glanced down at the *cornetti*, a kind of Italian croissant. Nearby were trays of *cantucci*. And there was so much more. She wanted one of everything.

"*Posso aiutarla?*" asked a friendly-looking woman from behind the counter.

"Uh," said Guin, still staring at the case.

"You are American," said the woman. It was more a statement than a question.

Guin nodded.

"*Sì.*"

The woman smiled at her.

"What can I get for you?"

"Everything looks so good," Guin sighed. "I can't decide. What do you recommend?"

"You should get a *cornetto*," said a familiar voice. "Their *cornetti* are the best, especially the ones filled with pastry cream."

Guin turned to see Chief Inspector Manetti.

"Okay," said Guin slowly.

"*Due cornetti, per favore,*" the chief inspector told the woman.

The woman picked out two of the Italian croissants from the case and placed them in a white pastry box. The chief inspector paid, and she handed him the box.

"*Grazie,*" he said.

"How much do I owe you?" asked Guin after they had stepped outside.

"Nothing. It is on me, as you Americans like to say."

He turned and headed to the police station carrying the box of *cornetti*. Guin wasn't sure what to do. The chief inspector stopped and turned around.

"Are you coming?"

"I... uh... Where are we going?"

"To the police station. I received a message saying that you were looking for me. Come."

The chief inspector led her to a small office on the second floor.

"I am borrowing it," he explained.

He placed the box on the desk, opened it, and indicated for Guin to take a *cornetto*. She hesitated.

"Go on. It will not bite."

"Do you have a napkin or a piece of paper towel? I don't want to leave crumbs."

The chief inspector rummaged in the desk and produced a napkin, which he handed to Guin.

"*Grazie*," she said. She lifted out the *cornetto* but didn't take a bite.

"So, what is it you wanted to see me about?"

"I wanted to know if you had made any progress on the case, and when I can get my passport back."

The chief inspector took a bite of his *cornetto* and thoughtfully chewed.

"Also, I have information."

He swallowed and looked over at her, waiting for her to go on.

"When I walked by the kitchen that night, I think one of the people I heard had an Italian accent."

"You are sure?"

Well, when he looked at her that way...

"Pretty sure."

"Hm," he said, once again looking thoughtful.

"Do you think that could have been the killer?"

"It is possible. What time was this again?"

Guin was pretty sure the chief inspector knew exactly what time it was as Guin had already told him. But she told him again.

"Around ten-thirty."

"Hm," he said.

Guin wondered if Bridget had confessed that she had been in the kitchen that evening and had overheard Julia arguing with Vera. She was tempted to ask him, but she didn't want to risk getting Bridget in trouble if she hadn't said anything yet.

"So, who do you think killed her? You have any suspects?"

"I am afraid I cannot discuss the case with you, Signora Jones."

"You must have at least a couple of suspects."

"Everyone at the hotel that evening is a suspect."

"But you must have narrowed down the list. You can't possibly think I could have done it. Or Glen."

He was looking at her, and Guin shifted in her seat. It was those coal-black eyes of his. It was like he could see what she was thinking.

"As I said, everyone is a suspect." He looked down at the untouched pastry in front of Guin. "You have not tried your *cornetto*."

Guin looked down at the pastry then back at the chief inspector. She picked up the *cornetto* and took a bite. The dough was the perfect flakiness and a dollop of pastry cream oozed out onto her tongue. Guin heard herself moan. She looked up to see the chief inspector smiling at her and she felt herself blush.

"It is good, no?"

Guin nodded her head, wishing she had some water.

"Is there anything else I can help you with, Signora Jones?"

"You didn't say when I can expect to get back my passport."

"No, I did not."

"You must have some idea. You can't keep us here forever."

He looked amused.

"I promise, I will not keep you here forever. Though there are worse places to stay, no?"

Guin frowned. He was toying with her.

"Are we talking a few days? A week? Longer?"

"I will give you back your passport when I feel it is safe to do so."

"It's safe to do so now. You put that tracker on our phones. So you can keep track of us."

"Ah, yes. But what if I give you your passport back and

you turn off your phone or remove it?"

"What if I promise not to?"

Though Guin already knew what he was going to say.

"As pleasant as this has been, Signora Jones, I have work to do. So…"

Guin knew she was being dismissed. She rose and headed to the door.

"Signora Jones," called the chief inspector.

"Yes?" she said, turning around.

"You forgot to take your *cornetto*."

Guin walked back over to the desk, picked up the *cornetto*, took a bite, making sure that he saw her, then turned and left.

CHAPTER 33

Guin finished the *cornetto* and purchased a bottle of water for her walk back to the hotel. When she arrived, she was surprised to see a strange woman speaking—or rather arguing—with Oliver and Rosa at reception. Was it a new guest? Though Rosa had said there wouldn't be any new guests checking in while the police were still investigating Vera's murder.

Guin knew it was probably none of her business and that she should head back to her room, but her reporter's curiosity got the better of her.

"And I am telling *you*," the woman said to Oliver, "I am not leaving here without my sister!"

Ah, so this was the sister. Guin regarded the woman. She vaguely resembled Vera, at least in the way she was frowning at Oliver.

"I would be happy to find you a room at a nearby hotel while we wait to hear from the chief inspector, Signora Weber," said Rosa, trying to placate the woman.

Mrs. Weber frowned.

"But I don't have a car."

"I can see about renting you a car or arrange for a driver."

"And how much is all that going to cost me?"

"The hotel will pay for it," said Rosa. "It is the least we can do."

That seemed to mollify the woman.

"Very well."

Rosa excused herself, saying she would be back soon and for Mrs. Weber to make herself comfortable.

"Really, Mrs. Weber," said Oliver in an oily voice. "There's no need for you to stay. Just tell them they can release the body to me, and I'll take care of everything."

"Like you took care of Vera? No, thank you. I'll see to Vera's body myself. Now how do I get in touch with this chief inspector?"

"Excuse me," said Guin.

Mrs. Weber turned to look at Guin, eyeing her suspiciously.

"And who are you?"

"I'm a guest here at the hotel, and…"

She saw Oliver gesturing to Mrs. Weber, shaking his head.

"What on earth is the matter, Oliver?"

"She's a reporter!" he blurted.

"You say that as though she had some sort of disease."

"I assure you," said Guin, "I'm perfectly healthy. And I just spoke with the chief inspector in charge of the case." Mrs. Weber looked interested. "And I'm sure he'd be happy to speak with you."

"Do you know how I can get in touch with him?"

"I'll give you his cell phone number."

"I'm sorry, I didn't catch your name."

"It's Guinivere, Guinivere Jones."

"That's an unusual name. And you're a reporter? You don't work for one of those horrible tabloids, do you?"

"Oh no, I work for the *Sanibel-Captiva Sun-Times*. It's a small local paper in Southwest Florida."

"Sanibel, you say?"

Guin nodded.

"I used to go to Sanibel with my husband and daughter back in the day. We would go beachcombing and watch the dolphins."

Guin smiled.

"You should go back."

"What are you doing here? Are you on vacation?"

"Actually, my colleague and I are covering the cooking course for the paper."

"Do a lot of people on Sanibel visit Italy?"

"I'm sure they'd like to. And the editor thought it might be fun to add a Travel section to the paper. So…"

"I see," said Mrs. Weber. "So you must have met my sister, Vera."

"Yes. Though I didn't get to know her very well. She mostly kept to herself and, well…"

"No need to explain. Vera wasn't exactly the friendly type. Thought she was above everyone."

Guin didn't know how to respond, so she remained quiet.

"Oliver here said it was a burglar who killed her," Mrs. Weber continued.

Guin raised her eyebrows and looked over at Vera's agent.

"Did he now? I believe the police ruled out a burglary."

Oliver looked like he had eaten something rotten.

"Something wrong, Oliver?" said Mrs. Weber. She turned back to Guin. "How do you know that?"

"As I said, I just met with the chief inspector. He seems to think it was someone here at the hotel."

Mrs. Weber raised her eyebrows and once again looked at Oliver, who began to sputter.

"You can speak with the chief inspector yourself," said Guin. "I'll give you his contact information."

"Thank you," said Mrs. Weber.

Guin found a piece of paper and wrote down the chief inspector's email address and phone number. Then she handed it to Mrs. Weber.

"If you can't reach him or there's a problem, you can try

contacting the U.S. Consulate in Florence."

"Thank you."

"You're welcome. Is there anything else I can help you with?"

"Do you know where I could get something to eat? I haven't eaten since before I left Chicago."

"You must be starving," said Guin sympathetically. (She always got cranky when she hadn't eaten.) "Let's go to the kitchen. I'm sure they can fix you something."

"That's very kind of you. I'm not taking you away from anything important, am I?"

"Not at all," said Guin. She turned to Oliver. "Do you want to join us?"

Guin saw Mrs. Weber glaring at him.

"I need to make some calls," he replied.

Guin turned back to Mrs. Weber.

"The kitchen's this way."

"Vera should have fired that odious man years ago," groused Mrs. Weber as she followed Guin.

"What makes you say that?"

"All he cared about was making money."

"Isn't that what a good agent does, make his client money?"

"More like making himself money."

That didn't surprise Guin.

"If you don't mind my asking, were the two of them on good terms?"

"Why do you ask?"

"Well, it's just that... they always seemed to be arguing about something."

"To be honest, I don't know Oliver that well. I met him just a few times, at functions. Book signings and the like. Though he didn't leave a very good impression. And Vera constantly complained about him."

"Oh? What did she say?"

"That he didn't deserve his fee. That he was a horrible negotiator. That he should have done better with this or that."

"Did she ever mention firing him?"

"Several times. But I think it was just talk on her part. Vera wasn't the easiest person to get along with. I don't think anyone could have lived up to her high standards. And Oliver had been with her a long time."

"I see," said Guin. "And had she mentioned anything about a new cookbook?"

"She emailed me about it just before she left. Couldn't resist bragging about it."

"Any idea what happens to it now that Vera's…" Guin struggled to find the right word. "Now that Vera's no longer able to do it?"

Mrs. Weber frowned.

"I don't know. You'd need to ask Oliver. I supposed he could find someone else to do it if the publisher was still interested."

Guin immediately thought of Bridget and made a mental note to speak with her and with Oliver.

"We're here," said Guin, stopping in front of the kitchen. She peered inside. She didn't see anyone at first. Then she spied Leo.

"Leo!" she called.

He stopped and turned around. Guin went over and introduced him to Mrs. Weber.

"I am very sorry about your sister," he said.

"Thank you," said Mrs. Weber.

"Mrs. Weber just arrived at the hotel and hasn't eaten since yesterday. Could you fix her something?"

"Of course," he said. "What can I make for you?"

"Do you have any coffee?"

"You would like an espresso or a cappuccino?"

"Whatever you've got. Just make it strong."

A woman after her own heart, thought Guin.

"And what would you like to eat?" Guin asked her.

"I'd be fine with a sandwich."

"I will fix you my special prosciutto, buffalo mozzarella, and tomato sandwich," said Leo. "Sound good?"

"Sounds delicious," said Mrs. Weber.

"I agree," said Guin. "Would you mind making me one too?"

"No problem," he said with a smile. "If you would like to sit on the dining terrace, I will have Francesca bring out the food when it is ready."

"Oh, and could we get a bottle of Pellegrino, Leo?"

"*Certo!*"

"*Mille grazie*," said Guin.

They headed outside and took a seat at one of the tables. Mrs. Weber sighed as she sat down.

"You must be tired from all your traveling," said Guin. "You said you flew here from Chicago?"

She nodded.

"My daughter thought I was crazy to just pick up and come here, but… Vera was my only sister. Even if we weren't that close. And after I received the message from Oliver, I thought I should be here."

"Does your daughter live in Chicago with you, Mrs. Weber?"

"No, she lives in New York. And, please, call me Lena," which she pronounced *LEH-nah*.

"Okay, Lena. And please, call me Guin."

Lena smiled at her, and Francesca stepped out onto the dining terrace with their sandwiches and drinks.

"*Grazie*, Francesca."

"Can I get you something else?" she asked them.

Lena was sipping her coffee.

"I'm good," Guin told her. "Lena, do you need anything?"

Lena shook her head, and Francesca departed.

"I'll say this for the Italians," said Lena. "They sure know how to make a good cup of coffee."

Guin smiled.

"I agree. I'm thinking of smuggling some home in my suitcase and getting an espresso or cappuccino machine."

They ate their sandwiches in silence, though Guin had a few questions she wanted to ask Lena about her sister. Finally, once Lena seemed sated, Guin spoke.

"You said Vera emailed you just before she came here. Did she write to you at all while she was here?"

"Just once, to tell me how glorious this place was and what a shame it was I was stuck working in a dingy library."

"Oh, you work in a library?"

Lena nodded.

"Going on thirty years now."

"Impressive," said Guin.

"I don't know about impressive, but I like it."

"So Vera didn't mention anything about the course or the people here?"

"No, at least not to me. Though she may have said something to Joanna."

"Joanna?"

"My daughter. Vera was very fond of her. Jo spent a bunch of time with Vera and her family growing up. She and Vera's son Christian were just a couple of years apart. The two of them were more like brother and sister than first cousins."

"I read about Vera's son. Such a tragedy."

Lena nodded.

"It was. We were all devastated, Jo especially. She adored Chris."

"I read it was a drug overdose."

"That's what the doctors said. But none of us could believe it."

"How come?"

"Jo said he didn't do drugs. That he thought they were a crutch."

"Though he could have changed when he was in Italy, fallen in with a bad crowd."

"That's what Vera said. She didn't care for his roommates or that woman he was seeing. Thought they were fast. But Jo said they were all right."

"She met them?"

Lena nodded.

"Jo did her junior semester abroad in Florence so she could spend time with Chris. He died not long after she came home. She cried for days. I think she blamed herself for not being there for him."

"Though it wasn't her fault. Surely, she must know that."

"She was young and sensitive."

"I imagine it must have been very hard for Vera too. He was her only child, yes?"

Lena nodded again.

"The sun rose and set with that boy. He could do no wrong in Vera's eyes. Well, until he became besotted with that model and wanted to stay in Italy. Vera and Nicholas were none too pleased about that. She even made Nicholas fly over there to talk to Chris."

"She did?"

Another nod.

"I told her it was a mistake. But did she listen to me? Still, Nicholas somehow managed to convince Chris to come home. Then they found him, dead, just before he was to fly back."

"And now Vera's dead too."

They were silent for a minute. Then Lena looked at Guin.

"Do you really think someone here murdered my sister? I know she wasn't the easiest person to get along with, but... to kill her?"

"I know," said Guin.

"Well, if someone here did it, my money's on Oliver."

Guin raised her eyebrows. She was surprised by how quickly Lena pointed the finger at Vera's agent.

Just then Francesca reappeared to take their plates and asked them if they would like anything else.

"A nap would be nice," sighed Lena.

That reminded Guin, what had happened to Rosa?

"I should go find the manager," she said.

Guin had just gotten up to look for Rosa when she saw Glen walking across the lawn with Beatrice and froze.

Lena saw where she was looking.

"Who is that woman?" she asked Guin.

"That's Beatrice. She was in the class with us."

"She looks familiar."

"Oh?"

"And who's the man with her?"

"That's my colleague, Glen. He's a photographer with the paper."

"He reminds me of my nephew, Chris. They have the same coloring and build."

"Chris as in Vera's son?"

Lena nodded.

"I imagine that's what he would have looked like had he lived. Though that man seems older."

Guin saw Glen and Beatrice walking towards them. She wanted to hide but knew that was silly.

"Hey," said Glen, smiling at the two women. "You having lunch?"

"We just finished," said Guin. She saw Glen looking at Lena. "This is Vera's sister, Lena Weber. She just flew in from Chicago."

"Nice to meet you," he said. "My condolences. Vera was a great lady."

Guin thought he was laying it on a bit thick but didn't say anything.

"Thank you," said Lena. Then she looked over at Beatrice.

"This is Beatrice," said Glen. "She was in the cooking class with us."

"So Guin said. Do I know you?" she asked Beatrice. "You look familiar."

"I do not think so," Beatrice replied.

"You're Italian."

"*Sì.*"

"Well, we should get going," said Guin, not wanting to hang around. "We need to go see Rosa about a hotel room. Would you excuse us?"

"Of course," said Glen.

Lena got up and followed Guin to reception. On their way there, they ran into Rosa.

"I am sorry to have taken so long, Signora Weber. Things are very busy in Chianti right now. But I found you a room at a nice pensione very close to here."

Lena frowned.

"A pensione?"

"*Sì,*" said Rosa.

"A pensione is like an Italian B and B," Guin explained.

Lena did not look thrilled.

"I assure you, the pensione is very nice," said Rosa. "And Lucia, who runs it, is a very good cook."

"Very well," said Lena. "How do I get there? Were you able to rent me a car? Though I don't have an international driver's license."

"Matteo will drive you."

"Who is Matteo?"

"He works at the hotel," said Rosa.

They walked over to Rosa's desk. Matteo was waiting for them with Lena's suitcase.

"By the way," Guin said to Lena. "Bridget, our instructor, is teaching a pastry class this afternoon. Would you care to join us?"

"But I don't have a car."

Guin looked at Rosa.

"I could ask Matteo to wait for you and drive you back here."

"That's okay," said Lena. "Cooking's not really my thing."

"It's not?" said Guin.

"Vera was the cook in the family. I prefer to read about food rather than make it."

"Well, if you change your mind… Bridget is an excellent teacher, and everything we've made has been delicious."

"I'll think about it."

"I am sure Lucia can arrange a ride for you if you would care to join the class," said Rosa.

"Thank you," said Lena. "And now, I'd like to see this pensione and contact this chief inspector."

"Of course," said Rosa.

"This way," said Matteo, taking Lena's bag.

"Here's my card," said Guin, handing one to Lena. "Feel free to message me if you need anything."

Lena looked at the card, then put it away.

"Thank you," she said. Then Matteo led her outside.

CHAPTER 34

It was nearly three o'clock. Time to head to the kitchen for the pastry class. Guin hadn't heard from Lena and had thought about reaching out to her, only to realize she didn't have Lena's contact information. Oh well. If Lena needed a lift, she could always ask her hostess for one.

She stepped into the kitchen and was surprised to find everyone already there. She took her place next to Glen, relieved he hadn't chosen to work next to Beatrice.

Bridget came in a minute later.

"*Ciao ragazzi!*" she said, a smile on her face. She saw the Americans looking confused. "That means *hi, everyone* in Italian. Technically, *hi, guys*. I'm happy to see you decided to join me! Are you ready to make some Italian pastries?"

There were several nods.

"*Bene!* Let's begin."

Just then Lena peeked her head into the kitchen.

"Am I too late?"

"Not at all," said Guin going over to her. "Everyone, this is Lena Weber, Vera's sister. I didn't think you were coming," Guin whispered to her.

"I changed my mind."

"Welcome, Lena," said Bridget. "There's a spot over there."

Lena went and stood next to Oliver. Neither looked happy about it. Guin again thought how Lena's look of disapproval was the same as Vera's.

"Are you familiar with Italian pastries?" Bridget asked the newcomer.

"I've had cannolis and tiramisu."

"Both of which are delicious," said Bridget. "However, today we are going to make *cantucci*, also known as biscotti, and crostatas, an Italian tart made with jam or fresh fruit."

"Sounds yummy," said Julia. Guin agreed.

"I suggest you work in pairs, with one member in charge of the *cantucci* and the other in charge of the crostata. Or you can work together on both recipes. It's up to you."

Guin glanced around the room. The Adamses were of course going to work together. And no doubt Beatrice and Domenico would work together too. And her and Glen. That left Oliver and Lena, who were both frowning.

Guin turned to Glen.

"Would you mind working with Oliver? I don't think he and Lena like each other, and…"

"No problem."

"Thank you."

He went over to where Lena and Oliver were awkwardly standing and told Lena to take his place by Guin. Guin could sense Lena's relief from several feet away.

"Okay," said Bridget, once everyone had paired up. "Both recipes are in your binder. And for those of you making a crostata, we have apricot and raspberry jam for the filling. Or, if you're feeling adventurous, we have some freshly picked nectarines."

"What about the *cantucci*?" asked John.

Bridget smiled at him.

"Those don't require jam or fruit. Now go ahead and start. Leo and I will be over to check on you. But if you need help, don't be shy."

"Which recipe do you want to make?" Guin asked Lena.

Lena looked at Guin's binder.

"I'm thinking the *cantucci*. If that's okay with you. They seem easier."

"That's fine. I'll make the crostata."

"What are you going to use for the filling?"

"I think I'm going to keep it simple and use jam."

"Which one?"

"Hm," said Guin. "Maybe raspberry? Though I like apricot too."

"I prefer raspberry myself," said Lena.

"Then I'll make it with raspberry. Shall we go get our ingredients?"

Lena nodded, and they went to fetch what they needed from the pantry along with eggs and butter.

"All right," said Guin, eyeing the crostata recipe. "Let's do this."

She measured out flour, sugar, and baking powder and began mixing them. Then she made a well in the dry ingredients and added a lightly beaten whole egg plus a yolk. Next came the butter, which she had cut into little pieces.

"How's it going over here?"

It was Bridget.

"Good, I think," said Guin, showing Bridget her mixture.

Bridget nodded.

"Just be sure to mix it until you can form the dough into a soft ball."

Guin nodded.

"And how are you doing, Lena?"

Lena showed Bridget her dough.

"Looks good. Did you remember to put in the orange zest?"

"No, I forgot about that."

"No worries," said Bridget. "I'll go get you an orange."

She returned a short time later with an orange.

"Here you go."

Lena took the orange but looked confused.

"Is there a problem?" asked Bridget.

"How do you zest it?"

"My bad. I just assumed… Let me get you a zester."
Lena sighed.

"This is the problem with having a famous cookbook author for a sister. Everyone assumes you can cook."

Guin felt for her.

"Here you go," said Bridget. "You just rub the orange against the rough side until you have around a teaspoon of zest. Then add it to your mixture. And if you're feeling a little wild and crazy, you can add a shot of amaretto."

Lena looked at Guin, who had been watching.

"I say go for it!"

"Where's the amaretto?"

"I'll go get it."

When Bridget returned, Lena added the orange zest and amaretto and stirred everything together as Bridget watched.

"Good," said Bridget. "Now add the almonds."

Lena did as she was told.

"Now roll the dough into two even logs. Then place them on a parchment-lined baking sheet and bake them for thirty minutes."

"Okay," said Lena, rolling out the dough.

Bridget turned her attention to Guin.

"You need any help?"

"I think I'm good."

"Okay, I'll leave you two to it then."

Bridget left, and Guin began working her dough.

"What do you think?" She asked Lena a few minutes later.

"Looks good to me. But what do I know?"

Guin thought about getting Bridget then decided not to.

"Now into the fridge with you," she said, after wrapping the dough in plastic wrap.

"Now what?" said Lena, after placing her logs in the oven.

"We wait until they're ready."

Lena looked down at the *cantucci* recipe.

"It says my logs need to bake for thirty minutes. I should check in with Jo. Would you excuse me?"

"Of course," said Guin.

She watched as Lena made her way out of the kitchen and noticed her pausing to look over at Beatrice. Then she glanced around the room, looking to see how everyone else was doing. It seemed like Glen had also made *cantucci*. She went over to get a closer look.

"They look good," she told him.

"You think so?"

"Definitely."

"Okay. Time to put these babies in the oven."

She watched as he placed the baking sheet in the oven then noticed that Oliver wasn't in the kitchen.

"Where'd your partner go?"

"He went to make a call. His phone's been buzzing nonstop. I told him to silence it, but he wouldn't."

"Is he making the crostata?"

"Yup."

"Where's his dough?"

"In the fridge."

"Wow. That was fast."

"I guess working with Vera, he picked up a few things."

"No doubt. You want to step outside, get some fresh air?"

"I'd love to."

As she and Glen strolled around the grounds, Guin saw several of their classmates doing the same. Though why did Beatrice look upset? Had something happened? She was saying something to Domenico, gesticulating wildly. She just hoped Glen didn't decide to go over there.

Her phone began to vibrate and Guin saw it was her reminder.

"Time to return to the kitchen!"

Lena was already there when she walked in, standing in front of the oven. Guin went over to her.

"Do you think they're done?" she asked Guin.

"Only one way to find out."

Lena took out her baking sheet.

"They look good to me!" said Guin. "But if you're concerned, ask Bridget or Leo."

Lena took the baking sheet over to their station then looked down at Guin's binder.

"According to the recipe, they need to cool for ten minutes. Then I have to cut them into half-inch diagonal slices and place them back into the oven for another ten to fifteen minutes. Doesn't seem too difficult."

"I'm sure you can handle it," said Guin.

Lena smiled.

"How's your crostata dough?"

"I was just about to go get it."

Guin walked over to the refrigerator and removed her dough ball. She took it back to her spot and began to knead it. Then she rolled it out until it was about an eighth of an inch thick.

"Okay," she said. "Now to get you into the tart pan."

She gingerly lifted the rolled-out dough, holding her breath. Then she let it out as the dough neatly filled the tart pan, though there was some dough hanging over the side. She would trim it off and use it to top her tart. She picked up a fork and gently pricked the bottom of the crust so it wouldn't puff up when she baked it. Then she added the jam.

"Now a few strips of dough on top and…"

Bridget had returned.

"Looks good," she said. "Have you done this before?"

"Nope, first time. Though I've made plenty of apple pies."

"Well, you could have fooled me."

Guin enjoyed the compliment. Though she wondered if Bridget was just being kind. Still, she was proud of her crostata.

"If you like, you can brush the top with a little bit of egg or milk to give it a shine."

"Okay," said Guin.

She took a pastry brush and lightly brushed the dough with a little egg. Then she placed the crostata in the oven. The tart would need to be baked for 25 to 30 minutes. She set a reminder on her phone.

Lena placed her *cantucci* in the other oven.

"Those look good," said Guin.

"We'll see how they taste."

"I'm sure they'll be yummy."

"We'll find out soon enough."

Guin saw Lena looking over at Beatrice again. She was frowning.

"Is everything all right?"

"Hm?" she said, turning back to Guin.

"I saw you looking over at Beatrice."

"I just know I know her from somewhere."

Beatrice had to be at least twenty years younger than Lena.

"Could she be a friend of your daughter's? Didn't you say your daughter studied in Italy?"

"Maybe," said Lena, still looking at Beatrice.

"You could always ask her. Joanna, that is."

Just then Guin felt her phone vibrating in her pocket. She had turned it to vibrate after she had set the reminder. She took it out and saw she had a message from Ginny.

"Would you excuse me?"

"Of course."

"I'll be right back. It's just my boss, probably wondering if I'm ever going to return to Sanibel." *Or send her another article*, Guin said to herself. Then she headed out of the kitchen.

CHAPTER 35

Guin called Ginny as soon as she stepped outside. Three rings later, Ginny picked up.

"Oh, good. You're alive. I was beginning to wonder."

Guin rolled her eyes.

"I've been busy."

"Working on articles for me, I hope."

"Of course," Guin lied.

"Any news about your passport?"

"Not yet."

"Surely, they can't think you had anything to do with it."

"I don't think so. It's just a precaution. They still haven't arrested anyone."

"Well, don't get too comfortable over there. We need you back on Sanibel."

"Things busy there?"

Though during the summer things were typically slow on Sanibel and Captiva. Winter was the busy season.

"Still have to put out a paper. And I could use my star reporter."

"Though you have plenty of freelancers. Or are they all away?"

"Are you saying I don't need you?"

"No, just that you have options."

"So, when are you going to send me another article?"

"Soon. I'm finishing up a pastry class. You want me to write about it?"

"Sure, why not? What are you making?"

"*Cantucci* and crostatas."

"Come again?"

"*Cantucci* are Italian almond cookies. And crostatas are a kind of tart filled with jam or fruit."

"Is Glen taking pictures?"

"I assume so." She hadn't really been paying attention. But she knew he never went anywhere without his camera.

"Well, tell him to send me stuff. I've been getting raves about his photos. You should tell Bridget to come to Sanibel."

"Would the paper pay?"

"Let's not get carried away. Hold on a sec."

Guin heard Ginny talking to someone. Then she was back.

"So, no update on the murder investigation?"

Ginny loved a good crime story.

"Not really. Though Vera's sister just showed up."

"What's she like?"

"A bit like Vera but nicer. Though she doesn't know how to cook."

"Huh."

Guin heard someone speaking to Ginny again.

"I need to go," Ginny informed her. "Get me that article about the pastry class, and get back here as soon as you can."

"Will do," said Guin.

They ended the call and Guin headed back to the kitchen.

All of the *cantucci* and crostatas were now out of the ovens and displayed on the center island, where Glen was photographing them. Guin had to admit, they all looked pretty good.

When Glen was done taking pictures, Bridget stood in front of the class.

"Great job, everyone. All of your desserts look good enough to serve at Dante's."

"I don't know about that," Guin heard Julia mumble.

"Shall we give them a try?"

Everyone nodded, and Bridget and Leo began cutting up the crostatas.

"Okay. Grab a plate and help yourselves," Bridget told them.

"Who made that crostata?" Guin asked Glen, looking at the one made with nectarines.

"That would be Oliver."

"It looks quite professional. Maybe Vera did rub off on him." Guin looked for Vera's agent and spied him on his phone. "Another business call?"

"Who knows? Let's eat."

He placed a slice of Oliver's crostata on his plate.

"Would you be okay sharing?" Guin asked him. "I don't think I can eat four slices of crostata and a bunch of *cantucci*."

"That's fine. I probably shouldn't eat four slices either."

Glen put a piece of Guin's crostata on his plate next to Oliver's, adding a couple of *cantucci*. Then Guin put slices of the two remaining crostatas on her plate, along with two more *cantucci*.

"Could I have your attention?" said Bridget as everyone was about to dig in. "You can't have dessert without a little prosecco." She held up a bottle of the bubbly and opened it, pouring the liquid into glasses. "Come up and take one."

When everyone had a glass, Bridget raised hers.

"To all of you," she said. "I know I said it before, but it bears repeating. You've been a great class. And I appreciate your help testing my recipes. *Salute!*"

"*Salute!*" they echoed back, raising their glasses.

"I think I could get used to drinking prosecco," said Guin.

"It's a little too sweet for me," said Glen.

They put down their glasses and Guin looked at their plates.

"What should we try first?"

"I want to try Oliver's crostata."

They each took a forkful.

"Wow," said Guin. "That's really good."

Glen nodded.

"I'm honestly surprised. Though I guess I shouldn't be. Okay, how about we try yours next?"

Guin felt apprehensive.

"Must we?"

"It looks great. Come on."

They stuck their forks in.

"Mm," he said. "This is really good."

"I don't know about really good, but I have to admit it's pretty tasty."

Glen smiled at her.

They next tried the other crostatas, one of which was also made with raspberry jam, the other with apricot.

"They're all really good," said Guin. "Which one was your favorite?"

"Yours, of course."

Guin made a face.

"You're just saying that."

"I am not. Which one was your favorite?"

Guin studied the four crostatas.

"Hm… They were all good. All a bit different."

"But if you had to choose."

"It's a tie between Oliver's and Beatrice's. I liked the fresh fruit in Oliver's, but Beatrice nailed the crust." Much as Guin hated to admit it. "Shall we try the *cantucci*?"

Glen nodded, and they each picked up a *cantucci*.

"Whoa," said Glen after taking a bite of Lena's.

"You okay?"

"This biscotti tastes like amaretto."

"That's because she put a shot of amaretto in the batter. It was Bridget's idea. Here, let me have a bite."

"Go get your own," he said, polishing off the cookie.

Guin frowned and went to get one.

Several minutes later, after eating the *cantucci* and discussing which one was their favorite, they looked around to find several people had left. Only John and Julia remained.

Guin went over to them; Glen followed.

"So, what did you think?" she asked them. "Were you pleased with how your desserts came out?"

"I liked them," said John. "Not so sure about Julia." He leaned forward. "She's a bit of a perfectionist."

"I am not a perfectionist," said Julia. "I just like to do a good job."

"I rest my case."

"Which crostata was your favorite?" Guin asked them.

"I liked the one with the fancy top and the raspberry jam," said John.

That was Beatrice's.

"Not Julia's?"

"Hers was very good, but I prefer raspberry jam to apricot."

"What about you, Julia?" Glen asked her.

"I liked Oliver's. The nectarines were delicious."

"And what did you think of the *cantucci*?"

"I liked the one with the amaretto," said John.

"That was Lena's," said Guin. She looked at Julia.

"They all tasted pretty much the same to me." John was looking at her. "But, of course, I liked yours the best, dear."

John grinned.

"Speaking of Lena," said Guin. "Did you happen to see where she went?"

John and Julia shook their heads.

Just then they heard a scream and Francesca came

running into the kitchen. She looked terrified.

"Please," she said to Julia, taking her hand and leading her towards the back door that led outside.

Julia followed her out, John, Glen, and Guin behind her. They got outside and Francesca pointed. There on the ground was Lena Weber. Lying face down. She wasn't moving.

"What happened?" Guin ask Francesca as Julia knelt and felt for a pulse.

"I do not know," said Francesca. "I just came out here and saw her."

Guin looked down at Lena's prostrate form.

"Is she...?" Guin asked Julia.

"She's alive," Julia informed her.

Lena moaned.

"Lena, it's Julia Adams. Just take it easy."

Lena opened her eyes, tried to move, and winced.

"Where does it hurt?"

"My head..."

"Do you know what happened?"

"I was talking on the phone, then I felt something on the back of my head, and..."

"May I examine you?"

Lena nodded and winced with pain.

"I'll be gentle," Julia promised.

She carefully examined Lena's head and neck.

"There doesn't appear to be any blood," she reported.

"Well, that's good," said Guin.

"Do you think you can sit up?" Julia asked Lena. Lena nodded and winced. "Hold on," said Julia. She turned to Glen and John. "Can you gentlemen help me?"

They gently got Lena into a seated position. There was dirt on her face and clothing.

"Do you feel at all nauseated or dizzy?" Julia asked her.

"A little."

"What about your vision? Is it blurry?"

Lena squinted and blinked.

"I think it's okay. It's really my head. It feels like my skull is cracked."

Julia gently felt Lena's head again. Lena winced at her touch.

"It seems okay. Though there's a bump. Do you think you can stand? We should get you inside, someplace where you can rest." They helped her up. "Where are you staying?"

"At a pensione not far from here."

"By yourself?"

Lena nodded and winced. Julia frowned.

"You shouldn't be alone the next twenty-four hours. I'll ask Rosa if there's an extra room here."

"There isn't," said Guin. Julia frowned. "But she can stay with me."

They turned to look at her.

"There's a sofa bed in my room. I can sleep on it, and Lena can have my bed."

"I think that's a very sensible idea," said Julia.

"You don't need to give up your room," said Lena. "I'll be perfectly fine back at my pensione."

"I'm not giving up my room," Guin said. "We're sharing it. Just for tonight. To make sure you're okay."

Lena frowned.

"Doctor's orders," said Julia.

"You're a doctor?"

Julia nodded. But Lena still looked hesitant.

"What would your daughter say?" asked Guin.

Lena sighed.

"She'd probably tell me to not be so bull-headed."

Guin and Julia smiled.

"But what about my things?"

"We can ask Matteo to get them," said Glen.

Guin saw Lena frown again.

"I can go," she said.

"I'll drive you," said Glen.

"There, it's settled," said Guin. "Just tell us what you need."

CHAPTER 36

"Do you really think someone hit Lena on the back of the head?" Glen asked Guin as they drove to Lena's pensione.

"Why would she lie?" Guin replied.

"She could have just tripped and fallen. Julia said there was no blood."

"That doesn't mean someone didn't hit her with something. It just means she was lucky. Though she could have a concussion. She looked pretty shaken up."

Glen said no more, and Guin looked out the window.

When they arrived at the pensione, Lucia, the proprietor, was there to meet them. She had many questions, which neither Glen nor Guin could really answer. Finally, giving up, she showed them to Lena's room and left them there to gather Lena's things.

"You can wait outside," she told Glen. "I'll just be a minute." But he went in with her.

"How long was she planning on staying?" he asked as he watched Guin go through the drawers and armoire, picking out items. "There are enough clothes here to last a month."

"There isn't that much," said Guin. "She probably didn't know how long she would be here or if it would get cold at night and was playing it safe."

Guin finished removing the items Lena had requested, placing them on the bed. Then she went into the bathroom to retrieve Lena's toiletry kit.

"Okay, I think that's everything."

She looked at the things on the bed and frowned.

"What's wrong?"

"Where do I put all this stuff?"

Glen looked around and spotted Lena's suitcase.

"You could always use her suitcase."

Guin looked at it.

"It's awfully big, and there isn't that much stuff. I should have brought my carry-on."

"Maybe there's a laundry bag in the armoire. Or you could always use a pillowcase."

Guin frowned at that suggestion.

"Let's see if there's a laundry bag. If not, maybe we can borrow something from Lucia."

Guin opened the armoire. There was nothing of use.

"Let me go find Lucia."

A few minutes later, Guin returned with a large shopping bag.

"Success!"

She placed everything in the bag, and they left Lena's room.

Lucia met them as they were about to leave the pensione.

"Please tell Signora Weber I hope she is okay. And that I will make her my *minestra di pane* when she returns." Glen and Guin looked confused. "It is a soup," Lucia explained. "Very good for you."

"Ah," said Guin. "Thank you. We'll be sure to tell her."

"What do you want to do about dinner?" Glen asked Guin on the drive back.

"How can you think about dinner when we just ate all that crostata and *cantucci*?"

"We didn't eat that much."

Guin shook her head.

"Your ability to eat never ceases to amaze me. How do you do it and stay in such good shape?"

"Good genes, I guess. Though I don't eat that much, do I?"

Guin didn't respond, just looked out the window.

"You didn't answer my question about dinner."

Guin sighed and turned back to him.

"I'm supposed to be watching Lena, remember?"

"We could always take her with us. She's probably hungry."

"I don't know."

"Come on, let's ask her. She'll probably be happy to get out."

"What if she's not feeling well?"

"Then we'll bring her back something."

They parked in the lot and Guin grabbed the shopping bag with Lena's things.

"You don't need to come in with me," she said, stopping Glen at her door.

"I thought we were going to ask her about dinner."

"I'll ask her."

Glen gave her a look.

"And I'll let you know what she says."

"Fine. Just message me or knock."

"Promise." Guin knocked on her door. "Lena, it's me, Guin," she called, not wanting Lena to think someone was breaking in. "I have your things."

She entered the room, but there was no sign of Lena.

"Lena?" she called. She knocked on the bathroom door, but there was no answer. She opened it slowly, but Lena wasn't there. "Where could she be?"

She left her room and knocked on Glen's door.

"That was fast," he said. "What did she say?"

"Nothing. She wasn't there."

Glen looked confused.

"She's not there?"

"Unless she turned invisible."

"Did she leave you a note?"

"I didn't see one."

"Maybe you should double-check."

Guin turned and went back to her room, Glen following her. They searched the room but didn't find a note.

"Do you think something happened to her? Should we go find Julia? Maybe she wasn't feeling well and went to see her."

"Good idea."

They headed to the Adamses' room. Guin knocked on the door.

"Yes?" Julia answered.

"Julia, it's Guin. We can't find Lena."

Julia quickly opened the door.

"What do you mean you can't find Lena? Isn't she in your room?"

"No. We just got back, and she wasn't there. I thought maybe she wasn't feeling well and went to find you."

Julia frowned.

"I haven't seen her."

"Where could she have gone?"

"She couldn't have gone far," said Glen. "Unless she was kidnapped."

Guin scowled.

They heard a toilet flush, and John stepped out of the bathroom.

"What's all the hullabaloo?"

"Lena's missing," his wife informed him.

"Missing?" said John.

"We're heading out to look for her," said Glen.

"You coming?" Julia asked him.

"Give me a minute."

"We'll be right out," Julia said ushering them out of their suite.

A couple of minutes later, Julia and John joined them outside.

"Where should we start?" Guin asked.

"Let's check the kitchen," John suggested.

"The kitchen?" said Julia.

"Maybe she was hungry," he replied.

Julia looked doubtful.

"It's as good a place as any," said Guin.

The four of them headed to the kitchen, but there was no sign of Lena or anyone else.

"Where else could she have gone?" said Guin.

"Maybe she went to see Rosa?" said Glen.

They turned and headed to reception, but there was no one there either.

"Where is everyone?" said Guin.

"Let's check Rosa's office," said Glen.

The door was closed, but they could hear voices.

Guin knocked on the door.

"Rosa, are you there?"

The door was unlocked, so she opened it. And there were Rosa and Lena, having tea.

"Thank goodness," said Julia.

Lena and Rosa looked at the four of them.

"Is everything all right?" asked Rosa.

"We were worried about Lena, Mrs. Weber," said Julia. "She wasn't in Guin's room when they got back."

"And there wasn't a note," added Guin.

"I'm so sorry," said Lena. "I didn't mean to worry anyone. I got a bit thirsty and went in search of something to drink. I ran into Rosa, and she invited me to have tea with her in her office. I guess I lost track of the time."

"I'm just glad you're all right," said Guin. "I have your things."

"Thank you," said Lena. She saw Glen looking at Guin, motioning with his head. "Was there something else?"

"Glen and I wanted to know if you'd like to have dinner with us."

"Thank you," said Lena. "But I couldn't eat another thing after all that pastry."

"You go eat," said Rosa. "I will look after Signora Weber."

"Are you sure?" said Guin.

Rosa and Lena exchanged a look and a smile.

"Positive," said Rosa.

"Run along," said Lena. "We'll be fine."

"What about your head?" asked Guin.

"It's feeling better already."

Guin hesitated.

"Come on," said Glen. "She'll be fine."

Guin looked at Julia, who nodded.

"Okay, but if you feel at all dizzy or sick, go see Julia."

"I'll give you my cell phone number, so you can message me," Julia told Lena.

"See," said Glen. "All good."

"Fine," said Guin. "So I'll see you later?" she said to Lena.

"You will. Now go have dinner with your young man."

Guin wanted to tell Lena he wasn't her young man, but Glen was pulling her out the door.

They had wound up going to a little place in town that Glen had found online. The food had been good, not great, but Guin hadn't been that hungry anyway. And she was quiet on the drive back.

"Is everything okay?" he asked her.

"Everything's fine. Why?"

"You're just awfully quiet this evening, and you didn't eat that much at dinner."

"I told you I wasn't that hungry, and I have a lot on my mind."

"Like?"

"Like who hit Lena on the back of the head."

"For all we know no one did. She could have tripped and fallen."

"But then why was there a bump on the back of her head?"

"Good point."

"The question is, why would someone attack her?"

Guin looked at him, but he didn't have an answer.

"And who could have done it? John and Julia were with us in the kitchen. So it couldn't have been them. And Leo and Francesca were there too."

"You think it was someone staying at the hotel?"

"Or someone who works there."

"But why attack Lena?"

"That's what I want to know."

"You think it had something to do with her being Vera's sister?"

"It must be. But what?"

"Maybe she knows something?"

"Lena said she had barely heard from Vera since she got here."

"But maybe her assailant didn't know that. Maybe he thought Vera had told her something and was worried Lena would go to the police."

Guin looked thoughtful.

"You may be right."

They had arrived back at the hotel, and Glen walked Guin to her room. He stopped and looked over at Oliver's room, which was a short distance away.

"I don't like him being so close, especially with Lena bunking with you."

"You don't really think Oliver would try anything, do you?"

"Someone hit Lena on the back of the head in broad daylight. My money's on Oliver. He wasn't in the kitchen when it happened. He could have been outside, heard Lena say something, and hit her."

Guin stared at him.

"What?"

"I just can't picture Oliver clubbing anyone."

"Just do me a favor and be sure to double lock your door."

"Would you like me to put the armoire in front of it, in case he manages to pick the locks? Or what if he tries to sneak in the window?"

"Sarcasm doesn't become you."

"I'm sorry. Look, we'll be fine."

"Just call or text me if you hear anything."

"I promise."

CHAPTER 37

There was a knock on the door.

"Yes?" called Guin.

"It's Lena. Is it okay for me to come in?"

Guin quickly went to the door, unlocked it, and let Lena in. Lena looked around.

"Is everything all right?" Guin asked her.

"I thought your young man might be with you."

"He's in his room across the hall. And he's not my young man."

"Oh?"

"We just work together."

Lena didn't look convinced. Time to change the subject.

"How are you feeling?"

"Much better. Though my head still hurts."

"I have some acetaminophen. I think Julia said you could take a couple."

"Rosa gave me something for the pain. I think I just need a good night's rest."

"Speaking of Rosa, did you and she have a good chat?"

"Oh, yes. She's quite a woman. I couldn't have done half the things she has."

"Oh?"

"She raised three children, mostly on her own, and ran several hotels. And she was in the Olympics."

"She was?" Guin had no idea.

Lena nodded.

"Which sport did she compete in?"

"Fencing. Women's Foil."

"A foil is a bit like a sword, isn't it?" *Or a knife*, she added silently, thinking of Vera.

"A bit. Though it doesn't have a sharp tip."

"What else did you discuss?"

"Oh, this and that. Mostly we talked about our children. Rosa has a daughter around Joanna's age who's studying to be a doctor."

"Speaking of doctors, you sure you're okay? You should probably get your head examined if it still hurts in the morning."

"I'm sure I'll feel better in the morning."

"Do you remember anything more about what happened?"

"I wish I did, but... All I remember was being on the phone with Joanna, then being on the ground with you lot looking down at me."

"It happened while you were speaking with your daughter? Does she know that you're okay?"

"I'm pretty sure it happened after we hung up. Otherwise I'd have heard from her."

"So you haven't communicated with her since the accident?"

"No, I didn't want to worry her." She frowned. "Though I have a feeling there was something she was going to tell me. Something important." She sighed.

"Don't worry about it," said Guin. "I'm sure you'll remember after a good night's rest."

"I hope so. I hate not remembering things."

"Me too."

"Is it okay if I use the bathroom?"

"Of course!" said Guin. "Help yourself. And by the way, your things are in a shopping bag on the bed. Francesca changed the sheets."

"Thank you," said Lena.

"And Lucia said to tell you that she hopes you feel better and that she would make you her *minestra di pane* when you go back."

"*Minestra di pane*?"

"It's a traditional Tuscan vegetable soup made with day-old bread." Guin had looked it up. "She said it's good for what ails you."

"Ah," said Lena. "Sounds like something Vera would have made." She paused. "Well, I shouldn't be long. Thanks again for sharing your room."

"No problem," said Guin.

Guin slept fitfully that night. The mattress on the sofa bed wasn't very comfortable, and she had a lot on her mind. (She had double-locked the door but had not put the armoire in front of it.) As soon as the light began peeking through the window, she got up. She quietly made her way to the bathroom, so as not to wake Lena. When she was done, she peered into the bedroom. Lena appeared to be asleep. Or could she be dead?

You're being paranoid, she told herself. But to be on the safe side, she tiptoed in. Lena snorted and rolled over. And Guin breathed a sigh of relief. She quietly went over to the chest of drawers and removed underwear and a bra along with a pair of capri pants and a t-shirt. Then she went to get changed.

She left Lena a note, letting her know she had gone for a walk and would see her at breakfast if not before—and to contact Julia or Rosa if she needed anything. Then she grabbed her card key and phone and left, quietly closing the door behind her.

"Good morning."

Guin dropped her card key and nearly screamed.

"A bit jumpy this morning."

Guin placed her hand over her heart to calm herself down and turned to Glen.

"You scared me. What are you doing up?" Though she knew Glen was an early riser.

"I was going to go for a short walk before breakfast. Where were you heading off to? Shouldn't you be watching the patient?"

"She's asleep, and I left a note for her. Where were you planning on walking?"

"I hadn't decided. What about you?"

"I figured I'd just walk down the road and back. I didn't want to be gone for too long."

"Okay if I join you?"

"Of course."

They passed the main building and headed down the driveway.

"How's Lena doing?"

"She seemed all right when we said good night. She said Rosa had given her something for the pain. Did you know Rosa had fenced in the Olympics?"

"I did not. How did you find out?"

"Lena. Do you think...?" She trailed off.

"Do I think what?"

"That Rosa could have stuck that knife in Vera and was chatting Lena up to see how much she knew?"

Glen frowned.

"But why would Rosa want to kill Vera?"

"I don't know, but... I feel like there's something we're missing. And the more I think about it, the more I'm sure one of the people I heard that night in the kitchen had an Italian accent."

Glen continued to frown.

"Did Lena say anything, about the accident?"

"No. All she remembered was talking to her daughter.

Then everything went black. But I'm hoping she'll remember something when she gets up."

They continued to walk, neither saying anything.

"I should probably check to see if Lena's okay," said Guin a few minutes later. She took out her phone and checked her messages, then frowned.

"Everything okay? Is it Lena?"

"No. Just my mother."

"She's up awfully early."

"More likely she was out late."

Guin read the message.

"So, what does she have to say?"

"She says she's worried about me. But what else is new?"

"You should give her a call."

Guin sighed.

"I'll call her later." She loved her mother, but they had a difficult relationship, her mother not understanding why Guin chose to live on Sanibel and be single. "We should head back to the hotel. Lena's probably up, and I should check on her."

"Didn't you say you left her a note and told her to contact Julia or Rosa if she needed anything?"

"True, but we should still head back. I promised Ginny an article on the pastry class. By the way, she said everyone loves your photos and to send her more. She also talked about Bridget doing a class on Sanibel."

"That's a great idea! Should I ask Bridget about it?"

"Be my guest. Though the paper won't pay."

"I'm sure we could find someone to sponsor her."

He was probably right. Though if Bridget was arrested for Vera's murder, she wouldn't be going anywhere for a while.

They walked the rest of the way in silence.

"You want to grab some breakfast?" Glen asked her.

"I'm going to check on Lena first. But you go ahead."

Glen hesitated.

"Go on. I'll be there in a few. You can save me a seat."

"All right," he said.

Guin arrived back at the room to find Lena dressed, her bed made, and her things by the door.

"I take it you're feeling better."

"Much."

"So, are you going back to Lucia's?"

"After I have some breakfast. Then I plan on getting my sister released from wherever they're holding her."

Yup. She was definitely feeling better.

"If you need a ride, I'm sure Glen would take you wherever you needed to go."

"Thank you, but Rosa said she could arrange for a driver."

"Would you like to join me and Glen for breakfast?"

"I don't want to intrude."

"You're not intruding. Come, let's go. Glen's saving us a table."

Glen smiled as Guin and Lena approached.

"Good to see you up and about," he said to Lena. "We were worried."

"As you can see, I'm perfectly fine."

"Won't you have a seat?"

"Are you sure?"

"Positive," said Glen.

Francesca came over and they ordered coffee. Lena was staring at Glen.

"Is everything all right?" he asked her. "Do I have something on my face?"

"Sorry. It's just... You remind me of my late nephew."

"Vera's son Chris," Guin explained to Glen.

"Though you're older than him," Lena continued. "Or how old he'd be if he were still with us. Still, the resemblance is uncanny."

"He was a painter, yes?"

"That's right," said Lena. "A very talented one. He had his first show at eighteen."

"Wow," said Guin. "That's impressive. Glen's also an artist."

"Oh?" said Lena.

"I'm a photographer. And I do a bit of painting on the side."

"Don't be so modest," said Guin. "You're an incredible photographer and artist."

"I don't know about that."

"What do you photograph?" asked Lena.

"Mainly people these days. Though I shoot whatever catches my eye."

"Glen's been photographing the class."

Francesca brought over their coffee.

"Breakfast is self-serve," said Guin. "Help yourself."

"I'm not much of a breakfast person," Lena said. "But it does look rather good."

"It is," said Guin.

They returned to the table with their plates of food and Glen asked Lena about herself. She told him she was a research librarian at Northwestern University, just outside of Chicago, and that she was a widow.

As she was talking, Guin saw John and Julia enter the dining terrace and waved to them. They immediately came over.

"How are you doing this morning?" Julia asked Lena.

"Much better, thank you."

"No headache?"

"My head still hurts, but not as much as it did before."

"And no nausea or blurry vision?"

"No, thank goodness."

"Okay. Just let me know if anything changes. And take it easy today. Doctor's orders."

"Thank you. But I won't rest until I speak with this chief inspector."

"We could take you to see him after breakfast," Guin offered.

Glen looked at her, but Guin ignored him.

"You don't have to do that," said Lena. "I'm sure I can get a taxi."

"Nonsense," said Guin. "Besides, Glen and I didn't have anything planned for today, did we?"

"Uh," said Glen. He saw Guin and Lena looking at him. "I'd be happy to take you. Though I rented a convertible, and I'm not sure it can fit the three of us."

"You're welcome to use our car," said John.

They looked up at him.

"Are you sure?" said Guin. "Don't you need it?"

"Maybe we could trade for the day?" he suggested. "I haven't driven a convertible in years."

Guin looked over at Glen.

"I guess that's all right," he said. Though he didn't look happy about it.

"Excellent!" said Guin. "You two can trade keys after breakfast."

John and Julia excused themselves, and the three of them finished breakfast.

CHAPTER 38

Glen and Guin and Lena were headed back to their rooms when they passed Beatrice and Domenico. Lena stopped and was staring at Beatrice.

"That woman. I remember now."

"What do you remember?" Guin asked her.

"I was talking to Joanna, and I asked her if she knew a Beatrice Krueger."

"And did she?"

Lena frowned.

"I don't think so. I'm still a little fuzzy. But... I know! I said I'd send her a picture." Then she frowned again.

"What's wrong?"

"How am I supposed to get a picture of her?"

"You could always ask her," said Guin.

"Actually," said Glen.

They turned to look at him.

"I have lots of pictures of Bea." *Of course, he did*, thought Guin. "I'd be happy to send you some to send to your daughter."

"That would be wonderful. Thank you."

"No problem. The edited ones are on my computer. I'll email them to you. What's your address?"

She gave Glen her email, and he said he'd go do it right now.

"Do you remember anything else?" Guin asked Lena

after she let them into their room.

"I'm afraid not. Though… that man Mrs. Krueger was with also seems familiar."

"Well, his family owns a bunch of hotels, and he worked in the States for a while. It's possible you saw a photo of him somewhere."

"I guess." She sighed. "I just hate having this feeling, like a memory is just out of reach."

"I know how that feels," said Guin. "But maybe you'll remember it later."

There was a knock on the door.

"Who is it?" Guin called.

It was Glen.

"I just sent you a couple of photos to forward to your daughter," he told Lena.

Lena took out her phone.

"I don't see anything."

"It may take a minute. The WiFi isn't great in this part of the hotel and the files are a bit large, though I compressed them."

"We should head to the police station," said Guin. Then she remembered. "Shall we go see John, so you can exchange keys?"

"Must we?"

"We must. Don't worry. I'm sure Julia will make sure he drives carefully."

Glen sighed and they headed off to find John and Julia.

They arrived at the police station only to be told that Chief Inspector Manetti was not available.

"But we have important business to discuss with him," said Guin. "Can you tell him it's urgent?"

The officer raised his eyebrows.

"This is Signora Weber. She's the sister of Vera van

Leyden, the American who died. Chief Inspector Manetti is handling the case. And I know he'd want to speak with her."

The officer looked at Lena.

"I am sorry for your loss, Signora."

"Thank you," said Lena. "Will the chief inspector be available later? Or is there someone else I can talk to? I just want to know how to get my sister's body released, so I can take her back with me to the States."

"I am sorry, Signora. I am unable to help you."

"Could we at least leave a message for the chief inspector?" said Guin.

"If you wish."

"Lena?" said Guin.

Lena started to rummage in her bag for a pen and paper then stopped.

"Can he read English?"

"Oh, yes," Guin replied. "He lived in the States for a while and is fluent."

"Oh," said Lena. She retrieved a small notepad and a pen and began to write. When she was done, she handed the note to the officer.

"Please make sure Chief Inspector Manetti gets this."

The officer took the note, looking nonplussed, and Guin wondered if he would actually give the note to the chief inspector. Just to be on the safe side, she would message Manetti and tell him they had stopped by the police station.

They stood outside, deciding what to do next.

"Now what?" Glen asked the two women.

Guin saw Lena looking intently at her phone.

"Is everything okay?" she asked.

"Sorry, I was looking at the photos Glen sent me. They're very good."

"May I see?" asked Guin.

Lena handed Guin her phone. She looked at the photos. The first one was a picture of Beatrice posing against an old stone building. It was a full-body shot, and she looked quite seductive. The second was a closeup of her face. She was smiling. Guin couldn't deny Beatrice was gorgeous and felt a pang of jealousy as Glen clearly thought so too, at least judging by the photos.

"Thanks," she said, handing Lena back her phone.

"I'm going to forward these to Joanna."

They waited for her to finish. Then Guin asked her what she wanted to do next.

"I should probably go to the U.S. Consulate in Florence."

"We can take you," said Guin.

"We can?" said Glen.

"Of course, we can."

"What about the car?"

"I don't think John and Julia would mind us keeping it for another hour or two. Florence isn't that far." She turned back to Lena. "It's settled. We're going to Florence."

"Are you sure?" asked Lena, looking from Guin to Glen.

"Absolutely," said Guin. "Besides, I want to get my passport back. And the police haven't exactly been helpful. Maybe we'll have better luck at the consulate."

"If you're really sure…" said Lena.

"Let's go," said Glen. "I'd like to get my passport back too."

Guin grinned at him.

"Then it's settled. We're off to Florence!"

Guin looked back at Lena and saw her frowning at her phone.

"Is everything okay?"

"Hm?" said Lena looking up at her.

"You were frowning at your phone."

"Oh, I didn't realize. I just received an email from my daughter."

"Did she get the pictures?"

"She did. And now I know why that woman looked so familiar."

Guin and Glen waited for her to go on.

"She was Christian's girlfriend. When he lived in Italy."

"She was?" said Guin.

Lena nodded.

"Joanna's pretty sure. Of course, that was ten years ago, and her hair's a bit different, but Jo said it's her. Christian always referred to her as Bae. And her last name was Donati, not Krueger. That's why I didn't realize it was her.

"And I asked her about the man Bae was with. And she said it sounded like Nico, Christian's roommate."

Guin was staring at Lena.

"Are you okay?" Lena asked her.

"Domenico was Christian van Leyden's roommate, and Bea was his girlfriend?"

"That's what Jo says."

She turned and looked over at Glen, who was driving. He quickly glanced at her.

"It doesn't mean anything, Guin."

"Of course it means something! Vera hated them for letting her son die!"

"But it wasn't their fault."

"Try telling Vera that," said Lena from the back seat.

Guin tried not to look smug. She looked back at Lena.

"And your daughter is sure it's them?"

"I can ask her again, but Joanna has a good memory for that kind of thing. She's always been good with faces, unlike her mother."

"What if Vera recognized them?" Guin said to Glen. "And she threatened them somehow? Maybe that's what she and Domenico were going on about. Maybe one of them is the killer!"

Glen glanced at her again.

"You can't possibly think Bea or Domenico killed her."

"Well, we're running out of suspects. And now they both have motives."

"We don't know that. Christian died years ago. You can't possibly think Vera still held a grudge."

"You clearly don't know my sister," said Lena.

"See!" said Guin.

"But why kill her? Wouldn't she want to kill them? Assuming you're right about her blaming them for her son's death."

"Maybe she did," said Guin. "Maybe she threatened to ruin them or even tried to kill them. Maybe they killed her in self-defense."

"You don't really believe that, do you?" said Glen.

Guin didn't answer.

"What about this?" said Guin a few minutes later. "Beatrice's husband dies, and she goes back to Italy. She's depressed, and her good friend Domenico suggests she go with him to attend a cooking class at a little hotel in Chianti. She agrees. Then who do they see upon arriving there but Vera van Leyden, the woman who ruined Beatrice's life."

"I don't think her life was totally ruined," said Glen. "She did get married."

"I know, to Klaus. But he wasn't the love of her life. Now let me continue. So Bea and Domenico arrive here and see Vera, and Vera sees them and goes ballistic. She tells them to leave, that they killed her son, and if they don't go, she'll ruin them."

"Seriously, Guin? That kind of thing only happens in telenovelas."

"You watch telenovelas? Anyway, I'm not done. So after sniping at each other for days, Vera and Bea wind up in the kitchen late at night. They argue. Vera threatens Bea again, tells her to leave the hotel. Then she turns to go. In a fit of rage, Bea picks up Bridget's chef's knife and plunges it into Vera's back as Vera's walking away."

Glen was staring at her.

"Keep your eyes on the road!" Guin shouted.

"You don't really believe all that, do you?" he said. Guin gave him a look. "Fine. Let's pretend something like that did happen. But why couldn't it have been Domenico who Vera threatened in the kitchen? He has far more to lose than Bea, and he's a lot stronger."

"It's not a bad theory, but I'm sure the two voices I heard in the kitchen that night belonged to two women. And you're just defending Beatrice because you like her."

"I'm defending her because she's innocent."

Guin made a face.

"And even if it was Bea you heard in the kitchen, it doesn't mean she's the killer. Someone could have gone into the kitchen after her."

"Like who?"

"Like Oliver."

"Much as I would like to pin the blame on Oliver, wouldn't he lose a lot of money if his client died?"

"It may not have been rational," said Glen. "And besides, he probably has other clients. And he could always find new ones."

"Not from jail," said Guin. "And what about Vera's cookbook?"

"He could always find someone else to write it."

"Who?" asked Lena from the back seat.

"Bridget," Guin and Glen said simultaneously, looking at each other. Though that gave Bridget another motive for doing away with Vera.

They drove the rest of the way in silence.

The American Consulate in Florence was located on the
north bank of the Arno river. The inside was rather ornate
for a consulate, Guin thought, with its gilded stucco and
ornate molding. Then again, it had once been a palazzo. She
imagined what it must be like to work there.

She had read online that the consulate was the smallest
U.S. outpost in Italy, with only three foreign service officers
and 18 staff. Still, that should be more than enough to help
them.

They introduced themselves to the woman seated at the
reception desk, explaining the situation regarding Vera's
body. The woman listened, nodding her head. She seemed
sympathetic. Then she asked Lena for her passport and
proof that she was Vera's sister, which Lena had brought
with her.

Then the woman asked Guin and Glen for their
passports, and Guin explained that their passports were
being held by the police in Greve, which was why they were
there. The woman again looked sympathetic and said she
would have someone look into the matter. Then she turned
to Lena.

She explained to Lena that to transport Vera's remains
to the States, she needed to obtain a death certificate, which
she could get from the doctor who had examined Vera or
the hospital where she had been taken. The death certificate
would then need to be given to a funeral agent, who would
arrange to have Vera's body or ashes shipped back to the
United States.

Lena asked if the consulate could help her with both, and
the woman, who it turned out was from the town of
Panzano near Greve, said she would look into it. Would they
mind waiting? They immediately told her that was fine. The
woman then picked up the phone and began speaking in
Italian.

A few minutes later, a man appeared. The woman spoke

with him for a minute, then she turned to Glen, Guin, and Lena.

"I will be back shortly, but you are welcome to wait."

"Where are you going?" asked Guin.

"It is time for my break."

She left, and the three of them spoke quietly.

"Do we wait?" asked Lena.

"I think we should," said Guin. "How long could her break be?"

An hour passed, and Guin regretted not going for a walk.

"Do you think she forgot about us?" she asked Glen. She remembered what Oliver had said about his visit to the consulate.

"Just give her some more time," said Glen.

"How much more time? Maybe this gentleman can help us."

She went over to the man who had taken the woman's place at the desk.

"Excuse me," said Guin, smiling politely. "Do you know when your colleague will be back?"

"She should be back very soon," he informed her.

Guin was tempted to ask him to define *soon*. Instead, she took a seat.

"Let's give her a few more minutes, then we should probably go," said Glen.

Guin nodded her head.

A minute later, the woman appeared. She went over to the man at the desk and said something to him in rapid Italian. Then she went over to Guin, Glen, and Lena.

"Do you have news?" Guin asked her.

"*Sì*," she replied. "I made a few calls during my break, and the good news," she said, looking at Lena, "is I found the hospital where they took your sister."

"Does that mean I can get a death certificate?" said Lena.

The woman nodded.

"Now you must find a funeral agent. I have a name for you if you would like it. You can tell him I referred you. He can arrange to have your sister's body transported back to the United States. Or, if you prefer, he can arrange to have her cremated here, and you can take her ashes."

"Thank you!" said Lena. "Please let me know how to contact this funeral agent. I'll call or email him right away."

"I will write his information on the back of my card." The woman went over to her desk, reached into a drawer, pulled out a card, and began writing. "Here," she said, handing the card to Lena.

Lena looked at the card.

"Thank you, Signora Rossi. I'll contact Signore Ricci this afternoon."

"What about our passports?" said Guin.

"I am very sorry," said Signora Rossi. "The police want to hold onto them a bit longer."

"But we had nothing to do with Signora van Leyden's death!"

Signora Rossi looked sympathetic.

"I am sure that is the case, but... I will ask the Consul General to make an appeal on your behalf."

Guin was about to say something, but Glen laid a hand on her arm, stopping her.

"Thank you," he said to Signora Rossi. "Let me give you my card." He fished one out and handed it to her. "If you could ask the Consul General to contact me with any information."

"*Certo*," she said.

She looked down at the card then back up at Glen, eyeing him.

"You are a photographer?"

"I am."

"You look more like a model."

"That's kind of you to say," he said.

She pocketed the card and looked at the three visitors.

"I must now get back to work. The consulate will be in touch if we have any news."

"Well, at least you'll be able to take your sister home soon," said Guin as they left the consulate and headed back to the car.

"I hope so," said Lena. "I'll reach out to the funeral agent as soon as we get back."

"If only we could get back our passports so we could go home too," sighed Guin.

"Though there are worse places to be stuck," said Glen. "If we didn't have John and Julia's car, I'd say let's have a look around Florence."

Guin had thought the same thing.

"I should message them. They're probably wondering where we are."

As they were driving back, Guin received a message from Julia, asking when they'd be back. Guin replied "soon," that they were about to drop off Lena at her pensione and would then head to the hotel.

As they neared the hotel, Guin saw a police car go by.

"I wonder what that's about," she said.

They pulled into the lot, and Guin spied Glen's red convertible. Glen immediately went over to it.

"Looks to be all in one piece," said Guin.

Glen was still looking for scratches.

"It's fine. Come on, John and Julia are waiting for us."

And indeed, John and Julia were waiting for them in the lobby. But something was wrong.

"I'm sorry we took longer, but…"

"Never mind that," said Julia. "The police were just here, and they took Beatrice!"

Guin looked at Glen, as if to say, *I told you she did it!*

"Did they arrest her?" Glen asked Julia.

"I don't know."

"Where's Domenico? Did he go with them?"

"I don't know. We didn't see him."

"We should find him," said Glen. He turned to Guin. "You coming?"

CHAPTER 39

"First, let's see if Domenico's car is in the parking lot," said Guin.

They went outside and looked. His Maserati was there.

"Okay, so he should be around here somewhere."

They went back inside. Julia and John were waiting for them.

"Was his car there?" asked Julia.

"It was," said Guin. "So how did you know the police took Beatrice? Did you see them?"

"She's staying in the room next to ours," said Julia. "And we heard them banging on the door."

"They were speaking Italian. Though yelling was more like it," said John.

"We peeked out our door and saw them leading her away."

"And you didn't see Domenico?" Guin asked them.

"No. John went to knock on his door, but either he wasn't in or he didn't hear him."

"Though how he could have ignored that racket."

"We'll find him," said Glen. "We should check his room again. Maybe if he was out he's back."

Julia and John led them to Domenico's room, which was near Beatrice's, and Glen knocked.

"Domenico, are you there?" he called.

No answer.

"Knock louder," said Guin. "He could be on his phone."

Glen knocked a second time.

"Domenico, it's Glen Anderson. Are you there? We need to speak with you."

Still no response.

"I don't think he's there," said Julia.

"Where else could he be?" said Guin.

"He could be in the business center," said John.

"They have a business center?" said Guin.

"It's not really a business center. It's more like a closet with a computer, printer, and fax."

Julia was looking at her husband.

"What?" he said.

"Leave it to you to find the business center."

"We should probably split up," said Guin. "You two want to see if Domenico's in the business center?"

"What about you two?" said John.

"You want to check by the pool?" she asked Glen. "Or he could be in the kitchen."

"I'll take the kitchen, you check by the pool," he said.

"Fine," said Guin. "And let everyone know if you find him," she said to the group.

They split up and Guin headed to the pool. She gazed out at the rolling hills, taking in the scenery. Then she looked around. The lounge chairs were empty, as was the pool. She was about to go when she heard someone talking in one of the cabanas. She walked over and could hear a male voice speaking in Italian. It had to be Domenico. And he sounded angry.

She thought about knocking, but how do you knock on canvas? Instead, she poked her head inside. It was Domenico. He was pacing and running a hand through his curly black hair as he spoke. Guin tried to subtly get his attention. Finally, he saw her. He didn't look pleased. He put his hand over his phone and glared at her.

"Can I help you?"

"The police took Beatrice."

He stared at her for a beat then spoke into his phone. A few seconds later, it was in his pocket.

"What do you mean the police took Beatrice?"

"John and Julia saw them leading her away."

"When was this?"

"I'm not sure. Not long ago. We…"

He interrupted her.

"Thank you. I must go to her."

Guin followed him out of the cabana.

"Wait!" she called.

He stopped and turned to look at her.

"You and Bea knew Vera, didn't you?"

He studied her.

"Of course we knew her. We were in class together. Now if you would let me…"

"No, I mean before you took the class. You knew Vera because of her son, Christian."

"I do not know what you are talking about."

But Guin could tell that he did.

"You were his roommate, and Bea was Christian's girlfriend."

"You must be mistaken. I never met Signora van Leyden before this week. Now I must go."

Guin followed him.

"Bea killed Vera, didn't she? That's why the police took her. They probably found evidence linking her to the scene of the crime. And when they learn that she and Christian had been lovers and that Vera tore them apart…"

Domenico spun around and glared at her. Guin took a step back.

"That woman was evil. She cared for no one but herself."

"So you admit you knew her, and that Christian van Leyden and Bea were lovers?"

He continued to glare at her.

"There's no point denying it. Bea told Glen everything. Though he didn't realize she was talking about Vera's son. Lena helped us piece it together."

Some of the anger went out of him, and he slumped.

"It was all my fault. If I had never introduced them…"

Guin wanted to put a hand on his arm but refrained.

"Beatrice told Glen that Christian wanted to marry her. Is that true?" He nodded. "She also told Glen that Christian's mother, that Vera, forbid it."

"As I said, she was an evil woman."

"What makes you say that?"

"What woman tells her son to abandon the mother of his child?"

"Wait, what?! They had a baby?"

Domenico winced.

"I thought you knew. You said Bea told Glen everything."

"She must have left that part out. So, they had a child together?"

"Bea was pregnant. When Vera found out, she was furious. She said it must belong to someone else. But Christian knew the baby was his."

"Yet she insisted he break it off with her?"

Domenico nodded.

"*Sì*. But Christian refused."

"But then Vera had her husband fly over and speak with him, and he agreed to leave Beatrice and Italy. I don't understand. What changed?"

Domenico suddenly looked sad.

"Bea lost the baby. Vera had gone to speak with her. They fought, and Vera pushed her down the stairs. She didn't realize she had lost the baby until later. Bea was devastated, and Christian blamed himself. Then his father came. He convinced Christian that the right thing to do was to leave Italy."

"So he broke it off with Bea." Domenico nodded. "And then he killed himself."

"It was an accident. Christian would never kill himself on purpose."

Though Guin wasn't so sure about that.

"Where did he get the drugs?"

"I do not know."

"I read about the accident. The article I read said you and his other roommate were away when it happened."

"*Sì*," he said. "We had no idea he was so unhappy. Though I should have known. He kept asking us if he was making a mistake, leaving Italy and Bea."

"And what did you tell him?"

"That only he could make that decision."

"And then you found him."

Domenico nodded.

"It was terrible."

"And Bea? How did she take it?"

"She was inconsolable. She blamed us for not being there for him. But the real ones to blame were his parents. If they had not interfered…"

Just then Domenico's phone started to ring.

"I must go," he said. Then he hurried away.

"I just saw Domenico leave," Glen told Guin as she entered the lobby. "He looked to be in a hurry and didn't stop when I called him."

"I'm pretty sure he's on his way to the police station."

"So you told him."

She nodded. She wanted to tell Glen what Domenico had told her, about Beatrice, but now was not the time.

"We should go find the Adamses," she said.

"What about Bea? Do you think he can help her?"

"If anyone can, he can," she replied.

No one had heard from Domenico or Beatrice by dinner that evening.

"Do you think she's all right?" asked Glen.

They were having dinner in town with John and Julia.

"I'm sure Domenico hired her a good lawyer," said John.

"Do you think she needs one?" asked his wife.

"Everyone needs a good lawyer," he replied.

"You only say that because you're a good lawyer."

John harrumphed, and Guin couldn't help but smile. She enjoyed listening to John and Julia's banter.

"I messaged Bea, but she didn't get back to me," said Glen.

"They may have taken her phone," said Guin. "Let's ask Rosa if she's heard anything when we get back."

They agreed that was probably the best plan, though Guin could tell that Glen was frustrated. Did he care more for Bea than he had let on, or was it just his nature to care what happened to people he knew? Guin hoped it was the latter.

CHAPTER 40

No one said anything on the drive back to the hotel. And Glen didn't wish Guin a good night as they stood outside their rooms. Guin tried not to let his sullen behavior get to her, but it did.

That night she had a nightmare. She dreamed she was pregnant and had lost her baby.

This wasn't the first time Guin had had the dream. She used to have it regularly when she and Art, her ex, were trying to conceive. But she hadn't had it in years. And instead of Art being the father, it had been Glen. That shook her almost as much as losing the baby had.

The dream had been so real. She and Glen were together. Happy. They hadn't been trying to have a baby. It had just happened. And they were both excited, albeit a bit nervous too. Then Glen's mother had found out, and she was furious. She accused Guin of trying to trap her son and begged Glen to leave her.

Though it wasn't really Glen's mother in the dream. It was a woman who looked a lot like Vera. (Glen's real mother adored Guin and would have probably been thrilled to have a grandchild. She was always talking about how she wanted one.)

In the dream, Glen's mother had gone to see Guin. They had gotten into a fight, and Guin had fallen down a flight of stairs. Soon after, she discovered she had lost the baby.

Guin woke up feeling her heart pounding against her chest and was drenched with sweat. The dream had been so real.

She went to the bathroom and splashed cold water on her face. When she returned to bed, she turned on her phone. There was a message from Glen. She was almost too nervous to read it. Though she knew she was being silly. Finally, she opened it.

It was an apology for being such a Debbie Downer the night before and shutting her out. And he wanted to know if she'd have breakfast with him.

Guin immediately wrote him back, saying yes to breakfast. They would meet on the dining terrace at 8:30.

They were finishing breakfast on the dining terrace, John and Julia seated at a table nearby, when Rosa appeared.

"I have good news," she told them.

"Yes?" said Guin.

"Your passports have been returned."

"They have?" said Glen. "When?"

"Just now."

"All of ours?" said John.

"Yes, yours as well," said Rosa.

"Where are they?" he asked.

"In the hotel safe."

"Who returned them?" asked Guin. "Was it the chief inspector?"

"No, a policeman brought them a short time ago."

"Did he say anything?"

"No, he just handed them to me."

John placed his napkin on the table and got up.

"Well, let's go get them!"

"But we're not finished with breakfast," said Julia.

"You finish if you like. I'm getting my passport back."

Rosa looked over at Glen and Guin.

"Would you like to come too?"

Guin looked at Glen.

"I'll be there in a minute," he said. "You go."

"I've waited this long," said Guin. "What's a few more minutes?" She turned to Rosa and John. "You two go. We'll be up soon."

John looked over at his wife.

"You sure you don't want to come?"

Julia sighed and put her napkin down on the table.

"Coming," she said.

Then she and John left with Rosa.

"So, what's up?" Guin asked Glen. "Is this about Bea? Did you hear from her?"

"No. It's just... Do you think they locked her up? I don't know if she could handle that."

"Bea's strong. She'll be okay. Besides, Domenico probably got her out on bail or put under house arrest."

"I know Bea acts like she hasn't a care in the world, but she's more fragile than you think."

Glen had a hand resting on the table, and Guin covered it with one of hers.

"She'll be okay. Now we should probably go get our passports and let Ginny know."

"It's still early on Sanibel."

"I'll shoot her an email."

"She'll want to know when we'll be back. We should book a flight first, then tell her."

"Probably a good idea," said Guin. She gazed out at the garden and the grounds and sighed.

"What?" he said.

"I'm going to miss this place."

"You will? Despite what happened?"

She nodded.

"We could always come back," he said.

"We?"

"I hope if you came back here, it would be with me."

The way Glen was looking at her made Guin feel suddenly warm.

"We should go," he said.

"Where are we going?"

"To get our passports, then book a flight home."

They waited in the reception area for Rosa to return with their passports.

"I haven't seen Oliver recently," Guin said. "Have you?"

"Now that you mention it, I haven't either," Glen replied.

"Do you think he knows about our passports?"

"Though we don't know if the police returned his."

"True," said Guin. "Maybe the police took him in for questioning too. We can ask Rosa."

A minute later, Rosa reappeared.

"Here are your passports," she said, handing them to Guin and Glen.

"Thank you," they said.

"Have you seen Oliver?" Guin asked her. "We haven't seen him."

"He was here this morning when the policeman dropped off your passports."

"Did they take him in for questioning?"

"I do not believe so."

"So he's still here, at the hotel?"

"He has not checked out."

"Have you heard anything about Beatrice, Signora Krueger?" Glen asked her.

"I am sorry, no."

Glen frowned.

"What about Domenico, Signore Conti? Have you seen him?"

"Not this morning." She paused. "Now that you have your passports back, you will be leaving us?"

"As soon as we can book a flight," said Guin.

"Let me know if I can be of any assistance."

"Thank you."

"I should phone Lena, let her know we got our passports back," Guin said to Glen as they stood outside. "We should also tell her about Bea."

"But we don't know for sure if they arrested her, or if she's the killer."

"Considering the police returned our passports, I'd say it's likely they think she did it or was involved."

"I need to do some work," he said as they approached their rooms.

"Okay," said Guin. "I'll ring Lena."

They parted ways, and Guin went into her room. She pulled out her phone and entered Lena's number. Lena picked up after a few rings.

"Guin?"

"Good morning. I'm not waking you, am I?"

"Oh no. I've been up for a while."

"Did you not sleep well?"

"I slept okay. I'm just one of those people who rises with the sun, even with jet lag."

Guin could relate.

"Is everything all right?" asked Lena.

"I'm just calling to let you know that we got our passports back."

"That's wonderful! Did the Consul General contact the Greve police?"

"I don't know. Rosa just came over to us at breakfast and said the police had returned them."

"Did they make an arrest?"

"We're not sure. But John and Julia said the police came to the hotel yesterday to speak with Beatrice while we were away, and they took her with them. And no one's seen her since."

"Do they think she killed Vera?"

"Either that or they think she knows something. Domenico went to the police station to find out."

"Well, let me know if you hear anything. Though I can't imagine that young woman murdering anyone."

"So, did you get in touch with the funeral agent?"

"Yes! I'm meeting with him this afternoon. He said I should be able to fly Vera home in a couple of days."

"That's wonderful," said Guin, who was genuinely happy for Lena.

"Well, fingers crossed. I'm not sure I trust these Italians. So now that you have your passports back, will you be going back to Sanibel?"

"As soon as we can get a flight."

"Good luck to you. And thanks again for your help."

"Thank you, and good luck to you too."

They ended the call and Guin put away her phone. Then she took it out again. She started to type a message to Glen, then she stopped. Instead, she went to knock on his door.

"Is everything all right?" he asked.

"I just spoke with Lena."

"And?"

"She's meeting with the funeral agent this afternoon. He said she should be able to fly Vera home in a couple of days."

"That's good, right?"

"She seemed optimistic."

"Anything else?"

"We should book a flight home."

"You want to do it? I'm a bit busy."

"Oh. I was thinking we could do it together."

Glen saw the look on Guin's face.

"You want to come in? I'll just be a minute. Then we can look for flights."

"Are you sure?"

"Positive."

He opened the door wider and gestured for Guin to come in.

Guin glanced around as Glen did something or other on his computer. She hadn't been in Glen's room before. It was the mirror image of hers, though the décor was different. She gazed at his camera equipment, which occupied a portion of the living area, and saw his computer on the desk, just like she had hers. She was curious to see if his bedroom was the same as hers but didn't want to seem nosy.

"You want the guided tour?" he said, as if reading her mind.

"Was it that obvious?"

He smiled.

"So, as you may have surmised, this is the living area," he said, gesturing around the room with his arm. "Which also doubles as my office."

"I would never have guessed," said Guin, smiling at him.

He then led her to the bedroom.

"And this is the bedroom."

Either the maid had been in while they were eating breakfast or else Glen had made his bed and tidied up as the room was exceptionally neat.

"And here is the bathroom," he said, opening a door.

It looked identical to hers.

"Very nice."

"Shall we go back to my office? We can look up flights on my computer."

Guin took a seat next to him and watched as he searched for available flights. There were no direct flights to Fort

Myers or even Miami from Pisa. But Glen managed to find them two seats on a flight from Pisa to Frankfurt and then another flight from Frankfurt direct to Fort Myers in a few days.

"Does that work for you?" he asked Guin.

"Doesn't seem like we have much of a choice."

"So shall I book it then?"

"Book it, Glen-O."

Glen smiled at the *Hawaii Five-O* reference and went to book the flights.

"Done," he said when he had finished. "Let me know when you receive your ticket. I put in your email address."

"Thanks. Let me know what I owe you. So, should we let Ginny know? She's probably going to be annoyed that we won't be back for a few more days."

"I'll write to her."

"Thanks."

Guin knew Glen had a way with their boss.

"Also, I was thinking…"

"Uh-oh. I recognize that expression."

"What expression?"

"That expression you get when you're thinking about something that you don't think I'm going to like."

"I have a specific expression?"

He nodded.

"I'll have to be more careful. Remind me not to play poker with you. Though I don't think you'll object to what I'm thinking."

"And what's that?"

"I'm thinking we should see if Domenico is back."

They knocked on Domenico's door, but there was no answer.

"I don't think he's back," said Glen.

"Wait," said Guin. "I thought I heard something. Let's knock again."

She knocked again, louder this time, and called his name. She definitely heard something, and a few seconds later, he opened the door.

"*Sì?*" he said. His eyes looked bloodshot, he hadn't shaved, and his hair looked unkempt. If Guin had to guess, she'd say he'd been up all night.

"Did you see Bea?" she asked him.

He shook his head.

"They would not let me see her."

"Did they arrest her?"

"They are holding her."

"They don't really think she killed Vera, do they?" said Glen.

Domenico didn't answer.

"Do they have proof she did it?" asked Guin. "Did you speak with the chief inspector?"

Domenico sighed.

"I spoke with the chief inspector, but he did not say much. I was just on the phone with the lawyer."

"You hired a lawyer already?"

He nodded.

"Now, if you will excuse me, I have more calls to make."

"Of course," said Guin.

They moved away.

"They can't really think Bea killed Vera," said Glen. "What motive did she have?" He saw Guin's expression. "What is it?" he said. "You know something. Tell me."

"I…"

"Tell me what you know, Guin."

CHAPTER 41

Guin told Glen about Beatrice and Christian. Although he already knew most of the story, he hadn't known that Bea had been pregnant or that she had lost the baby.

He looked horrified as Guin relayed what Domenico had told her.

"No wonder she hated Vera."

"I would hate her too," said Guin. "To lose both your child and the man you loved... If I had seen Vera again, I might have wanted to plunge a knife into her too."

"We still don't know if she did it though. It could have been Domenico. It sounds like he hated Vera too."

"But the police arrested Bea. They must have found some evidence."

"What could they have found?"

"A hair, a fingerprint, a piece of clothing... If this had been Sanibel, I could have asked Detective O'Loughlin. Or Craig could have found out." (Craig was the paper's crime reporter and had connections.) "But I doubt Chief Inspector Manetti would tell me anything."

Glen frowned.

"It just seems unfair."

"Life is rarely fair."

They saw John and Julia. They had their suitcases out.

"Are they leaving?" asked Guin.

"It looks that way."

They walked over to see what was up.

"Are you leaving?" Guin asked the Adamses. "How did you get a flight out so soon?"

"We didn't," said Julia. "We're going to Milan for a few days. Then we leave from there. What about the two of you?"

"Glen found us a flight out of Pisa, but it's not for a few days. Everything was booked."

"So will you be staying here?"

"I don't know." Guin hadn't thought that far ahead and made a mental note to go see Rosa. Though she wouldn't mind staying someplace else for a few days.

"Well, I wish you safe travels. If you ever find yourselves in Boston, please, look us up."

"We'll do that," said Guin.

Julia turned to Glen.

"And I'd love to see the photographs you took of the class. You should post them someplace, so everyone can see them. I'd like to order a few."

"I can do that," said Glen.

"Thank you."

"And let us know when the two of you make it official," said John.

"Official?" said Guin.

"You two can't fool me. But I understand wanting to hide your relationship, professionalism and all that. Though I'd never say anything."

Guin stared at him.

"We're not…" Guin began.

"Come along, dear," said Julia.

Then they headed to reception.

"What was that all about?" Guin asked Glen after the Adamses had left.

"I think John was saying we make a nice couple. And I agree with him."

"I thought we agreed to just be friends."

"I don't recall agreeing to that," he said.

He was giving her that look again, and Guin felt her face grow warm.

"So, what do you want to do the next couple of days while we wait to go home?" Glen asked her. "Fancy a visit to Florence or Siena?"

"I'd like that," said Guin. "That is if we can find two rooms someplace."

"Hm, good point," said Glen. "Let me poke around, see what I can find. If I can't find us a place in Florence, how do you feel about Pisa?"

"Either is fine."

"Okay, I'll do some investigating and let you know."

With Bridget's help, Glen was able to reserve them a room at a boutique hotel in Florence that was run by a friend of a friend. And even though Guin had wanted them to stay in two rooms, Glen told her that they were lucky to find one. However, the room had two beds, which pacified her, somewhat.

They checked out of the Albergo Dell'Incanto, thanking Rosa and the staff for everything. Then they went to visit Bridget and Dante to say goodbye. While they were there, Bridget revealed that Oliver had offered to represent her and Dante in the States and have her cookbook published there.

"He said it was sure to be a bestseller."

"What did you tell him?" Guin asked her.

"We told him we would think about it. But I can't imagine working with that odious man."

"And he wanted fifteen percent!" said Dante.

Guin couldn't help smiling. She also still wondered if Oliver had been involved in Vera's murder. Though the police hadn't arrested him.

Then Glen told Bridget that their boss wanted her to come to Sanibel to do a cooking course.

"I'd love that!" said Bridget. "Though I imagine it's expensive to stay there."

"We'd find a sponsor," said Guin.

Then it was time for them to leave. They hugged and promised they would visit again. Though Guin had no idea when that would be. Then they headed to Florence.

The hotel Glen had booked was charming. It was located on a quiet street, and their room, which was located on the top floor, had a view of the Duomo. It was perfect. However, Guin was still nervous about spending two nights in a room with Glen, even with two beds.

They dropped their bags, not bothering to unpack, and immediately headed out to see the city. They spent the next two days seeing the sights. They visited the Duomo, the Piazzele Michelangelo, the Boboli Gardens, the Uffizi Gallery, the Ponte Vecchio, whatever they could cram in, only taking time out to eat, drink, and sleep. It was two of the nicest days Guin had ever spent. And she wished they could have stayed longer.

They were at the airport in Pisa, about to board their flight to Frankfurt, when they received an email from Ginny. It contained a link to an article in the *Boston Globe*.

"Thought you'd want to know," she had written.

They immediately clicked on the link and began to read. When they were done, they turned and looked at each other.

"It's horrible," said Guin.

"They made Bea sound like some kind of she-devil," said Glen.

"And they made Vera seem like some kind of saint."

Glen scowled.

"This must be Oliver's doing," said Guin. "Where else

could they have gotten the story?"

"If I ever see that weasel, I'll wring his neck."

"Just don't plunge a knife into him." She paused. "I wonder if Domenico knows? I should have gotten his cell phone number or an email."

"You can probably find it online. Just look up the Conti Group."

"Good idea. I'll do it when we get to Frankfurt."

Guin gazed out the window as they flew over Northern Italy and the Italian Alps.

"They're beautiful, aren't they?" said Glen, leaning over her. Guin had taken the window seat and Glen the aisle.

"They are," she sighed.

"We could always come back. I've always wanted to visit the Italian lakes."

Guin turned and looked at him.

"You said *we* again."

"Wouldn't you like to go? I hear the Italian lakes are beautiful. We could say hi to George and Amal."

"Don't tell me you know the Clooneys."

"Maybe," he said with a smile.

Guin looked at him. Was he telling her the truth or pulling her leg? She wasn't sure.

She looked down. Glen's hand was resting on hers. It felt warm and right.

"By the way, I communicated with Ginny," he said, removing his hand. Guin immediately felt its absence.

"You replied to her email?"

"No, this was a different email."

Guin waited for him to go on.

"You going to tell me what you two talked about?"

"It's about the Travel section. She said it was a big hit, and she's thinking of making it permanent."

Guin immediately felt guilty. She still owed Ginny a couple of articles. She would lock herself in her house when she got back and bang them out.

"She is?"

Glen nodded.

"She also said we make a terrific team. So, you game?"

"Game for what?"

"For going on more trips together."

"For the paper?" He nodded. "Will they pay?"

"It sounded like it."

Guin sat back in her seat. A travel section. Guin had always wanted to travel the world. She just never had the time or the money. But would this mean constantly leaving Sanibel? She had felt in a bit of a rut before she had left for Italy, having grown a bit weary of interviewing store and restaurant owners. But in her heart, she loved Sanibel and wasn't ready to leave.

"What are you thinking?" he asked her.

"I was thinking visiting places and writing about them could be fun."

"Especially if we went together," he added.

Guin felt her face grow warm again as he looked at her. She could think of worse people to travel with.

"Let's talk to Ginny when we get back."

"Let's do that," he said. "And Guin?"

"Yes?" she replied.

"Ginny was right."

"About?"

"Us making a good team."

"We do make a pretty good team, don't we?" she said with a smile. Then she closed her eyes and leaned against the window, drifting off to sleep.

EPILOGUE

Guin periodically checked to see if there was any news about Beatrice or a trial, but she didn't see anything, at least in the U.S. media. She finally sent an email to Bridget asking if she had heard anything. Bridget explained that the Italian justice system moved slowly, but she would keep an eye out for news about Beatrice.

Several months later, Bridget sent her a link to an article in *La Nazione*, a newspaper based in Florence, along with a link to an English-language paper. Beatrice's trial had caused a minor sensation. The beautiful young widow had made quite an impression on the judges. (Unlike in the United States, criminal trials in Italy were determined by a panel of professional judges, not peers.)

Beatrice had told them about Christian and the baby and how Vera was responsible not only for causing her son's death but for causing Beatrice to lose her child, which had struck a chord with both the female and male judges.

Then she had described that fateful night in the kitchen. She claimed Vera had lured her there under false pretenses, claiming she wanted to make amends, when in fact she had lured Beatrice there to berate and threaten her. Then, Beatrice claimed, Vera had attacked her. To defend herself from the madwoman, she had picked up a knife. Though she claimed not to remember plunging the knife into Vera's back.

Domenico had spoken on Beatrice's behalf, confirming her story and telling them that Beatrice was a good Catholic and would never hurt another human being unless her own life was in danger. And even then, he found it difficult to believe she would intentionally hurt another soul.

Reading Domenico's testimony made Guin wonder if it was Domenico, not Beatrice, who had killed Vera—and had knocked Lena unconscious outside the kitchen, something that hadn't come up in the trial. But the police must not have had proof that Domenico was responsible for either assault.

And despite there being holes in Beatrice's story (Guin wondered how it could have been self-defense when the knife was in Vera's back), the judges believed her, and she was not convicted.

While Guin wasn't sure if justice had been served, she was somewhat relieved to hear that Beatrice would not be spending the rest of her life in jail. Though she knew she was letting her emotions get the better of her.

She thought about forwarding the articles to Lena. But no doubt Lena was already aware of what had occurred or would soon know. And despite the two sisters not being close, Guin couldn't help thinking that Lena would be disappointed with the outcome of the trial. Though Lena hadn't thought Bea was the killer.

She wondered if Glen knew. She would ask him that evening. The two of them were having dinner together, something they had been doing regularly since they returned from Italy. They hadn't talked about Beatrice in a while, and Guin discovered she was no longer jealous. She knew Glen cared for her, and she had grown to care for him as something more than a friend.

But she wasn't going anywhere that evening until she finished her article for Ginny.

Acknowledgments

First, I'd like to thank *you* for reading this book. If you enjoyed it, please consider reviewing or rating it on Amazon and/or Goodreads.

Next, I'd like to thank my first readers, Robin Muth and Amanda Walter. Amanda and Robin have been with me from the beginning of my writing journey, and I value their insights and typo spotting. Thanks, too, to Kristen Renfroe, for fact-checking my Italian and descriptions of Tuscany.

I am also indebted to Sue Lonoff de Cuevas—my mother and a former professor of English and Writing—for proofreading the manuscript, Rita Sri Harningsih for designing a gorgeous cover, and Polgarus Studio for formatting the interior. It really does take a village to produce a book.

And as always, thank you Kenny for keeping me well-fed and for nurturing my creative spirit. *Ti amo*.

About the author

Jennifer Lonoff Schiff is the author of the popular Sanibel Island Mystery series and the rom-com novel *Tinder Fella*. A former journalist and world traveler, Jennifer has always loved Italy and all things Italian.

For more information about *Something's Cooking in Chianti* and Jennifer's other books, visit www.ShovelAndPailPress.com.